Praise for

PROMISES *to* KEEP

National Bestseller

"At once dizzyingly romantic and tremendously adventurous, this novel also serves as a poignant reminder of the senseless toll the violence of war can take—and the incredible lengths of heroism humans will go to in order to survive and rescue the ones they love."

—*Toronto Star*

"Fascinating, harrowing, illuminating, this is a gripping love story. Graham sheds light on a dark chapter of Canadian history, immersing the reader in 1755 Grand Pré, making vivid the flames and the pain of the Acadians deported from their idyllic homeland."

—Beth Powning, bestselling author of
A Measure of Light

"In this beautifully written, meticulously researched novel of the Acadian expulsion from Grand Pré in 1755, Genevieve Graham crafts an uncompromising glimpse into the anguish of war and the eventual triumph of love. A must read for fans of Canadian history."

—Kaki Warner, bestselling author of *Pieces of Sky*

Praise for

TIDES *of* HONOUR

National Bestseller

"[Graham] has delivered a book that reads like a love letter to a time and place that figures largely in our national identity: Halifax in 1917."
—*The Globe and Mail*

"Fans of Gabaldon and other historical fiction/romance writers will lap this up for the classy, fast-moving, easy-to-read, and absorbing book that it is—with some Canadian history to boot."
—*Winnipeg Free Press*

"Evocative of place and time, a novel blending tragedy and triumph in a poignant and uplifting tale that's sure to leave its mark upon your heart."
—Susanna Kearsley, bestselling author of
A Desperate Fortune

"Audrey is a strong female character, a hallmark of Graham's books."
—*The Chronicle Herald*

"Travel back to 1917 and explore a world of suffragettes, Bolsheviks, and the Great War—and the love story that illuminates them all."
—Jon Tattrie, author of *Black Snow*

"A moving Maritime story of love, loss, and the human spirit."
—Lesley Crewe, author of *Relative Happiness* and *Kin*

ALSO BY GENEVIEVE GRAHAM

Promises to Keep
Tides of Honour
Under the Same Sky
Sound of the Heart
Somewhere to Dream

COME

from

AWAY

Genevieve Graham

Published by Simon & Schuster

New York   London   Toronto   Sydney   New Delhi

SIMON &
SCHUSTER
CANADA

Simon & Schuster Canada
A Division of Simon & Schuster, Inc.
166 King Street East, Suite 300
Toronto, Ontario M5A 1J3

This book is a work of fiction. Any references to historical events, real people, or real places are used fictitiously. Other names, characters, places, and events are products of the author's imagination, and any resemblance to actual events or places or persons, living or dead, is entirely coincidental.

Map of Nova Scotia Library and Archives Canada / e010694188

This Simon & Schuster Canada edition April 2018

SIMON & SCHUSTER CANADA and colophon are trademarks of Simon & Schuster, Inc.

For information about special discounts for bulk purchases, please contact Simon & Schuster Special Sales at 1-800-268-3216 or CustomerService@simonandschuster.ca.

Manufactured in the United States of America

7   9   10   8   6

Library and Archives Canada Cataloguing in Publication

Graham, Genevieve, author
Come from away / Genevieve Graham.
Issued in print and electronic formats.
ISBN 978-1-5011-4289-5 (softcover).—ISBN 978-1-5011-4292-5 (ebook)
I. Title.
PS8613.R3434C66 2018   C813'.6   C2017-906859-8
C2017-906860-1

ISBN 978-1-5011-4289-5
ISBN 978-1-5011-4292-5 (ebook)

For Dwayne

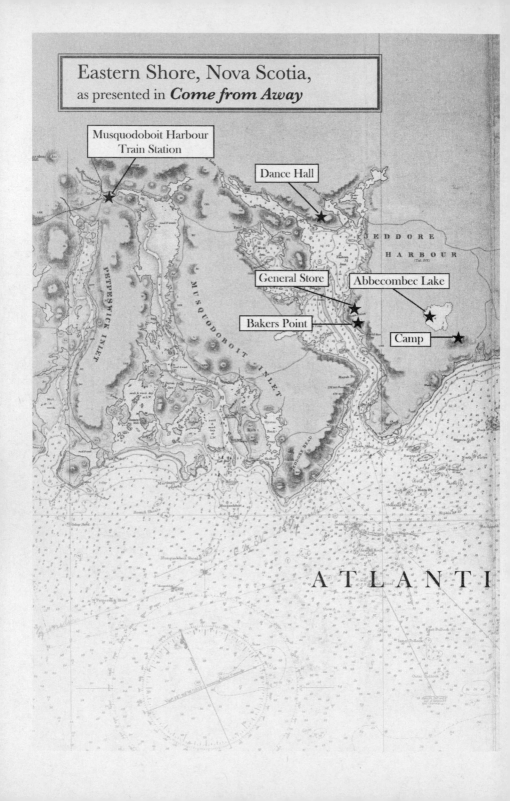

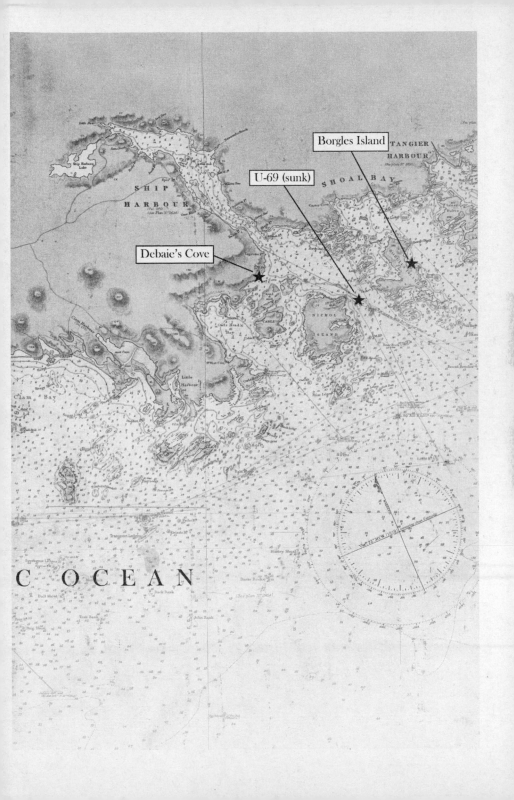

Borgles Island

U-69 (sunk)

Debaie's Cove

A Note to the Reader

During the Second World War, U-boats (*Unterseeboot*, or "undersea boat") were called the greatest threat to Allied victory, and it was common knowledge that "wolf packs" of U-boats patrolled the many nooks and crannies along Canada's east coast. In May 1942, U-213 navigated the great Fundy tide and quietly delivered Lieutenant A. Langbein, a German spy, to a tiny inlet in New Brunswick. The same month, U-553 surfaced in the Saint John Harbour and spied for five days, sending wireless transmissions to Germany every night without anyone taking notice. Between 1942 and 1944, fifteen U-boats infiltrated Canadian waters, sinking twenty-three ships. This became known as the Battle of the Gulf of St. Lawrence.

Along the Eastern Shore of Nova Scotia, legends persist about U-boats skulking in our deep harbours, and one tale in particular offers an interesting twist. The locals tell an unlikely—but ostensibly true—story about a dance in late 1942 that was attended by a few unexpected guests. Evidently craving social interaction outside their own crew, a half dozen or so German sailors left their U-boat one chilly evening and took advantage of the opportunity to temporarily forget about the war and enjoy a night of entertainment instead. How could their commander have allowed this unorthodox lapse of discipline? We don't know. What conversations might the sailors and the locals have had in that dimly lit community hall? Did anyone risk a dance with the visitors? Again, we'll never know. But we can imagine the possibilities.

PROLOGUE

September 1939

The bittersweet truth these days was that there was a lot less laundry to hang. Standing on tiptoe, Grace clipped her father's blue-checked shirt to the line, then reached for the next. The wind saw her working and rushed in to help, turning the shirts to balloons and flapping the sleeves so they seemed to wave towards the sea, and she paused from her work to appreciate the moment.

Sunlight sparkled off the water like diamonds, and a fishing boat drifted by. Grace had seen all kinds of boats in her twenty-one years living on Bakers Point. She'd watched the small in-shore fishing boats leave before sunrise and return in the dark of night, and she'd been aboard dories, schooners, rowboats, and canoes. Most were simple crafts past their primes, badly in need of paint and patching, but others were more impressive. These days all of them were overshadowed by the distant silhouettes of destroyers patrolling the shoreline. Those were quite a sight, and one Grace could not bear to watch.

Once upon a time her parents had sailed from Halifax all the way here, to East Jeddore, on a small white schooner with three young orphaned boys they'd rescued from the shattered debris of the Halifax Explosion. A few months later, Grace had come along and become their sister. As a family they'd built the fish plant, which supported not only them but the fishermen along the shore. Things sure had changed since then.

Grace picked up another shirt, pinned it roughly to the line, and reached for the next.

Her brothers were all grown up now, riding ugly metal ships somewhere, taking separate paths to a faraway war, while she stayed home to gut fish and babysit.

Harry was with the merchant marine, transporting supplies for the Allies. Blinded in one eye by the Halifax Explosion twenty years before, he hadn't been able to join the Royal Canadian Navy like his twin brother. Eugene was aboard the destroyer HMCS *Sackville*. His job was to hunt the greatest threat in the war: the German submarines. Just thinking of U-boats made Grace shudder. The creatures reminded her of sharks, the way they prowled silently beneath convoys of merchant ships like Harry's, shadowing their prey until they could take them out one by one.

The twins had always loved the sea, rode it like they were born to it, but their younger brother Norman stayed away from the water whenever he could.

"I don't like not knowing what's under my feet," he said once. "The ocean's black and deep and filled with creatures I don't want to meet. Sure, I can live by the water, but when it comes right down to it, I'd rather not live *on* it."

So he'd chosen the army. Her father had tried everything to talk him out of it, even speaking unexpectedly about his own horrible experiences in the Great War. He'd said the glory of invading the land was nothing when compared to the hell of being left to die on a burnt-out field, his severed leg lying a few feet away.

But Norman's mind was set. "I'm not you, Dad. You'll see. I'll come back in one piece. But I won't do that until I've blown a few Nazis to kingdom come."

And off he'd gone to enlist.

How could it have only been two weeks since they'd all gathered around the Halifax Harbour and said goodbye?

"Come on, Grace," Norman had said. "No more crying. I'll be back before you know it. Hey, maybe by then you'll have finally found a man. But don't get married without me, okay? I want to be at that party."

She'd almost laughed at that. Some of her friends were already married with children. Grace, well, she'd never even been kissed. Worse than that, she'd never met a boy she *wanted* to kiss. To make her brother happy, she'd wiped her tears and smiled bravely up at him. Then he'd turned and boarded his ship.

The three Baker boys waved farewell from the decks, standing sharp and proud in their uniforms, their copper hair shining in the sun. Everyone on the docks flapped white handkerchiefs, then used them to dab away tears. Long after she'd lost sight of her brothers, Grace stood watching, wondering what they were thinking. She knew they were courageous, and she understood that their efforts to defeat the hateful German forces were important. She was so proud of them. They were much braver than she could ever be. Really, they were much more *everything* than she was.

With them gone, what am I supposed to do?

Tucking her hair back under her kerchief, she bent to pick up her basket, then hoisted it onto one hip. She scanned the water one more time, but she knew she wouldn't see the answer she sought.

She'd never promised Norman she'd stop crying. Couldn't have promised that in a million years. But she'd smiled through the agony as she'd waved farewell to him and the others. She'd smiled for the children and their parents when they were weak.

But when she was alone—which felt like most of the time—she let the tears come.

Everyone said the war would be over quick. That they'd be home soon. Grace tried hard to believe them, to convince herself it wasn't so bad. But as she made her way to the house, she felt a familiar sinking sensation in her gut. It was hard to believe anything would ever be the same again.

PART ONE

Grace Baker

ONE

August 1942

The heat was a living thing, and cicadas screeched maniacally from hidden perches. Sunlight streamed through the leaves overhead, painting polka dots on the road under Grace's feet, and she felt a bead of perspiration run down her back. July had been wet and miserable, but the closer they got to the end of the summer, the hotter and drier it became. Like summer figured it was running out of time and had better make an impression while it still could. The only thing that had saved her during her long shift at Gardner's Store today was the brand new General Electric fan, all sixteen glorious rotating inches of it. If she could have stood in front of that thing the entire day she would have, not the least bit worried about how it tangled her hair. After all, it wouldn't matter if her hair was a mess if she died from overheating, she reasoned.

By the end of her shift she had become so attached to the fan that she'd decided to buy one for the family and carry it home. In these days of patched dresses and mended stockings, it felt good to buy something new. She wished they could take care of a few more things, like change the wallpaper in the sitting room, do more than cover the hole in the couch with a blanket, but times were tight and manpower was scarce. The damn war had raged on for three years and it was hard on everyone. At least today, she could replace their broken fan.

She paused in the middle of the road to set down the box and wipe sweat off her forehead. The fan was heavy, but it'd be worth it. Her parents would be so relieved—once they got over the shock of her spending a week's wages on this kind of luxury. They could put their feet up after a long day and relax in the refreshing cool air, just like the whole family used to do. Except it would only be the three of them this time. *How long before Eugene, Harry, and Norman feel the wind of this fan on their faces?* she wondered.

Her family tried not to talk too much about the boys, about what they might be doing, feeling, seeing. And often that meant they didn't talk at all. A few months after they had gone, the oppressive silence had gotten so much heavier because her uncle Tommy had gone and done the unthinkable: lost at sea. He'd been out fishing like the Bakers had done for generations, but his boat had come back empty, carrying nothing but stories it couldn't tell.

"The sea can be a cruel, cruel mistress," her stiff-lipped father had said at the funeral, "but my brother loved her anyway. Maybe she just—" He'd pressed his fingers hard to his brow, then taken a determined breath before speaking again. "Maybe she just loved him so much she couldn't do without him anymore."

Lost at sea, they called it. Lost. Grace could almost imagine what that had been like for him, because for the past three years that's how she had felt. Like her mind had filled with the same cold, unrelenting murk that had swallowed her uncle, and she couldn't see her way through.

The war was not going well. The Nazis had taken over much of Europe, and America still wasn't fighting. It seemed Canada was the only ally providing any help at all to the struggling British. In the summer of 1941 Germany had attacked Russia, breaking an earlier pact, but Russia had refused to crumble. Then December had come, and Japan had roared through the sky and dropped screaming bombs on Pearl Harbour. Her father said the Japs had hoped to cripple American forces with that attack, but they had done just the opposite. Finally, *finally*, the American hive had been jostled enough, and the red, white, and blue hornets had burst out of their nest to fight back with a vengeance.

But nothing had changed for her brothers. Harry and Eugene were still floating on the Atlantic, and Norman was somewhere in Europe, getting shot at. Did they ever get used to it? To the explosions and bullets intended for them? How could anyone? She got letters from all three boys fairly regularly, but as much as she loved the missives they were still just pencil on paper. She would give anything to wrap her arms around the real things, to listen to them tease and laugh. That was the one thing she prayed for: to have them home again.

"Remember," she muttered to the sky, "I'm talking about all three brothers. Just sending me one or two will not do."

Not much had changed for Grace, either, other than working at the store. She woke up before the sun had risen, got dressed, fed herself, did her chores, then went to work and came home again in time to help her mother make supper.

"Men are dying by the thousands, and I sell groceries," she grumbled to the trees. "My brothers are being shot at, and I do laundry."

She got to a break in the trees and the heat from above hit her full force, as did a hovering throng of black flies. Flapping one hand around her head and hanging tight to the fan with the other, she sprinted far enough that the vicious bugs couldn't keep up, but it was too hot to run any farther.

When she finally walked into the house she spotted her father on his favourite chair in the sitting room, reading the paper. The radio was halfway through "Sleepy Lagoon" and Harry James's trumpet was soaring. Her father looked so comfortable she debated disturbing him, but then she noticed the sweat trickling down the side of his face.

"Do I have a surprise for you!" she declared. She crouched with her back to him, not wanting him to know what was in the box yet.

"Good day at work?" he asked, turning a page.

"Oh, sure. Same old thing. But this," she said, whirling around with the fan in her hands, "is going to change everything!"

His reaction was worth much more than what she'd paid for the fan. Quick as she could she plugged it in and aimed it directly at him. He closed his eyes and exhaled, long and satisfied.

"Better?"

He closed the rattling newspaper. "My darling daughter, you are a genius."

The Bakers were one of the few families in the area lucky enough to have electricity. Just before the war started, her father, brothers, and uncles had helped build the power line coming from Lakeville, setting poles through Jeddore. The first time the family had gathered around that brand new lamp, they had pulled the chain, then cheered when electric light filled the room. It was still an extravagance, and she loved it.

Grace settled in the chair next to her father's and shut her eyes as well, savouring the cool air as it tickled her face. They sat in blissful silence for a few moments, but the quiet reminded her—as it always did—of all the voices she didn't hear anymore.

"I miss them, Dad. Still."

"Three years is a long time," he agreed, "but not long enough to forget, thank God."

She wasn't looking at him, wasn't looking at anything really, but from the corner of her eye she was aware of him watching her. Now was as good a time as any to ask what she'd been wondering for so long, but the words were harder to say than she'd expected.

"Do you wish I'd gone too?"

She'd asked herself that question so many times. Should she go? Did she *want* to go, or was she too afraid? Or was it simply that she was selfish?

Her father sat up taller. "Absolutely not."

"I mean I still could," she went on, staring at her lap. "Not actually fighting, obviously, but a lot of women are volunteering as Wrens, doing whatever's needed. Should I do that?"

"Is that what *you* want to do?"

"Sometimes I think maybe I should." She slumped. "It's not like I'm doing anything important here. I just work at a store. Everyone else is fighting for our country, making a difference."

"What do you wish you were doing?"

"I don't know. Something useful."

"We need you, Grace. You are essential around here. When you're not at the store, you're working here, helping your mom, your aunts, the children. You help me at the plant, too. I can't think of a single aspect of this place that you don't help with."

"Really?"

"Certainly." He cleared his throat. "And when all the work's done, the truth is I feel better knowing you're safe here with us. So I guess you're helping me that way, too. Of course, I really don't know what your mother would do without you."

"Maman would be fine."

He thought about that. "She's strong, but she needs you."

Maman needed her. The children, the aunts, the business, the store, all needed her. If that was true, then why did she feel so guilty all the time?

"Does it ever bother you that I'm not married?"

"No. You'll marry when you've found a man that means something to you. The truth is, none of the boys out here are good enough for you."

That was nice to hear, but it didn't really help.

"When you get around to it, my Grace, your babies are going to be beautiful."

"Dad!"

He winked. "Don't worry. Someone's gonna come around sometime, and he's going to knock your socks off."

"You really think so?"

"Sure. But he's gonna have to knock *my* socks off, too. I'm not letting you run off with just any Tom, Dick, or Harry. You're too special for that. You're my girl."

Was it silly for a woman of twenty-four to still cherish those words from her father? She didn't care. She leaned over and gave him a quick peck on the cheek. "Thanks, Dad. I love you."

"I love you too, princess."

There was a knock at the door. "I'll get it," she said, rising and heading down the hall.

Grace opened the door, giving the pale young delivery boy standing there a cheery hello. Then her eyes fell to his hand.

"Dad?" she whispered. She tried again, louder this time. "Dad?"

She heard him get up, grab his crutch from beside his chair. He came down the hall towards her: *step, tap, step, tap,* his pace quickening when he spotted the figure in the doorway. When he finally stood before him, the boy wouldn't meet his eyes. He placed a small envelope in her father's hand, touched his cap, then turned and fled.

Her father's expression had gone completely blank, and he wouldn't look at Grace. He opened the envelope, his fingers moving very slowly, as if there was nothing in the world to worry about. She knew he didn't want to scare her, but he couldn't help that now. She had heard of these telegrams. She had prayed they would never, *ever* see one in her house. But here it was.

He read the paper; it trembled in his hand. "Get your mother, Grace."

She flew out the door to find her, and moments later the three of them crowded together in the hallway.

"What is it, Danny?" Audrey asked.

"Norman was at Dieppe," he said, lifting his eyes. In minutes, he had aged ten years. "He's dead."

TWO

Norman is dead.

Those three words whispered through Grace's head, squeezed through the crack in her heart. After three months they were still there, pushing and tearing, building scars upon scars. They would always be there. But not Norman. Norman was buried in a cemetery in France along with hundreds of other dead Canadian soldiers. Norman was never coming home.

The house felt like a tomb. These days her mother spent a great deal of time in her room, behind a closed door. Her father stayed out at the plant, sometimes not coming in until long after dark. Norman's widow, Gail, rarely looked anyone in the eye anymore. Life within the old walls had never been this quiet.

Outside those walls, the war had gotten louder. It crept closer every day, practically washing up on their beach. Just a month ago, a Nazi sub had sunk the SS *Caribou*, the passenger ferry that travelled between Newfoundland and Sydney. A hundred and thirty-seven souls lost, mostly women and children just trying to get home. That attack had made front-page news across the country. It had convinced the rest of Canada—any who hadn't figured it out yet—that they truly were at war.

To make everything worse, winter was on its way. Most of the time it felt like everything around Grace was smothered under a mantle of cold, clammy fog—or maybe it was she who was stuck inside, barely seeing out. The long stretches of grey days wore her down. The only place she felt alive was at the store. There she could distract herself with sweeping and dusting, stocking shelves and placing orders, listening to customers' stories when they were offered. Only then could she remember briefly what it felt like to be herself. She tried very hard not to let her unhappiness show. People already had more than enough troubles these days, and she was determined to keep hers to herself, to bury them whenever she was around people. On her walk home from work she dropped the mask for a while, but she always made sure to slip it back on as soon as she opened the front door.

"I've invited Linda for supper, Maman," she called, closing the door behind them. She and her best friend crowded into the front hall, peeling off wet coats and hats and slipping out of their boots. Being around Linda helped sometimes—when her friend was in a good mood, anyway. When Linda was down she dragged everyone with her, but she was cheerful that night, and Grace hoped her mood could rub off on her a bit. "We bumped into each other at the store."

In the sitting room, Gail and Grace's mother were sitting with Catherine, Eugene's wife. They were already tucked in for the evening, knitting by the fire, the little ones playing at their feet. The Philco played big band tunes in the background, and the comforting aroma of corned beef and cabbage filled the air.

"How nice," her mother said. "How are you, Linda?"

"I'm fine, thanks, Mrs. Baker."

"The new Eaton's catalogue came in," Grace offered brightly. She and Linda settled in next to baskets filled with big skeins of grey yarn, and Grace handed her friend a pair of needles. They'd all been knitting socks for years; after they finished outfitting the local fishermen, the rest were sent overseas.

Linda set her needles to the side and picked up the Eaton's catalogue instead.

"How was work today, Grace?" Catherine asked.

"The same as always, I guess. I moved things around a little."

"Mrs. Gardner doesn't object when you change things?"

"She probably doesn't even notice," Linda muttered, flipping a page.

Grace shot her friend a look. "She lets me do what I want for the most part. I convinced her a while back to take catalogue orders for customers, and I rearrange the shelves so whatever's in demand is easy to find. I like doing things like that. And Mrs. Gardner, well, she—"

"She's talking to herself more than to the customers these days," Linda finished for her.

Leave it to Linda to bring up the elephant in the room.

Her mother cleared her throat. "Life gets more difficult as you get older, and Mrs. Gardner's been alone for so long, what with her husband's passing ten years ago. What a sin that God never chose to bless them with any children. I can only imagine how tiring it is for her, being on her own. I'm sure she appreciates your help."

For a while now, Grace had had a bad feeling the sweet old woman was more than just tired, but she was glad the bulk of the responsibilities at Gardner's General Store had fallen on her shoulders. It was a popular place around the area, and she enjoyed keeping it that way. The store's shelves were always full to the brim with everything from a needle to an anchor, apples to butter. Gardner's had it all, and if it didn't, Grace was always happy to order it.

"Would you look at these dresses?" Linda gushed, tapping the page. "How lovely!"

Her mother peered over, and the lamplight caught the

faded line of her scar. Grace hadn't noticed it in a while. A shard of glass had cut straight across one cheek during the Explosion, narrowly missing her mother's eye and taking part of one ear. The cut had healed cleanly, but every time Grace saw it she felt a twinge of sympathy for the girl her mother had been.

"They're nice," Audrey acknowledged, "but there's nowhere to wear them around here."

"I bet those Wren girls wear things like this when they're not working."

"Wren?"

"Oh, you know about them, Maman. The WRCNS—Women's Royal Canadian Naval Service." Grace scowled at a tangle in the wool, plucked it free with a finger. "They're doing the odd jobs now that the men are all gone."

"Not just odd jobs," Linda clarified. "Women drive trucks and cabs, too. Even work with secret codes! Wouldn't that be exciting?"

"They're still hiring switchboard operators," Grace reminded her. "Ever think of joining them?"

Linda shook her head, traded the catalogue for the wool. "Who would take care of us up here?"

"What's it like, running the switchboard?" Gail asked, surprising everyone by speaking up. "And being by yourself all day."

"I like it," Linda replied. Not a lot of places along the shore had telephones yet, but any that did went through the local switchboard. It was run by Linda's family out of their house, which also served as the post office.

"Don't you get lonely?"

"Lonely? No, no. People call me all day long. I'm never alone."

"Oh, I see. Of course," Gail said. "I hadn't thought of that."

Catherine's mouth twitched. "You must hear some pretty interesting things in your job."

"Oh, I hear plenty of things I probably shouldn't."

"What kinds of things?"

"Oh, you know. Some people just say hello, and I connect them to whoever they want, but others are just ridiculous. They act as if they have a big secret, then they tell me all about it as if I had asked. And that's before they even ask to be connected. After that I'm certainly not the only one who hears things. People are always picking up on the party line even when they aren't being called. People are *always* listening in when they're not supposed to."

Catherine lifted her daughter onto her knee. "I imagine you hold a lot of secrets in that head of yours, Linda."

Audrey clucked her tongue with disapproval, and Grace rushed to defend Linda.

"It's entertainment, Maman. Just like the stories on the radio. You know that show *Nazi Eyes on Canada* that we listen to every week? That Nazi spy they talk about, Colin Ross, isn't real. None of the stories are true—"

"Thank heavens for that!" Gail interjected.

"—but loads of people tune in to listen. Imagine those people who call Linda, sharing all their stories and secrets."

Grace and Linda glanced sideways at each other. "Sometimes it's fun to think of doing it, you know? Writing them down, I mean."

Her mother's hands fell to her lap. "You would never do that, would you, Linda?"

"Of course I wouldn't. Don't you worry about me, Mrs. Baker. My lips are sealed." She paused. "But speaking of secrets, did you hear what Captain MacLellan said the other day about security? He said that so many people in Halifax and Dartmouth are blabbing on about our defences that the German spies probably have to hire extra people to write it all down."

"Well, he's right," Audrey said shortly. "No one should spread rumours, whether they're about the war or not. People are entitled to their secrets."

The side door squawked open. "Everything is very quiet in here," Grace's father said warily, entering the room. The familiar reek of fish clung to him like the scales he handled all day long. His arms and hands were powdery white, cracked by salt. "Always makes me nervous when you ladies aren't going on about something." Danny turned towards Audrey. "How is my beautiful wife?"

Her fingers were still working, but her face relaxed. " 'Beautiful' indeed. You need your eyes checked."

"Most beautiful girl in the world," he said fondly.

How he loved her, Grace thought. Her father could be a hard man, stubborn as well, but when he looked at her mother he softened. Sometimes Grace wondered about their story. She knew it had been traumatic—they'd met during the Great War, then lost each other during the Great Explosion—but a small part of her thought it must also have been exciting and romantic.

"Any mail?" her father asked.

"Oh!" Grace hopped to her feet and ran back to the door. She'd been too distracted by the catalogue and Linda's stories. She handed the envelope to Catherine. "How could I forget? A letter from Eugene."

Catherine lit up as she opened the envelope. She drew out two folded letters and handed one to Audrey.

"This one is for you, Mrs. Baker. You should read it to the family. Eugene sent me a separate one."

"What a thoughtful husband," Audrey said, smiling at the

paper in her hands. "Well, at least stay and listen to this one before you go."

"Of course. I never get enough of his letters."

Audrey's eyes lifted to Danny's. "Eugene." It was more of a sigh than a statement.

"The children will be hungry," Gail said, getting swiftly to her feet and reaching for her sweater.

There was no reason for Gail to stay and listen. Her husband would never send her another letter. Grace thought of the stack of letters Norman had sent to the family. They were all tied up tight with a blue ribbon now, gathering dust in her parents' bedroom.

No one said anything until the door creaked closed behind Gail, and even then it took a moment. The sense of awkwardness she left in her wake was still new to the family. When Norman had been alive, Gail's laughter had rung through the house and across the yard. Just one more sound that no longer echoed through their days.

Her mother stared at Eugene's letter until Gail's footsteps had faded away, then she opened the envelope and stared a few seconds longer, savouring every pencil stroke. Grace sat on her fingers, lips glued together. She was impatient to hear the words that said he was safe, that he was all right. When her mother cleared her throat, Grace closed her eyes, trying to hear her brother's voice while her mother read aloud.

November 15, 1942
Dear Family,

I hope this letter reaches you before Christmas, because then I can say "Merry Christmas!" and not sound like a dolt. Feels like it's already passed, with all the parcels I got from you this week.

Thanks loads for the new socks, Maman, and I know that sweater was from you, baby sister. Thanks to you two, I'm toasty even on the coldest nights. I already sent Catherine a letter thanking her for her package. Did you know she sent me a book and a cake as well as shaving cream? What a girl. I'll be all clean shaven and smelling good for a change. Too bad I can't say the same for some of the other boys!

It looks like I'll be on the water for Christmas Day. Some of the others are staying in England, but I'm posted on the next ship. I'm hoping Father Christmas brings us nothing but clear sailing all the way. Rumour has it we'll be feasting on chicken with all the trimmings. It's not Maman's delicious spread, but it's better than nothing. Maybe next year I'll get to sit at that table with you all again.

Just wishing for that makes me think of Norman. I know it's not cheerful Christmas talk, but I can't help thinking of him. Out here every one of us knows guys who won't go home again, and in general we don't talk about that. Almost like it's a curse if we do. But I'm hoping that doesn't count in a letter home, because writing to you is almost like talking to you, and I miss that a lot. Every time I think of home, I think of Norman and feel that big empty space where he should be. I'm so sad for Gail and the kids, and I'm so sad for the rest of us. Norman was one of the best men I ever knew, and this Christmas I hope he's looking down on us and missing us even half as much as we miss him.

Hard to believe we've been out here three years. If you asked, I'd say that sometimes I'm actually glad I signed up, because I can't imagine sitting at home and watching the war from the couch. But most of the time I'm calling myself a fool. I'd love to be miles away from all this right now, even if it meant I was stinking of fish. Don't get me wrong. I'm fine, really, and I'm safe. But it does get tiresome. I miss you all like nobody's business, and I hate knowing that me and Harry make you worry so much. Keep your chins up. It's not so bad most of the time.

If I don't get a chance to write again before the big day, I wish you all a very festive holiday. Please give little Claire and baby Susie an extra special hug and tell them that their daddy misses them very much. Maybe next Christmas I'll be home to hug them myself. That would be a gift indeed.

I'd better sign off before the others see me getting all soft.

Love to all,
Eugene

P.S. Grace, I know I promised you a present from jolly old England, and you're probably wondering where it is. Sorry I didn't get around to shopping this time around, but you never know what might happen in the new year.

Grace let out a small laugh for the benefit of everyone in the room, but even to her own ears it sounded flat. She didn't want anything from jolly old England except her brothers, and nothing would ever bring Norman back. Was she supposed to feel hopeful about the approach of 1943? All she'd seen this year was death and destruction. All she'd felt was loneliness and grief. What could the future have in store? That was the scariest question of all.

THREE

The Christmas Dance offered hope, or at least a distraction from all the sadness. It was a much-needed opportunity to step outside the day-to-day realities, if only for a few hours, and Grace was determined to make those hours special.

"I bought myself some dark red velvet," Linda confided. "I've made a skirt of it, and a matching bow for my hair. Won't that be the cat's meow?"

She'd stopped in while Grace was working, and they were enjoying a cup of tea at the counter. The poster for the dance said everyone had to wear something red, even if it was just a sweater. That was almost as exciting as the dance itself, since the whole world seemed to dress in nothing but blacks, browns, and greys those days. Grace didn't tell her friend that she'd actually purchased a brand new dress from the catalogue. Not velvet, but a lovely, deep red cotton sprinkled with cheerful white polka dots. She'd bought it on impulse, and she wasn't sure where she'd ever wear it again after the dance, but she didn't regret it.

"You look hotsy-totsy in everything, Linda." Grace tilted the teapot, added steaming tea to each of their cups. "So tell me what you're hearing on the switchboard. Do you know who's going to the dance?"

"Oh, everyone, really." Linda blew on her tea, then looked

up at Grace from under her dark eyelashes. "Was Harry able to get time away? You said he was trying."

His letter had arrived the day before, and the whole family had been ecstatic. Maman had spent all night planning his favourite meals.

"He is. He'll 'escort' me, he says."

The corners of her friend's eyes creased. "I hope he'll escort *me* onto the dance floor."

Grace was uncomfortable talking about her brother in a romantic context, so she said, "I'm bringing marble cookies and ginger snaps. You?"

Linda lifted her chin a little, and Grace realized she'd just started a competition.

"I'm bringing my chocolate cream pie."

"You're not!"

"Sure am."

It was easier to concede the point than to come up with a more difficult recipe she could make in time. "That pie is so good, Linda. You'll put the rest of us to shame."

When the next customer arrived, Linda got to her feet and shrugged into her coat.

"That's my cue," she said, fastening the buttons. "I better get going. See you tonight!"

The rest of the afternoon seemed to pass in a minute. The bell over the door never stopped ringing. Every customer wanted to talk about what they planned to wear and who might be there. Many blinked anxiously at the sky and fussed that there'd be too much snow, though it looked to Grace like it might stop soon.

Grace was fidgety too. She kept tucking her pin curls under her cap so they would be fresh for the dance, not limp from a busy day behind the counter. She knew she'd be exhausted by the time she finally hit the pillow that night, but as long as she could keep her eyes open it didn't matter. Adrenaline, she hoped, would carry her through.

After she closed the store, Grace ran almost all the way home, surprised by her own eagerness. When was the last time she had felt excited about a dance? In the three years since the war started, she had come no closer to falling in love. She was bored with the boys there, tired of the endless cycle of taking fish from the sea, processing fish in the plant, delivering fish to the buyer. Fish, fish, fish. All these boys wanted was to be like their fathers: to fish, work lumber, pick up odd jobs, then fish again. What Grace wanted was something entirely different. She wanted something she could find only in magazines, or occasionally in radio shows. Something far, far from here.

Out of breath, she burst through the front door and closed it behind her, stomping snow off her boots.

"Is that you, Grace?" Her mother came around the corner. "I have bad news, I'm afraid."

Grace stopped stomping. Her mother's tone didn't make it sound like *terrible* news, but still. "What's happened?"

"Harry won't be coming, I'm afraid. Too much snow in Halifax. The train's waiting it out."

"Oh no! Did Linda telephone you?"

"No. Her father was looking after the switchboard."

"She'll be awfully disappointed."

"Poor dear. We all are."

"At least the tracks should be clearer tomorrow. He'll be home then."

An hour before it was time to go, Grace sat in front of the mirror, finger combing her curls out. She loved the fat curl that flipped up from the bottom, loved the shine of her bangs when she rolled them tightly under. After she'd coated her hair with spray, she pulled out a new tube of lipstick and slid it over her lips. It matched her nail polish exactly, just like the catalogue had promised. The folds of her skirt were perfectly creased, the bright red bodice tight and flattering around her chest. She was as ready as she was going to get.

"My, you look lovely in that dress, Grace," her mother said as she came downstairs. "The lipstick's a bit much, but I suppose that's what girls are wearing these days."

She turned around, gave her mother the full view. Audrey lifted one eyebrow when she saw the line drawn down the back of Grace's leg.

"It's all the rage," Grace explained.

"Don't you have any nylons?"

"No, and there weren't any in stock." She shrugged. "Everyone's doing it. Isn't it stylish?"

"It's . . . different."

She knew that tone, and her heart tugged. She and Norman used to share a secret signal every time their mother spoke that way. She could almost see him standing there, wiggling an eyebrow at her while keeping one protective arm around their mother's shoulders. He'd had a gift for keeping a straight face that Grace had always envied.

"You look pretty, Maman," she said quickly. "Norman always loved that dress."

Her mother ran her hands thoughtfully over the skirt. "I don't get to wear it nearly often enough."

Outside, her father started singing "Jingle Bells" in his warm baritone, and more voices joined in as their extended family arrived at the door. Her mother paused at Norman's portrait in the hallway, then she walked outside. Grace was alone in the house. She stood a moment, studying her big brother, her heart aching.

"Won't be the same without you there," she whispered. "But I'm not going to cry." She shook her head, jaw tight. "Nope. If you were here, you would want me to dance the night away, so that's exactly what I plan to do."

Still, she blinked a few times to clear her vision. Forcing a smile back in place, she joined the others already bundled in coats and blankets on the sleigh. It was a fine, clear night, and the stars seemed close enough to touch. A wonderful night to be alive. For just a little while, Grace did what she could to put the war and all its ugliness out of her mind.

The hall was just starting to fill with guests, and their eyes were as bright as the flames dancing on every lamp and candle. No one had installed electricity up this far yet, and it always made Grace feel a bit smug when she thought of her own house, with its electric lights and heaters. Here at the hall, though, the flickering lamps were cheerful and more than enough. A small band had set up at the front of the room, and the fiddle player was tuning his strings to the accordion. Grace wasn't sure she knew any of the musicians, but a couple looked vaguely familiar.

"Isn't this wonderful?" Linda eased up beside her, setting her chocolate cream pie on the tablecloth right next to Grace's cookies. She was beaming, looking everywhere at once. "So many people! Where's your brother?"

"Harry's not here. Too much snow in Halifax." She scowled at her friend. "Quit pouting. At least he'll be here for Christmas."

"I've been writing him letters, you know."

"What? Why, you've been keeping secrets from me! Does he write back?"

Linda's grin was back, quick as the fiddler's fingers as he started up a jig. "He sure does!" She spun away, laughing. "Oh well. Doesn't matter that he's not here. We're gonna have a great time anyway. This place will be full of fellows wanting to dance with us!"

Music and conversation escalated as more guests arrived, and before too long Grace had to raise her voice to be heard. She didn't mind. She hadn't enjoyed anything this much in a long time. Some of the older folks started the dancing since the others were too busy talking and gawking to coordinate themselves. Grace and her mother stood with Linda, watching everything and everyone.

"What are the finest women in the room doing over here on their own?" her father asked, appearing beside them.

"We're not alone anymore," her mother said. "We have you."

Grace rolled her eyes. "Linda and I are a little thirsty, I think. We'll leave you two."

As she was walking away, she heard her father say, "C'mon, Audrey. Let's dance."

Grace might feign exasperation, but every time she saw her father show his romantic side it made her happy. From her spot beside the cider table, she watched her parents move together, enchanted by the sight. Her father's missing leg gave him some trouble on the rocky shores, but here on the dance floor he seemed comfortable. He always stood tall, proud as a peacock when Maman was on his arm, and she gazed up at him, rapt as a young girl with her first crush. After more than twenty years of marriage, they still looked at each other that way, still recalled shared memories, still needed to touch each other for reassurance. That was what Grace wanted.

She surveyed the room, spotted a lot of the familiar boys from the area; some had come all the way from Musquodoboit

Harbour or Sheet Harbour or places in-between. A group of young men Grace didn't recognize stood in the back corner, out of the light. They seemed to be enjoying the desserts and the view. She was about to mention them to Linda when one of them approached her.

He was tall and sturdy with short golden hair and pale blue eyes, and at first Grace just stared. He was the most handsome man she'd ever seen. He seemed a bit uncertain when he held out a hand in invitation, but she surprised herself by accepting it with barely any hesitation, and he led her onto the dance floor. Some of his steps were unfamiliar to her, but she caught on, determined not to embarrass herself. He was a marvelous dancer, smooth and confident, and his warm hand on her back eased her past any missteps. When she peeked up at him, he was smiling slightly, looking a bit like a movie star. She couldn't help but blush. Who was this man?

The song came to an end far too soon, and everyone clapped for the band. Not knowing what to say or do, Grace started to turn away, but he touched her arm, then led her to the cider table, indicating to the woman that he wanted a glass for each of them.

"Thank you," Grace said, taking a sip.

"You are welcome." He had a nice voice. A little husky, which made it difficult to hear over the noise, so she leaned in a bit closer than would have made her mother happy.

"I haven't seen you before. Where are you from?"

He answered, but she couldn't hear what he said.

"Pardon me?"

"East of here."

Lots of people lived "east of here." She lifted her chin toward the back of the room. "You and your friends came down just for the dance?"

"Yes."

Grace was used to the people around here, to the open conversations and sharing of gossip. She felt kind of clumsy around someone she didn't know. She scanned the crowd, catching Linda's eye. Her friend gave her a knowing look.

"You live here?"

His unexpected question startled her. "Me? Oh, yes. I live in East Jeddore."

"With your husband?"

"What? No, no. I'm an old maid."

"Old maid?"

"You know, old and not married."

"But you are beautiful."

Her cheeks burned. How should she react to such flirtatious remarks from a tall, handsome stranger? "Well, I—"

"She is, isn't she?" Linda chimed in, stepping right into the conversation as she always did. Thank goodness for her friend, the switchboard girl. She always knew what to say. "It's nice to see new people around here. Are you enjoying the party?"

He lifted one hand and rubbed the back of his neck, but his gentle expression didn't falter as he adjusted to Linda's bold manner. Nice big hands, Grace noticed. She kind of wished they were still dancing.

"Yes. Very good."

"They're from 'east of here,'" Grace explained to her friend.

"Huh. Are you sailors?"

"Trapper," he said quickly.

"Oh, well then, I'm sure you'll find lots to talk about tonight. Loads of men like you around these parts. I'm glad you're having fun." She hooked her arm through Grace's. "Would you excuse us? We have to go see someone."

"Nice to meet you," Grace said over her shoulder, letting

Linda lead her away. She gave him her brightest smile. "Have a good night."

He bowed slightly in reply, and something about the movement gave her a little thrill. Not enough to tempt her to run back, but enough to keep the flush on her face as she crossed the room.

"Your escort sent me over," Linda muttered into her ear. She tugged her to the side of the room, but Grace was still watching her mysterious dance partner head back to his friends. He had a kind of swagger to his step, like Eugene did when he was particularly proud of something he'd done. Had dancing with her put that swagger into his step? She liked that thought.

"Grace?" Linda said, breaking through her reverie.

"Sorry. Wasn't listening. Um, my escort?" she replied. "Who?"

"Tommy." Linda pointed. "He's over there. Surrounded by girls, as usual."

Her cousin had become the centre of all the single women's attention now that the other, older Baker men were married or overseas. He didn't respond to it like they had, though. Tommy's smile was strained, his hands deep in his pockets, and Grace felt bad for him. Since his dad had died three winters ago, Tommy's favourite company was his own, and though he tried hard at these parties, she knew it was difficult for him.

"Poor fellow. Maybe I'll go help him out." She left her friend and crossed the room. "Hey, Tommy," she said.

One corner of Tommy's mouth curled up at the sight of her. "What's buzzin', cousin? You're looking like a pin-up girl."

"Sweet of you." She set a hand on his shoulder. "Come dance with me."

Tommy took her hand. "Say, who's the fellow you were dancing with? Never seen him before."

The group in the corner of the room was standing in a bunch, talking to each other. Her dance partner's back was to her now.

"Says he's a trapper. Not much of a talker."

"Hmm. Maybe his friends are."

Nerves skittered down her neck at the thought of approaching them. "Well, I'm not going to go over and find out."

"Maybe I will."

That made her laugh. "What? You're going to start up a conversation on purpose? What has gotten into you, my shy cousin?"

"I'm curious. You don't normally see a group of young guys like that—fighting age, I'd call them—showing up out of nowhere."

"You've been reading too many spy books. Have you read the latest by Helen MacInnes?"

"*Assignment in Brittany*? Sure. You?"

"No, can I borrow yours?"

"Anytime."

The party continued well into the night. Everyone danced, laughed, and ate until they all were fit to burst. Tommy never did go over to the group in the corner, but Grace couldn't help peeking over at the young man every once in a while. His eyes would meet hers and they both would smile shyly, then look away, but as the party continued they grew slightly bolder.

She lost sight of him and his friends when the organizing committee politely began to usher guests out the door. She figured he'd head back east right away, and she'd probably never see him again. She would have liked a few minutes more, a second dance perhaps, just to see if they could hold a real conversation away from all the noise.

"Come on, slowpoke," Tommy said, nudging her on his way past. "Grab your coat. I'm gonna get the sleigh ready."

With a sigh, she headed to the cloakroom. "That's mine over there," she told the young girl behind the counter. "The brown one with the tartan scarf. See?"

While she waited, Grace scanned the crowd one last time. A moment later, she felt a touch on her shoulder. Her heart gave a little leap when she saw the young man waiting behind her, holding out her coat.

"Oh! Thank you." She slipped her arms into the sleeves, then reached for her scarf. "I hope you had a good evening," she managed.

"Very good."

They were each waiting for the other to say something more, but Grace couldn't think of anything except, "Well, it was nice meeting you."

So much for a real conversation.

But as she stepped outside, he stayed with her. His friends stood apart from the crowd coming out of the dance hall, waiting for him, she assumed. The tips of their cigarettes blinked like orange fireflies in the dark.

Linda shuffled from one foot to the other at Grace's side, and Tommy joined them after he'd hitched up the sleigh.

"Ready when you are, cousin," he said.

"In a minute," Grace told him, stalling.

"Did you have fun?" Linda asked the stranger. "You looked like you did."

"You see me?"

Linda waved a hand as if it were nothing. "I see everything."

The corner of Tommy's mouth twitched, and he focused on the man in their midst. "So you're a trapper, huh? Catching many martens?"

"Sorry?"

"Martens. You know. Them and mink." Tommy crossed his arms. "Should be a lot of them around here. They like to hunt squirrels, and we sure have enough of those. The general store'll buy 'em up if you're looking for a place to sell."

He blinked at Tommy.

No one said anything for a moment, then Tommy asked, "So are you selling?"

"Tommy!" Grace snapped, embarrassed at the cross-examination. "Don't be rude."

"Sorry?" the man asked again.

"Looking for a place to sell the furs?"

"Uh, no. Thank you."

This was beyond uncomfortable, Grace thought. She pressed Linda's arm purposefully, and her friend caught her signal. She waved towards the group of men who were obviously trying to get the young man's attention.

"Looks like your friends want to go."

"They can wait," he said, watching Grace. "Want to walk?"

The invitation set Grace's heartbeat racing. "Well, I—"

Linda elbowed her hard, bringing her back to reality. No matter how attractive he was, no matter how much she was tempted, the plain truth was she'd just met him. She couldn't go marching around the frozen woods with a tall, handsome stranger.

"Um, I don't think so. We're going home now. Thanks again for the dance." She put her hand on her lapel. "And for my coat."

"Short walk?"

Tommy stepped in then. "She said no."

Grace was mortified. "I'm sorry. It's late. Maybe I'll see you around."

"Time to go," one of the friends called.

"Yes," he replied, stepping back. He tugged his black cap on and held up a hand in farewell. "Good night."

As they walked away, Tommy asked, "Where's their sleigh?"

"Don't know," Grace said. "Maybe farther up the road." She hoped she was right. If she was, the Bakers would pass them on the way.

"I don't know about him," Linda said quietly, her teeth chattering with the cold. "He was kind of pushy, and he didn't even tell you his name."

"I didn't tell him mine, either."

"Linda's right," Tommy said. "Something about him makes me suspicious."

Grace hoisted herself into the sleigh and burrowed into the back, next to her mother. "You're being ridiculous. Just because he doesn't live around here doesn't mean he's a bad person."

Her cousin shook his head. "It's not just that."

"What do you think, Maman?"

"He seems nice enough. Just . . . persistent."

Tommy climbed up front, then chirped to the horses. As the sleigh jingled along the road, Grace peeked out, hoping to catch another glimpse of her mysterious dance partner. Tommy's sleigh should have caught up to them by now.

But the men were nowhere in sight.

FOUR

Why, oh why hadn't she gotten his name? She could have kicked herself for letting him leave the hall without at least telling her that. She could still think about him, imagine that they'd gotten another dance, but it would have been easier, somehow, if she knew his name.

To everyone else, Grace waved off any teasing that hinted at her being whisked off her feet, but truthfully, she was flattered. Out of the whole room, he had wanted to dance with *her*. Not Linda, not any of the other girls, just her. She'd felt the belle of the ball in that moment, swept up in the magic of the night.

Realistically, she told herself, it was probably good that he was from away. He hadn't talked much, and she had no idea what she would say if she ever met him again.

The excitement of the dance was eclipsed by Harry's arrival the next day. Tommy went to pick him up at the railway station in Musquodoboit Harbour, and when he poked his head through the door Grace practically flew to him.

"Hey, Gracie!" He was laughing, his arms around her. "You're gonna choke me! Get off!"

"Never!" she replied. "I'm gonna hang on and they'll never be able to take you again."

He pried her off. "Happy Christmas, baby sister."

"Best present of all, big brother. I'm so glad you're here!"

The family crowded around, hugging and peppering him with questions and exclamations. He laughed at all the attention and answered what he could, but Grace could see the exhaustion in his eyes. She hoped he'd have time to rest.

"How will they ever manage without you?" Linda gushed, her dark red lips drawn into a pout.

Linda had conveniently dropped by the house, saying she wanted to talk to Grace about something or other, but Grace knew she had ulterior motives. Linda had had a mad crush on Harry for years, but he'd married Beth, his high school sweetheart. Then Beth—and the couple's only baby—had died in childbirth six years ago, just about breaking him. Harry had always been a shy sort, hiding his scars, keeping his damaged eye from view, and grief had made it all worse. Linda had kept a respectful distance, but she never let Harry forget she was available.

Today, Harry didn't seem to mind Linda's advances. "Well, I just don't know," he replied, deadpan. "How will the Canadian Merchant Navy stay afloat without their one-eyed sailor?"

Linda's pout deepened to feigned concern. "Without you there, the Germans will run amuck all over the place!"

"Linda, you know what you need?"

"What's that?"

"A dance."

That was perhaps the first time Grace had ever seen her friend speechless, and it made her laugh out loud. Harry held out a hand, then whirled a stunned but elated Linda around the living room, dancing to Glenn Miller's "A String of Pearls."

"What do you think?" her mother asked Grace, appearing at her side.

"They are adorable together. Harry never says anything, and Linda never stops talking."

⌒

Harry was to stay until just after Christmas, and during those few days he was home, the family settled into an almost familiar pattern. As Grace dusted the living room one afternoon, humming a Christmas song to herself, she dared to dream that things might someday return to what they were before. But Norman's portrait, so lovingly painted by their mother so many years ago, stared back at her from across the room.

"It will never be normal," she quietly reminded herself.

No sooner were the words out of her mouth than she heard a muffled boom in the distance. She rushed to the window, but nothing seemed out of the ordinary. The sky was blue, the snow undisturbed. Then she noticed a cloud of black smoke rising over the far inlet.

The telephone rang just as two RCAF planes roared by, shaking the windows. She leaped back, stunned. What on earth were *they* doing out here? She picked up the receiver, still watching their smooth flight over the water.

"Hello?"

"Grace!" It was Linda, and her voice sang with excitement. "Did you hear that? Did you hear the explosion?"

"I did! What's going on?!"

"You're not gonna believe it."

"Try me."

"There was a U-boat out there."

"*What?*"

"A German submarine! By Borgles Island."

"Oh, come on."

"It's true! The boys at the logging camp out by Debaie's Cove spotted it yesterday, and they called to report it."

"What? We have Nazis here, and you didn't think to tell me until now?"

"They told me I wasn't allowed to say a word. You know, 'loose lips sink ships' and all that."

It didn't make sense. "Linda, why would a U-boat go there? It's just a boring little island with nothing to it. Not even the stupid Nazis would want it."

"For spying!"

"Oh, for Pete's sake."

"Grace, I'm telling you. That noise you just heard? Well, that was our plane blowing up the sub!"

Ever since the start of the war people living along the shore had seen things in the distance: flares in the sky, planes, ships of all sizes, but this was something completely different. Debaie's Cove was only ten miles from Grace's home.

When Harry walked quietly into the room, she pointed out the window at the smoke. Covering the telephone mouthpiece, she whispered, "Did you see that?"

He leaned slightly to the side to get a better view, then turned away without a word. That was odd. She'd expected him to at least react.

"But what about the men inside the sub?" she asked her friend, still watching Harry. "They're all dead?"

Linda paused. "I wouldn't think you'd have a thought to spare for them, Grace. They're Nazis. They're killers, remember? Don't worry about them."

Linda was right, of course. What she *should* be worried about was that the Germans had been so close, and she should be glad they had been thwarted. Except . . . she couldn't help feeling sick at the thought of their sudden, violent deaths. Was this really what war was like? Did her brothers see this sort of thing all the time? Worse, was it possible that they might sometimes *cause* it? She looked at Harry, still apparently unconcerned by the event, and wondered how he could live that way. Yes, that bomb had killed a boatload of Nazis—Nazis who had no place slinking around near her home!—but still . . . death was death, no matter which side they fought for.

PART TWO

Rudi Weiss

FIVE

Rudi Weiss's cheek was stuck to the ice. Other than that, he didn't feel any pain. Either he was numb, or he'd been extremely lucky. Moving carefully, he peeled his face off the ice and cracked his eyelids open. When his vision cleared he saw a bulbous mass of dark smoke rising from the water and filling the sky, turning the day black with confusion.

U-69 was gone. One minute he and the others had been climbing from the submarine onto the ice, and in the next, two planes had appeared. There had been no time to escape before the first rattled off a killing round of bullets, and the second dove low to drop its lethal load. How the hell had the enemy spotted them? This was a tiny, unobtrusive cove with no inhabitants. They should have been invisible. That was the whole plan: surface on the edge of the island, disembark, then set up a bunker from which they could monitor the comings and goings of enemy ships. But something had gone terribly wrong.

He rested his cheek back on the ice and closed his eyes—only for a moment—hoping for clarity. He needed to think straight, and quickly. The headache that had started to pound in his temples was no help. Where were the other men? A mix of just over forty officers and seamen had lived aboard that craft, but the ice around Rudi was bare. He listened hard for voices, but the explosion had deafened him. Nothing came to him but a high-pitched whine, nothing moved save the smoke. And yet . . . it couldn't be possible that he was the only survivor.

Except he was alone.

He hadn't been the first man to exit the ship, he knew. That meant some must have reached the island. Had Kuefer, the radioman, been ahead of him? Yes . . . yes, he remembered seeing him, hunched across the ice under the weight of his pack. If he'd made it out safely, maybe he could contact someone, get help. What about the others? Had there been anyone ahead of Kuefer? Otto had been behind him in the corridor, he recalled, chattering about family members who lived in Nova Scotia. Rudi had heard it all before, so he'd put Otto's voice in the background. If only he could ignore the predictably foul words coming from Franz, one of the senior officers.

"My brother said girls in Canada will go with anyone," Franz had said. "Easy pickings. Like the ones at that pathetic little dance. Rudi took the easy route, going to that brazen girl with the red lips. Like Rita Hayworth. She would've—"

"Shut up," one of the others cut him off, saving Rudi the trouble. "Let's just get out of here."

"Rudi?" Otto said, blinking through spectacles, his hands full of provisions. "Would you mind? I left my bag over there."

"Go ahead. I'll get your things."

He'd slung his bag and Otto's over his shoulder, then followed the others. More men were behind him, eager to get onto land at last, but . . . where were they now?

It came to him that the fire from the explosion would be visible for miles; locals would flock to see what was going on, and they certainly would not miss a lone U-boat sailor lying on the ice. He chanced a look around and realized he had landed surprisingly far from the sunken ship, close to the bush line of another island, halfway between Borgles Island and the mainland. A cluster of large granite boulders formed a kind of gateway to the shore, and beyond them waited a quiet forest, dense with winter trees. He hoped it was as uninhabited as it appeared. If he could just get—

Movement caught his eye: people emerging from an area up the shore. Behind them he noted a small cluster of roof-lines. How many lived here? How many would come to see the destruction? Did he have enough time to escape detection? Fighting dizziness, he started to rise, then collapsed again as pain shot through his side. His shoulder, he recognized, was dislocated again. Yet another reason to get moving right away. He gritted his teeth and got to his feet, then staggered a few steps to regain his balance before sprinting towards the rocks until his lungs burned.

The swish of his own breathing began to push through the whine in his ears as he ran, but his shoulder shoved a blade through him with every step, so he hugged that arm to his chest to stabilize it. Nearly there, and stars danced in his vision. He could barely see through his streaming eyes anyway. Would he make it? Could he—

One foot slipped from under him and he crashed onto his side, the momentum sweeping him all the way to the bank. Had he cried out? He didn't know, the pain was so bad. He watched the approaching crowd, listened hard, but no one was yelling or pointing in his direction—a stroke of luck.

His shoulder was seizing up, screaming for attention, and though he felt sick at the prospect, he knew what he had to do; he'd done it before. Biting down on the agony, he struggled back onto his feet and sought out the largest of the boulders. He leaned over and curled his fingers into a sharp crevice on the bottom of the granite, its surface slick with dormant li-chen. Gripping the rock hard, he twisted his body to the side, stretching the spasmed muscle to the limit, urging the joint back into place. The effort bathed him in clammy sweat, but he kept pulling and somehow managed not to scream. The eventual *pop!* brought instant relief. With his sore arm pressed against his body he scuttled farther up the bank, seeking shelter in the thick brush.

The instinct was to run, to leave this islet behind and lose himself in the relative safety of the mainland. He needed to get as far as he could from this place—except the small crowd of curious locals continued to advance towards the shattered ice between the sub's last position and the island, and the late-afternoon sunshine would illuminate anyone fleeing the scene. From his refuge behind the trees he counted twenty or so people in the group, suggesting this area was rather remote, but they could still catch him. He was cornered. He couldn't go back, couldn't go forward. Not yet, anyway.

He still saw no sign of any of his crewmates at the site of the disaster. If anyone from the boat was alive, he would assume Rudi was dead. He realized that for now, he might as well have been.

For more than an hour Rudi sat on the island, wondering what to do. The smoke still burned his eyes, but at least his shoulder was getting some rest. Most important, his heartbeat had slowed so he could think more clearly. Across the ice the fire was done, smothered along with the ship, and dusk had swallowed the smoke. And somewhere in the liquid cavity beneath rested the remains of the men he had known, the friends with whom he had laughed mere hours before. The hollow ache in Rudi's bruised chest constricted with guilt. How could he just leave them?

How could he not?

As afternoon dwindled so did the crowd, returning to their

homes in twos and threes. Rudi watched them go as the sun moved farther west, and wondered at his next step. The cold pressed against his coat and threatened to invade, sending a shudder through him. He couldn't stay here any longer or he risked freezing to death. It was time he found a place to dig in for the night, and it would have to be far from this useless little island. Vowing silently to return and search for his crewmates when it was safer, he stepped back onto the ice, then ran for the banks of the mainland.

A recent thaw followed by a hard freeze had turned the surface of the snow solid, so his boot prints through the trees were minimal, but being tracked was just one of his worries. He had nothing with him, no idea where he was going. The bitter night would come in fast, so he would have to find his way even faster. Once he was farther inland the crusty snow softened, and he discovered a well-used game trail. He checked behind him once more. The hole left by the explosion was in the distance now, and in the semidarkness Rudi's immediate fear of discovery eased. Walking more easily, he followed the path to an opening in the trees, paused at the edge of a snow-covered field, and took in his surroundings.

For most of his life, Rudi had lived in the city. He had gone to the best school, and his mother had ensured that his excellent education was bolstered by a deep immersion into culture. His uniform was always pressed and spotless, his manners just as impeccable, his discipline unquestioned. He could recite most of Wagner's libretti as easily as he could calculate mathematical equations or answer questions of politics. But if anyone had asked, he would have said that his favourite memories were of those rare times when his father had taken him away for a few days in both summer and winter, taught him to trap and hunt, to understand a whole different way of living.

Young Rudi had watched in awe as his father lit fires, trapped small animals, then skinned them without any apparent effort. He'd been nervous but eager—maybe seven or eight years old—when his father handed him his first knife, shown him how to fend for himself.

"Not like that, Rudi. Cradle the handle in your fingers like I am doing, you see? Put your thumb against the piece between handle and blade. That's the quillon. That way you have more strength behind you if you are cutting upwards. Now show me how you do it."

He missed his father with a physical ache. That knife had stayed with Rudi from that day until just a few hours earlier, when the world had exploded around him. Now it would rust at the bottom of the Atlantic.

"You must check your traps often, Rudi," his father had said, showing him how to walk a trapline. "That last rabbit was frozen. We were fortunate it had not been eaten already."

From twenty feet away he could see his next snare had been a success and dashed towards it. "Look, Father! I set that one!"

"You did, son. You're getting better all the time."

He stared down at the small corpse. "Do they suffer, Father?"

"Sometimes." His father swung his hands out to the side. "See how the snow here is messy? Looks like he struggled." With one finger he lifted the head, inspected the neck, then untangled the creature from the snare. "It panics, you see. Tries to get free, but it cannot. Its attempt to escape the snare hurts it the most in the end."

Young Rudi blinked hard. He wanted to be brave and strong and please his father, and he felt weak for pitying the creature. "Your sack looks heavy, Father," he said, burying his shame. "Can I carry this one?"

"You're right, mine is full. Put this rabbit in your pack instead, and you can carry any others we find."

With every catch it became easier to steel himself against the sight of dead animals. The rabbits became no more than items to place in the pack.

What would his father think if he knew those lessons would soon be tested in the Canadian wilderness? That his son would be forced to depend on them to survive? He'd certainly be relieved that Rudi was still alive, but what would he say of the circumstances? Of Rudi abandoning his sinking ship and crew then fleeing the scene?

But Rudi could not think that way. He had no time to wonder about such things. He had to get somewhere warm soon or he would die.

Once the sun was completely gone, there was less darkness than he'd feared. The snow reflected the rising moon, cloaking everything in a dull grey light. Rudi scanned the trees in the distance, needing some kind of structure to use as shelter, and after a while he spotted a broken-down log cabin that hadn't lodged anyone in a very long time. It looked barely capable of holding up for even one more night, but the age-blackened walls cut the chill, and Rudi hunkered down in one corner, piling spruce boughs on top of himself to serve as a blanket. He thought he would never fall asleep, then he worried he might never wake up, but adrenaline, pain, and exhaustion pulled him down, down, down, until he sank like his ship under the ice. He couldn't have surfaced even if he'd wanted to.

He awoke before the sunrise, weak with hunger. Every bruised muscle seemed frozen in place; when he stood, they shook uncontrollably from the cold. He shuffled toward the doorway and braced himself against its rotting frame, using his hand to shade his eyes against the sparkling snow. The snow, the trees, the sky . . . it all looked the same, and the unfamiliar landscape clearly went on this way for a long while. He needed to organize his thoughts, visualize a plan, but his attempts to think clearly were washed aside by a wave of panic. Where was he? What could he do?

His father's words came back to him. *If you are lost, find water. That is where the food will eventually go.*

He would not disappoint his father. Taking a wobbly step into the snow, he followed his own footprints back to the game trail, then considered the path. In the trampled snow he saw the split hoofprints of deer, and for the first time he felt a vague hope. If he followed them, he would most likely find water, and if there was water there would be game. With that, however, came the risk that he could also run into local hunters. He would have to proceed with caution.

You must always be careful, son. You might assume you are the hunter, but you can easily become the prey.

But if the hunters weren't around, there was a possibility he might find an unoccupied camp. Following the trail until it split, Rudi took the wider option until that path opened up as well. The forest was dense with spruce, pine, fir, and leafless maples, and everything was complicated with snow, but he felt confident that the broader the trail, the better chance he had of finding some sort of shelter.

Hours later he came upon a flat white meadow dotted with deer tracks, and farther on he discovered a frozen lake, its curving, tree-lined coast extending into the horizon. Optimism stirred in his chest; if he was right, a camp might be nearby. Using the shore as a home base, he began walking in one direction, then retracing his steps to the water, determined not to get lost. By his third attempt, the tips of his fingers were numb from the biting cold, and he was hungry to the point of dizziness. Worst of all, he was dangerously tempted to give in to his exhaustion. Darkness was closing in. He could only hope he wasn't wasting precious time with his search.

Then, as if in a dream, he saw it: a small, snow-covered shack mostly hidden in the trees. He rubbed his eyes to convince himself it was not a mirage, and when he dropped his hands the sturdy little place was still there, huddled in the dark, the snow around it undisturbed.

Rudi stumbled across the final few yards, checking the entire way for footprints and finding none. His frozen fingers fumbled with the latch until the door swung open, and he stepped through. Holding his breath, he braced himself for an attack, afraid to trust his good fortune. But he was alone, safe.

The one-room cabin was pitch-black inside, and the air within smelled as if no one had been there for a while. When his eyes adjusted to the lack of light, he could see the camp was dry and clean. A couple of bunk beds had been built against two walls, and grey wool blankets lay neatly folded at the foot of each. In the middle of the building stood a table, a couple of rickety chairs, pots and dishes, and—*Gott sei Dank!*—a wood stove with a box of matches set conveniently on top. Firewood was neatly stacked against the wall, accompanied by an axe.

He removed his gloves and knelt by the stove, setting the kindling clumsily with numb fingers. The dry birch caught quickly, as did its sap, and the resultant crackling warmed Rudi's spirit. At first he couldn't move, hypnotized by the promise of warmth, then his stomach cramped, reminding him he had things to do. He filled the pot on the stove with snow, and by the time it melted, the cabin's dull interior flickered gold. The warmth came straight from heaven.

In the belly of the U-boat, the men were always slick with sweat, stripped to undershirts and short pants, craving cool air.

The entire craft stank of body odour, months-old stored food, and diesel—among other things—and the smell only got worse under the constant, heavy blanket of heat. The difference between that life and this one was shocking; Rudi hadn't been prepared for this kind of cold. Even though he'd grown up with winters such as this, it took a long time before the fire could slow the vibrations running through him.

As his skin warmed, something trickled down the side of his face, and when he touched his brow, his fingers came away bloody. A long cut over his right eye still seeped blood, but after he'd cleaned his face with snow he determined the wound wasn't serious. He was more concerned about his shoulder. The joint was back in place now, but the muscles around it were so tender he held his breath as he slid his arm from his sleeve to inspect it. A furious red-black bruise spread across his swollen shoulder. There was nothing he could do to soothe it, and it would take days before his shoulder and arm would function at normal strength. But other than that, he was remarkably sound.

He sat on the bunk and surveyed the cabin, appreciating how fortunate he'd been in finding this place. After the last day of running blindly, he felt it almost unreal to be in a place like this: warm, dry, and safe—at least for now. The camp was a veritable treasure trove as far as provisions: traps of various sizes hung from one wall, and a couple of skinning knives wrapped in a burlap bag lay on a high shelf. Food wouldn't even be much of an issue, because beside those tools stood large tins containing staples: flour, oats, salt and pepper, even sugar. He could not have asked for better. When he'd first lit the fire he'd been concerned someone might spot the smoke rising from the chimney, but for now it was too dark for anyone to see. And really, he had no choice—he could either take a chance with the smoke or risk freezing to death.

As long as no one came along, he would be fine, and judging by the amount of dust in the place, he had nothing to worry about.

Rudi craved sleep, but his body needed food first. He boiled a cup of oats on the stove, then sprinkled some sugar on top. The first spoonful eased the furious cramps in his stomach. In the morning he would set a trap or two.

When the bowl was empty, he lay back on the bunk and closed his eyes, drifting. He let his thoughts go, followed them as they reached out to the men with whom he'd been living just a day before. Their faces already threatened to fade from his memory, but Rudi couldn't let them; they were all he had left. In his mind, he called each man's name, and their faces appeared. Grief and guilt swelled in his throat, then gave way to an unfamiliar flood of apprehension. Throughout his life he'd been part of a larger unit, had depended on others and proudly shouldered their reliance on him. But his world was different now. No one would come to Rudi's rescue out here.

He might be the only one who had survived, but now he was caught. Like the rabbits he had hunted so many years before.

It panics, you see, his father had said. *Its attempt to escape the snare hurts it the most in the end.*

Calm. He needed calm. *I am safe,* he reminded himself. *I am warm and fed. I am alive.*

The crackle of the fire, the silence of the night, comforted him. When he couldn't hold sleep off any longer he said a prayer, thanking God for protecting him, begging for peace for his lost comrades. And before his final *Amen,* he added one more plea.

Please, God, help me get home.

SIX

Rudi awoke after the sun had risen and was greeted by a silent stream of dust motes dancing in light—a far cry from the usual clanging of metal, foul breath, and clammy air. Every muscle rebelled when he tried to sit up, but lying motionless wasn't an option. With a groan he staggered towards the cooled ashes from the night before, hugging his injured shoulder against his chest. He relit the fire, then set a pot of melting snow on the still-warm stove, wishing fiercely for a cup of coffee. The closest he was going to get was hot water. Clear tea, he thought ruefully.

But man could not live on hot water and oatmeal alone. Grabbing a roll of snare wire from the wall, Rudi stepped outside and squinted against the blinding reflection of sun on snow, letting the door creak gently shut behind him. It was the lone sound in the forest. Naked winter branches criss-crossed over his head, the only barrier between him and the vast blue heavens, and the sight took his breath away. For so long his sky had been a curved metal ceiling, its clouds the endless paths of pipes and wires and knobs. At times, confined for so long beneath the surface, one could forget anything existed beyond the steel. Now all that was gone, and his soul rejoiced. He inhaled, inviting the cool, clean air to suffuse every starved cell in his body.

He had imagined Canada would be like this: an untamed,

sparsely inhabited, desolate beauty. From the submarine he'd not been able to witness the mountains as they passed Cape Breton, but he knew they were there from the map. Now that he actually stood here, the snow underfoot, the sleeping trees, the quiet wilderness—all of it was balm for his soul. Almost as if he were back home. At that, guilt seeped back into his thoughts. As a highly trained U-boat officer, he was a valuable cog in the German war machine. He should not be here, so far from his duty.

They'd had their first contact in these waters just three months ago, in October, while Rudi had been overseeing the radio room crew. The encounter was burned permanently into his memory, and its shadows still flitted through his nightmares. For weeks they had been hunting for convoys on the Gulf of St. Lawrence, and nothing had come their way. But on that day, at nearly four o'clock in the morning, Kuefer leaned in, concentrating, his hand held up for quiet. He froze like he always did when he thought he heard an anomaly running through the tiny, silent sounds of the sea, and the crew members held their breath in anticipation. Pressing his earphones firmly against his head with one hand, the radioman started moving the other with deliberation, turning the wheel on his hydrophone.

"Propellers," he whispered to Rudi. He listened again. "Yes. Small convoy. Seven ships. Ten knots. Fifteen hundred metres off port side. About sixty kilometres off Newfoundland, sir."

"So close," Rudi muttered. "A gift."

"Periscope depth," Kapitänleutnant Gräf said calmly, and the order was called down the voice tube to engineering. When they stopped the ascent, Gräf flipped his cap around, putting its peak behind him, and stared into the scope. He rotated the pipe all the way around to seek out possible enemy ships, then backed away, satisfied.

"It is not the grain convoy we wanted. Doesn't appear to be heading to Montreal, either. But it is good enough." He righted his cap and addressed Rudi, keeping his voice low. "Battle stations!"

The U-boat's tomblike atmosphere became an organized frenzy of activity—except no one spoke, no one made any sound at all; it was imperative they maintain silence so the target wouldn't pick up any noise that could give them away. Every man knew where he had to be; they emerged soundlessly from bunks, the toilet, or dinner, pulling on pants or life jackets as they ran.

"Surface," Gräf ordered.

Once they were on deck, Rudi and the other watch operators had a 90-degree zone to monitor. They pressed binoculars to their eyes, breaking contact with the view only when the sea washed over them like a giant, fluid hammer. Freed of the restraining water pressure, the U-boat coasted swiftly past the convoy, giving the crew better visual access and taking them out of range of the navy escort ships' sonar equipment. Here, above the surface, they could be easily spotted by a keen eye, but they hoped the darkness of night would hide them.

The captain lowered his binoculars and scowled. "Where are all the escorts?"

Rudi scanned the convoy, then pointed. "There, sir. One off the port side, thirty degrees. Minesweeper, Bangor class."

"Right. What is the target? I can't make out her lines."

Rudi agreed. "Too much diesel smoke to tell exactly."

"I think . . ." Gräf took a deep breath. "I see a sixty-five-hundred-tonne passenger freighter and a two-stack destroyer. Close in to four hundred metres. Prepare torpedo bays one and three."

When all was ready, Gräf issued the command. "Loose torpedo one!"

It was always a thrill, watching the phantom shape break from the ship and speed towards the target. When the missile was out of sight, Rudi's binoculars scanned ahead, following the path it would lead, and his heartbeat soared. Their patience was about to pay off. This was what they were here to do: win the war for Germany by ridding the Atlantic of enemy ships and by blocking essential trade routes.

The torpedo blasted into the side of the ship like a giant fist. Direct hit. The night flared orange, outlining the black profile of the vessel they'd just destroyed—and Rudi's stomach filled with ice.

"Sir, that ship—"

"I see, Lieutenant Weiss, I see."

The officers stared in horror; they were close enough now to see the fallout in the light of the fire. The target was about half as large as they'd estimated. Between the flames, distant profiles of passengers ran to lifeboats, even leaped into the frozen depths when they saw no other way out, and their screams were audible over the fire's roar. Another explosion cut through the noise, and the distinctly shrill cry of a panicked child calling its mother travelled over the water.

This was no merchant ship. The ship they had just sentenced to a watery grave was a small passenger ferry.

"Herr Kapitän! Destroyer!"

"*Tauchen! Tauchen!*" the captain roared as the four men dropped down the tower, water splashing to the floor with them. "Dive! Position the ship under the target!"

The U-boat plunged deep below the surface, safely out of reach of the depth charges booming overhead, and moved rapidly from the scene. Minutes later, they were invisible again and back on the prowl. Later, in his report about this attack, the captain would say the target hadn't been the ship they'd thought it was, but it was still an enemy ship. The German crew had done their job and lived to see another day.

Why, then, had no one cheered? Why was Rudi still haunted by that night's conquest?

Now was not the time to think of that. He must concentrate on the here and now, not the past. Crouching in the snow, he pushed the ghosts away and surveyed the small tracks on its surface. There was plenty of small game here; he would not starve. After brushing the area clear, he set a snare and moved on.

The forest around him was silent, and without a breeze not even the shadows moved. It was ethereal in its stillness; still, Rudi was uneasy. There was an eeriness to the calm, a reminder that he was completely alone in an unfamiliar world, and it made him feel exposed like never before.

Rudi knew fear. He knew the deep, bone-wrenching terror that came from being inside a submarine that *almost* didn't dive quickly enough or *barely* escaped a minefield. When the only barrier between him and the bottomless void of the sea had shuddered, blasting freezing seawater through weakened metal seams, he hadn't been able to breathe. He and the others had been like mice trapped in a giant metal fist, and the fingers were closing, squeezing the life from them. He had heard grown men weep and pray with everything they had, certain they were about to die. He had even been one of them. He knew that kind of fear, and he'd learned to live with it, because it was his duty to fight for his country.

But what he felt now was different, and in a way this was the most frightened he'd ever been. Rudi was utterly alone. His parents were most likely dead, his comrades as well. There was no one he could contact for help. He was lost and alone in the Canadian wilderness in the dead of winter—and here, he was the enemy. The silence which had delighted him at first now threatened to suffocate him. How long could he survive out here on his own?

Grace

SEVEN

For a while the sunken U-boat was all anyone could talk about, but the sudden, decisive arrival of winter meant life quickly got back to normal. After one particularly savage storm that buried the roads in snow, Mrs. Gardner said she wasn't sure it was worth the effort to open the store, but it was a Wednesday, two weeks before Christmas, and people had errands to run. Grace gave Tommy fifty cents, and he shoveled the road outside the store for her.

Days like this were Grace's favourites. Sure, it was freezing outside, but icicles hung like tinsel from every branch, putting to shame the silver foil namesakes people draped over their Christmas trees. The sky beyond the window was a sea of joyous blue, and the aroma of burning maple rising from the wood stove made her feel warm from the outside in. Grace turned on the radio, treating herself to music while she swept dust from the corners. The bell over the door jingled and a customer walked in.

"Good morning, Mrs. MacDonald," she said.

Her customer rubbed her mitts together, shuddering with cold, then tugged off her hat and tucked it under one arm. "Not a day for the meek."

"No indeed. I'm glad you could come keep me company."

"I've come to see if my Eaton's order arrived. I ordered one of those Little Angel dolls for my granddaughter, and I'm so afraid it won't be here in time for Christmas."

"Oh yes. It just came in yesterday." Grace retrieved the parcel from the back room. "She is going to love this. Is there anything else you need today?"

"Why yes, please. I'd like some cranberries, if you have them. And some of that V8 juice. Just put it on my account, if you would be so kind."

Grace packaged up the goods and recorded them in the daybook. She'd changed the accounting columns, made them easier to read, and she was pleased with the result. Even Mrs. Gardner had agreed it was better than her husband's ancient system. That reminded Grace that she had meant to stop over at the widow's house. Mrs. Gardner hadn't come out to the store in a week or so, which was unusual. Grace wanted to make sure she had everything she needed.

"Have a wonderful Christmas," she called as Mrs. MacDonald set out on her way.

The next person held the door open as Mrs. MacDonald left, absently stomping his boots inside the doorway. Grace tried not to scowl, but she knew who would be wiping up that mess after he was gone.

The day flew by with customers and conversation, but as the light faded, fewer shoppers came to call. Nelson Eddy's band played a soothing, sad "Silent Night" on the radio, and Grace sang along. She was up the ladder counting and sorting inventory when the bell over the door tinkled a welcome for the first time in a half hour or so. She grabbed the sides of the ladder with both hands and climbed back down.

A man in a heavy black coat had entered, winter cap pulled low over his ears, scarf over his mouth. She tried not to stare, but she was curious. Grace knew everyone around here, but she didn't recognize this man.

"Good afternoon," she said.

"Good day," he replied, not looking at her. She noticed he made no move to take off his hat and scarf, as most customers did.

"Cold out there, isn't it?"

He said nothing, only gave a brief nod and turned away, facing the shelves.

"Please let me know if you can't find what you are looking for."

His hands were stuffed in the pockets of his bulky coat. He seemed to be about her father's height, but that's all she could see. He went directly to the shelves, picked out his own groceries, then set two large cans of tomatoes and a sack of potatoes on the counter.

"Is that everything?"

"Tea?"

She was caught for an instant by the crystal blue of his eyes, bright over dark half moons of exhaustion. Most of his face was covered by his scarf, but the skin she could see was windburned a chalky burgundy. A small cut was healing over his right eye. Maybe it was her imagination, but she thought he seemed familiar.

"Just tea, tomatoes, onions, and potatoes?" she asked cheerily, fetching his request.

"Tea, tomatoes, onions, and potatoes. *Ja.*" He picked up a newspaper. "And a paper. Oh, and a book."

He held up a comic he'd picked off the display, and now she could tell he was purposefully keeping his eyes averted. It was strange behaviour for anyone around here, to be sure. Of course that wasn't the only strange thing about him. She couldn't quite put her finger on it, but something about the way he talked was odd. He didn't say much, but what he did say sounded unusually stiff. Or was it an accent of some kind? Whoever he was, she figured he was most likely heading right back out into the cold, lonely woods again, and from the haggard look on his face she thought he could use some kindness, so she wrapped up a bit of chocolate and slipped it into his sack as well.

The scarf fell away. "Thank you," he said, appearing surprised by the gift.

She could hardly believe her eyes. "It's you!" Heat surged into her cheeks. "From the dance, right? Do you remember me?"

"Of . . . of course. Most beautiful girl there."

They stared at each other while Grace desperately searched for something to say. She instantly recalled how he had been great at compliments but lousy at conversation.

"So . . . so you've been trapping?"

He held up a bag. "You buy them?"

She peered in and identified rabbit pelts. "How many?"

He held up five fingers.

"Sure we do."

Actually, the store hadn't taken a lot of furs lately, but she could always sell them to Colin Bonn, the trader, when he passed by next time. This fellow probably wouldn't have any idea who Mr. Bonn was, so it was easier for everyone this way. She flipped through the daybook, coming to the page she'd created for any new customers who might just be passing through, and recorded the five pelts in the credit column. Then she considered all his items, realizing there wasn't quite enough to cover his purchases. If she knew him, she could let him pay later, but it would be irresponsible to offer credit to a stranger.

"I'm sorry. It's not quite enough." She held up the tea, gestured back towards the shelf.

He shrugged, then strode swiftly to the door, his groceries clutched in one hand.

"Nice to see you! Thanks for—"

Before she could wish him a good night, he was opening the door, heading into the cold. She watched through the window, but the wind whipped up snow in his wake and closed around him like the train of a cape.

As soon as he had disappeared, she picked up the telephone. "Linda? You won't believe who was just here! You remember the other night . . ."

Rudi

EIGHT

Rudi tucked the bag of provisions under one arm and practically ran down the road towards the trail, jaw clenched. He'd known he'd have to speak with someone at the store, but *her*? Did it have to be her? What was she thinking now? She must have heard his accent, though he'd done everything he could not to speak. Would she tell anyone that she'd seen him?

He never should have danced with her. He should have stayed in the background with the others and been satisfied with admiring her from across the room. All he'd wanted was some innocent fun, a little humanity for a change. Dancing with her had been impulsive, and that slip could ruin him. What would these people do if they realized they had a Nazi living right here in their woods? He knew nothing about Canadian laws. Did they execute their enemies here?

But he was here now. There was nothing he could do about that, and worrying about what might happen only made everything worse. Just in case, he turned around to check that no one was following, but he was alone. He'd lived in the camp a week already, and though it was lonely, it was going all right. He was warm, he was fed, and he was off everyone's radar— except hers. If nothing went wrong, he imagined he could keep this up for the rest of the winter, but trappers—*Canadian* trappers—would probably be out this way by spring. By the time the snow melted, Rudi planned to be somewhere else, though he had no idea where that might be.

Despite the danger, he had to admit it had been nice to see her face again. He hadn't been exaggerating at the dance; she was stunning. Like the princess in the German fairy tale "Snow White," with her long black hair and ruby lips. And that smile—it was contagious. If only he'd met her at another time, in another place.

He peered back once again, then stepped onto the trail to the camp and disappeared into the shaggy spruce. Maybe he was still okay. Maybe he would survive this somehow. Maybe she wouldn't tell.

As he walked, a familiar melody came to mind. He'd heard it on the radio in the store.

Stille Nacht, Heil'ge Nacht,
Alles schläft; einsam wacht . . .

So strange, to hear the carol in a language other than his native tongue. He remembered other words for the melody as well: the new German lyrics his mother had taught him five years earlier.

"For your protection," she had explained. "We must all learn the new way."

Holy infant, so tender and mild. Sleep in heavenly peace, sleep in heavenly peace

had quietly been changed to

Only the Chancellor steadfast in fight watches o'er Germany by day and by night,

and the part about

Round yon Virgin, Mother and Child

was now

Adolf Hitler is Germany's wealth.

Over time he'd noticed how everything people said or did made it seem as if the coming of Jesus was being replaced by the coming of Hitler. Especially at Christmas. As a boy he'd witnessed the transformation of Christmas first-hand. His mother had—quite rightly—followed all the instructions printed on the twenty-page Nazi leaflet, replacing the star at the top of the tree with a swastika ornament, baking cookies in the shape of swastikas or sun wheels, ensuring the correct number of baubles was hung from the tree branches. The family learned through Nazi teachings that the true reason for celebration was not the birth of a Jewish baby, but the arrival of the winter solstice. The true Christmas traditions, they were told, stemmed from the much older, more important pagan rituals, and when his mother lit the candles on the tree she was actually summoning light for longer days.

Der Führer was the future; the world would adjust. It was an exciting time, an end to obsolete concepts which could only hold his country back, and Rudi had been proud to be a part of that change, a valued member of the German military machine.

A branch overhead twitched and snow showered over him, bringing him back to the present. Another storm was rolling in; he needed to get to the camp before dark. This was no place to be stranded. Along the way he checked a couple of the traps he'd set out that morning and came up with two more rabbits, not yet frozen. As he entered the chilly cabin, he decided to cook them up in a pot of *Hasenpfeffer* using some of the tomatoes he'd just bought and a bit of flour from the cupboard. A poor man's feast, but he wasn't much of a cook. Never had been. His mother and sisters had always taken care of the kitchen. What he wouldn't do for a bite of *Apfelstrudel*. There'd been delicious sweets at the dance the other night. Which one had Snow White made?

As he stirred his supper, he thought of her standing behind the counter, white apron tied over her plain brown dress, kerchief covering most of her hair. It didn't seem to matter how she dressed. Once he'd recognized her, he had trouble taking his eyes off her—and he hadn't missed the pink of her cheeks when she'd recognized him, either. He liked to believe that meant she found him attractive as well—though it could have just been surprise. How might she react if he went back to see her again sometime? Of course he couldn't do that until he felt safe enough, but he would need more staples in time.

Thinking back on their brief conversation at the store, he was disappointed in the part he'd played. If he knew more of her language he could have said something more intelligent than yes or no, but he didn't. As usual, his mother had been right. Rudi had always been more interested in his father's lessons than hers.

"You are a smart boy," his mother had insisted. "When you concentrate you have a very nice accent. Almost like an English person. Come on, Rudi. You can learn this. It will be good for you as you get older."

"The school doesn't see the value in teaching any other languages, Mother, so why must I learn? Besides, I have tried."

"Not very hard."

"I think Father wants to see me."

"One more hour. Then you can go."

After that hour he would fly from the kitchen and seek out his father, who never stayed in the room when the lessons happened. Rudi got a sense that he disagreed with his son learning English, but when Rudi asked him to interfere, his father raised an eyebrow.

"You will respect your mother, Rudi. I am disappointed to hear you questioning her."

"But the teachers say—"

"To respect your parents. Enough. I will hear no more of this."

Rudi's sisters were better at learning English. They were smart and attentive and could string sentences together almost from the beginning. Rudi was smart too, but he would rather be with the men, learning to shoot and fight and march.

"Pay attention," his mother constantly said.

With a sigh, he'd put his forehead in his hands, plunge his fingers into his thick blond hair, and stare at the page. She'd point at a sentence in an English book while his sisters held their breath in anticipation. They seemed to get great joy out of his mistakes.

"What does it mean, Rudi?"

"It makes no sense."

"It does, and it is not difficult. Tell me what it says."

"The boy . . ."

"Yes, yes. Good pronunciation with the 'th.' Go on. What about the boy?" his mother pressed.

He muttered something that made no sense at all, and his sisters burst out laughing.

"You're so stupid!" Helga shouted.

"You're not even close!" Marta howled, doubled over.

More often than not, he stormed out after that, frustrated and humiliated, but his mother refused to end the lessons. Instead, she changed tactics. Since she knew what he liked to read in his native language, she went in search of similar material printed in English: comic books. She started with *Terry and the Pirates*, a comic book full of adventure and drawings, and the challenge proved to be irresistible even to Rudi. Ever since then, his English vocabulary had come from comics and newspapers.

But tonight, as he flipped open the comic he'd bought at the store, sleep pulled at him like tar. Not even the pirates would have been able to keep him awake. He set the comic on the floor and closed his eyes, hoping to bring back images of earlier Christmases, but that was not what he saw. Instead he fell asleep with his mind on a girl with ebony hair and ruby lips, dressed in a red polka-dot dress.

Grace

NINE

A week or so before Christmas the quiet trapper from the woods returned, bundled head to toe against the cold. As before, he'd waited until dusk closed over the village, then swept like a shadow into the store.

She was a little bit surprised at how happy she was to see him. "Good evening," she said, trying to still the nerves dancing in her chest. "It's nice to see you again."

He managed a shy smile, but he looked exhausted. The bruises she'd seen under his eyes before seemed even darker.

"Good evening," he echoed, walking towards the shelves of canned goods.

Curiosity was not a ladylike quality—her mother always said that—but she couldn't help herself. "I imagine it gets lonely. Out there in the woods, I mean. It must get pretty quiet."

His hands stilled for a breath. "Yes, quiet." He got back to his browsing. "Knife?"

"Sure. We have a good selection on the wall there."

He went to where she was pointing, then took one in his hand, testing its weight. "Apples?"

"Yes, over there." Barrels of cabbages, beets, potatoes, and well-polished apples stood in the corner. "I keep them away from the stove so they stay fresh. A pound?"

"Please."

Grace had had a chill earlier, so she'd added an extra log to the stove and now the store was quite warm. Her guest slipped off his gloves and cap, tucked them under one arm, then scrubbed his blond hair. It was such a brilliant shade of gold, even more golden than she remembered from the dance. She took the opportunity to admire him as he studied the top shelves, turning his head so slowly it looked as if he were reading every label. In fact, he stared at them hard enough that she began to wonder if he could actually read. What if his poor conversational skills had something to do with not knowing English? That idea intrigued her even more. It was rare for any strangers to come out this way, but a young, foreign—and handsome—man appearing in their quiet village was more than a little intriguing. No wonder Tommy had been suspicious.

He caught her watching, and her cheeks burned.

"I'm so sorry," she sputtered, collecting the apples. "It's just . . . I didn't mean to stare, but . . ." He was watching her intently, not even blinking. She lifted her chin. "Now *you're* staring at *me*."

"Sorry." He scratched the side of his short beard, not looking the slightest bit sorry.

"What?"

"Nothing." Appearing pleased with himself, he picked up a new comic and walked towards the counter. "I have more rabbit today, squirrel, two of these . . ."

She peered in. "Two martens, you mean? Okay. That will more than pay for all this." She checked the daybook, then opened the cash register and counted out some coins. "Let me give you some actual money. I imagine you could use some of that."

His confident, almost smug expression didn't fade as he reached into his sack and held his cupped hands towards her.

"I make for you."

There it was again, that strange way he had of speaking. Like English wasn't his first language. If she could only keep him talking, maybe she could figure out the accent.

"You made me something? Why?"

"Thank you for *Schokolade*."

"Shocko . . . Oh! The chocolate! You're very welcome."

"And is Christmas."

The small wooden shape fit perfectly into her palm. It was a moment before she recognized his version of a ladybug, obviously created with a great deal of care. The chunk of wood had been carefully whittled and shaped, and since he'd had no paint he had pared small dips into the creature's round back, suggesting spots.

"It's beautiful," she said, and it was. Not just the workmanship, but the thought that had gone into it. He'd been thinking of her, out there in the woods.

"You also are beautiful," he replied.

Once again blood surged into her cheeks, and she stumbled to think of an intelligent reply. "How, uh, how are your friends?"

The shine faded from his eyes. "I do not know. They . . . go home. I stay."

That was odd, but it made her feel even sorrier for him. He really was alone out there.

"You . . . you have an accent," she ventured, hoping she wasn't being rude. "Where are you from? Are you French?"

His jaw flexed. "I—"

The doorbell rang, interrupting.

"Hello, Mrs. Gaetz," Grace said a little too cheerfully, wishing the sweet woman would turn around and leave. She needed more time so she could at least learn his name. "I'll be with you in a moment."

From the corner of her eye, she saw him pull on his cap and step away from the counter, leaving his small sack of furs by the register.

"No trouble, dear. I seen you got icing sugar. I come for that."

"Certainly. Just a moment."

"Okay then. I'll take a look 'round while you get that."

In the second that it took for Grace to fetch the sugar and bring it to the counter, his scarf was back in place, his hat and gloves on. He tucked his newly purchased knife into one deep pocket, the apples into another, then folded the comic into his bag.

"Uh, we don't call this a book," she told him, pointing. Anything to keep him there just a bit longer. "We call it a 'comic.'"

"Comic?"

"Yes. When they have all the drawings and words in bubbles, those are comics."

"Okay. Thank you."

She wished she had a hundred more pieces of information to give him just so he'd keep talking to her. "You . . . you don't have to leave, you know."

"It is dark. I am to walk far."

Of course. How silly of her. "Well, thank you so much for the gift. It's very, very special."

"You are welcome."

"Maybe I'll see you again."

She could tell he was smiling from the way his eyes crinkled above his scarf. "Maybe."

"Wait!" she said as he stepped away. "Have a happy Christmas."

"Yes," he said. "Happy Christmas."

"Oh, Grace?" Mrs. Gaetz called.

She reluctantly turned away. "Yes, Mrs. Gaetz?"

"Do you have cherries?"

"Of course. One can?"

The bell rang, and freezing air rushed inside. The stranger stood in the door frame for a moment.

"Good night, Grace," he said, then he was gone.

TEN

Christmas 1942

It was snowing again, a soft, hypnotic snow, and frost clouded Grace's bedroom window. She breathed a view through the ice and wiped it clear, then she watched the flakes trickle down. Everyone these days was singing Bing Crosby's "White Christmas," and here it was, right before her eyes. But Grace wasn't dreaming about snow, didn't care if Christmas was white or not. The peace she saw out there, the careless snow drifting lazily from a ceiling of white as if nothing out of the ordinary was happening, brought tears of envy to her eyes.

Christmas made everything harder. Eugene hadn't been home last Christmas or the one before. And Norman—well, her memories of him laughing at the dining room table were fading, the echo of his voice so much farther away.

They should be here.

Somewhere across the sea, in a land she'd only ever heard of and would probably never see, a small-minded dictator had stepped onto a stage and started a war. Grace suddenly felt sure he would succeed. The Germans would march right up to her front door and kill them all, just as they did in the radio stories.

The frost crept back over the circle she'd cleared, and she sank onto her bed. The only good thing in her life in that moment seemed to be the trapper, and how was she supposed to feel happy when she knew nothing about him? In the darkness of her room she reached for the wooden ladybug on her night table, and her thumb stroked its smooth back, riding the memorized pattern of spots. Where was its handsome creator that night? Was he watching the snow? Was he thinking of her? She raised the ladybug and stared into its empty eyes.

"You know him better than anyone, little bug," she whispered. "Who is he?"

He'd been an unexpected Christmas gift, a cause for smiling despite all her unhappiness, and a puzzle she wished to solve. She had been sure Linda would have learned more, but when she'd telephoned to ask, not even her snoopy friend had any information. Now that it was Christmas, the store was closed, and Grace clung to the hope of seeing him again afterwards. Would he stay after the holiday, or would he disappear along with the tinsel and carols?

The cozy aroma of Christmas dinner wafted up the stairs, but not even that could cheer her. It had been a strange, restrained kind of morning. Uncomfortable, even. Christmas had changed, and Norman's missing presence loomed over them all. The children, of course, had been oblivious to everything but the season, and their glee had been refreshing. The adults acted as if they shared their excitement, but pretending took a lot of energy. Grace feared her mask was slipping.

She set the ladybug back on the table and headed downstairs with a certain reluctance. Maybe supper would distract them from their sadness, if only for a while. The children sat quietly around the tree, reading new books or playing with spin tops. Little Claire, Eugene's oldest daughter, examined a toy boat her father had carved for her. Inside that tiny boat Grace imagined a tiny Eugene, far away, out of reach.

The tree was lovely, but even it was different from the ones she'd loved as a child. The delicate glass ornaments they'd always used had been made in Germany, so she'd been given the task of getting rid of them and ordering replacements. No one, including Grace, wanted to be reminded of Germany at Christmas. But somehow she hadn't had the heart to throw the treasures away. She'd buried them in a crate packed tight with sawdust, then she'd hidden the crate at the back of the shed. The ornaments might have been German made, but they were also shiny with memories. They were just as much a part of her Christmas as the stockings hanging from the mantel, and it was comforting to know they were still there. Would they ever come out of storage? Would Christmas ever feel normal again? She doubted both.

Grace corralled the worn-out children to the table where they sat dutifully in their places, blinking like dazed little owls as the adults settled into the evening's feast. The ham was moist and delicious, the turnips, carrots, and potatoes a perfect medley. Harry walked around the table and filled everyone's wineglass, then their father stood for a toast. For this moment at least, they could all come together and be happy.

Maybe it was the wine, or maybe the welcoming sound of laughter around the table was too difficult to resist, but for whatever reason the blond man from the woods appeared in Grace's thoughts. Wouldn't it be nice to have him sitting here, his blue eyes sparkling at her over a glass of wine? Once the dishes were cleared, maybe he'd hold out a hand and ask Grace to go for a moonlit walk, and this time no one would object. She'd follow him into the night and they'd dance under the stars.

She must have looked happy, because Harry lifted a teasing eyebrow. She dropped her eyes, feeling guilty.

"It's okay to enjoy yourself," Harry told her quietly. "Maybe you forgot, but it's Christmas. You're supposed to be having a good time."

"How can I?" she whispered back. Her daydream was gone, kicked to the side by reality. "I mean . . . what is Eugene doing right now?"

She shouldn't have asked. "What do you want me to say, Grace?"

"Nothing. I'm sorry. It's just that I wish I knew more about what was going on."

He didn't answer, and when she followed his gaze she understood why. Their father was watching them, a stern look on his face. She should have kept her voice down.

Harry cleared his throat. "It's not so bad. We have a job to do. You just have to be ready all the time." His shoulders rose and fell. "Sometimes that's a pretty tall order."

The volume around the room dropped noticeably. Catherine and Gail were studying their hands, but Tommy gave Grace a sympathetic smile. He'd been sitting quietly throughout the meal but paying close attention to the conversation. He might only have been sixteen, but he knew what was going on. He was the man of his family now that his father was gone.

With a sigh, her mother set down her fork. "Let's not talk about this."

"Please, Maman," Grace said, holding tight to her frustration. "I want to know what it's like out there."

"Now is not the time."

Grace was so tired of being silenced. U-boats were being blown up ten miles from where she sat, and she wasn't supposed to talk about the war? "It's *never* the time, though. The little I know about the war is tearing me apart. It's like I can hear people screaming but I have no idea why. It's terrible, not knowing. Don't you ever feel that way?"

Her mother's voice hardened. "You forget, Grace. I already know war. So does your father. We don't want to talk about it."

Grace clenched her hands under the table. "Well, then let's talk about Germans."

"What about them?"

"What could make a whole country of people so terrible?"

"Come now, Grace. They're not all terrible," her mother said. "You're looking at it the wrong way."

"What other way is there to see it?"

She'd tried to hold her tongue, but what good was that doing? Every time she thought of Norman, she thought of the men who had killed him in France. Of the guns and bombs she read about in the newspaper, of the vicious German soldiers they discussed on the radio. Why on earth would her mother want to defend them?

She leaned forwards, her fingers curling over the table's edge. "Germans killed Norman, and they're trying to kill Harry and Eugene. In my books, that makes them the worst people on earth."

At the mention of Norman's name, the room went silent. Gail bunched her serviette in her hands and shifted in her seat, looking almost desperate to leave the table.

"Grace, you're speaking out of turn. I know a few Germans, and so do you," her mother said slowly. "Some of them have lived out here twenty years or more. You grew up with them. All good people. People I call my friends."

"Hard workers, every one of them," her father agreed.

This was silly. They knew what she meant. Why were they trying to turn her words around? "Those are different. They live here. They're not Germans anymore. They're Canadians."

"They are Canadian *Germans*, Grace."

"I'm talking about *German* Germans. Nazis. Are you defending *them*?"

Her father scratched his chin, thinking. "I won't defend

the war, but I will defend the men who are forced to be in it. The men in uniform didn't start it. They're just following orders."

She couldn't accept that, but she couldn't think of a response, either.

"I understand what you're saying, Grace," her mother said softly, "but that kind of thinking doesn't help anyone. You have to look at it differently. I learned that twenty years ago."

"Oh? There's another way to look at it? I'm all ears."

"Watch your tone," her father warned. "We're having a conversation, just like you wanted."

"Sorry." But she wasn't. Not entirely. This was not the conversation she wanted.

Harry said, "Some people call what we're doing the 'game of war.'"

She huffed, taken aback to hear him joining their side. "Some game."

"Your brother's right," her father said. "It is a kind of game."

His jaw was tight, but Grace didn't think her father's anger was meant for her. She wondered—not for the first time—if he'd always been this tough. He'd been about her age, at the prime of his life, when he'd been ordered into the trenches. He'd seen his friends killed before his eyes and had his leg blown off, but he never talked about any of that. Yet there he sat, defending the Germans.

"Those men you're talking about," he said, rubbing his brow, "they signed up to play the game, and their country expects them to win. But a game requires at least two teams. Ours is just as determined as they are, and we are fighting back." His mouth twisted wryly. "Of course every team has a captain, and unfortunately, the captain of the German team happens to be a dictator who wants to rule the world."

"This game should be called off. Permanently," she snapped. She knew she sounded like a petulant child, but she said it anyway. "I want Eugene back home right now."

"I bet there are more than a few German families wishing the same thing right now," her mother said quietly.

"Stop that!" Grace slammed her palms onto the table, making everyone jump. "Stop talking about them like they're the same as us. This whole war is their fault. I hate them."

Harry put one warm hand over hers. "Problem is, hate's what got us into this mess in the first place."

"Don't patronize me." She pushed her chair back and reached for the nearest dishes, aware that she was moving too quickly.

Harry followed. "Gently now," he muttered as the kitchen door closed behind them. "Don't break the china."

She couldn't even look at him, she was so upset. "I think I'm losing my mind."

"It's just that war's not a subject for family conversation," he said. "You know that. Especially around Maman, and especially at Christmas." He lowered his voice. "Ask me what you want now, and maybe I can answer."

Now that the offer was on the table she almost couldn't think of what to ask. Carefully, she set the dishes in the water.

"Do you ever see Eugene?" came off the tip of her tongue.

"Actually, yeah. I've seen him a couple of times through binoculars. And when they're loading and unloading we occasionally cross paths."

"How is he?"

"He's good, I'd say. I think he's up for a promotion."

"I bet he misses you."

"When he has time. I imagine so." He peered closely at her. "What about you, Gracie? How are you?"

She stared at the dishwater, blinking against tears. She didn't want to complain. Not to him. "I'm fine."

"I know you better than that."

The concern on his face was so sincere it would have been lying to tell him she was all right. She dried her hands on her apron, took a deep breath.

"I don't know, really."

"Tell me what's in your head."

It had been building for so long, and until that night she'd kept the fears, the confusion, mostly to herself. But keeping secrets was a lot like lying, in her opinion, and she'd never been able to lie to her brothers.

"All right," she said slowly. "It's like, well, it's like I'm safely packed away in a box, and I can't see or hear anything. Or like I'm watching a movie in a theatre, except I know all the actors and I'm separate from them, which tears me apart." A sob caught in her throat. "Oh, the worst is Norman. He was one of those actors, and it's like the director just yanked him from the screen with no explanation. I'll never know what happened to him. I'll never know if he . . . if he . . . " She tried very hard to still her wobbling chin. "I feel useless. That's what it is. Useless and alone."

"Come here."

He held her tight, letting her cry against him until she reluctantly pulled away, wiping at her eyes and nose with the back of her wrist.

"I'm sorry to put all this on your shoulders," she managed. "But when you and Eugene are out there, I . . . all I can think is that they killed Norman and they won't stop until they've gotten both of you as well. And I couldn't bear to live without you."

"We will be fine," he said after a moment. "All of us."

If only she could have believed him.

That evening she stood by the water's frozen edge and stared out at the horizon, bumpy with the distant profiles of small islands and massive chunks of broken, refrozen ice. The earlier snowfall had buried everything under a smooth, soft layer, but the storm was over now and the stars were out. She'd done this before: standing alone in the night air, praying for the ships she couldn't see and all the men on board. But tonight she was distracted and felt oddly disconnected from the night.

Were her father and Harry right? Would the war be easier to comprehend if she envisioned the other side as regular men simply wearing different uniforms? Could she even do that? Her thoughts went to the U-boat that had exploded the other day, of the sudden violence that had dropped those men under the ice. Such a terrible, terrible waste.

An infinity of stars peeked through the branches, sparkled over the frozen expanse of sea in a magnificent, endless reminder of how very small she was. How every human being in the world, no matter who or where he or she was, was no more than a speck in the universe. How they were all equal in that.

No, she decided. She couldn't do it. Imagining the enemy that way made the war seem *worse*. So much more complicated. If it were true, that meant the people fighting on the other side were the same as her: living day-to-day, trying to survive the madness. And she couldn't stand the thought of so many people hurting like she did.

ELEVEN

Down came the tinsel, the decorations, and the lights, off went the Christmas music, and the last of the shortbreads were eaten. Gardner's General Store was back to normal, and Grace made work for herself by moving boxes, packing things away, and bringing out more stock. Anything to keep her distracted. When everything was done, she leaned on the counter and flipped through the newspaper, reading the stream of depressing narratives. Diphtheria, scarlet fever, and the mumps were on the rise in Halifax. Liquor was being rationed again. The Nazis were fighting the Russians. Nothing ever got any better, she thought ruefully, closing the paper.

Then there he was, walking through the door, his pale hair and eyes lit by the late-afternoon sunshine.

"Hello there," she said, trying to appear nonchalant. "Happy New Year!"

His beard had grown in, but he seemed better-rested than before. "Hello, Grace," he said. "Yes. Happy New Year for you."

Butterflies swooped through her stomach. "Did you have a happy Christmas?"

"Christmas. Yes." He slipped off his gloves, walked slowly towards her. "Thank you."

What was it about his casual, confident stride that set her heart thrumming?

"Your ladybug was my favourite gift," she admitted. "I'm curious. Why did you choose to make a ladybug?"

She wondered if she'd said the wrong thing, because he didn't answer at once.

"This is *Marienkäfer*," he explained, watching her reaction. "In German means good things come."

She hoped her hesitation was brief enough that he didn't notice, but she wasn't sure she could hide her shock. Of all the people in the world, did he have to be *German*?

"Good things come?" she echoed, pushing away the niggling in her head.

Maybe it wasn't so bad. After all, she was well aware that a number of Germans lived along the Eastern Shore, and just like her father had said, they were *Canadian* Germans. They'd been here for years. She had to accept the fact that she was wrong about blaming "all" Germans for the war.

"So do you mean ladybugs are lucky?" she asked, trying to recover. "Ladybugs make good things happen?"

"Good things. Yes."

"We think of them as lucky, too," she said.

They regarded each other shyly, unsure, then she watched him go to the shelves, collect a few cans of vegetables and a bag of oatmeal. At least now she understood why he took so long to read the labels. And maybe that was why he seemed reticent whenever anyone else came into the store. After a moment he picked up some sugar and canned peaches, then returned to the counter.

"We got some new comics," she said, remembering, "and I saved this one for you. *Johnny Canuck*."

"Canuck?"

"Yes, it's another word for Canadian."

"Yes, Canuck. Thank you." He flipped through the first couple of pages. "Is good." He dug into his pocket and set some coins on the counter between them. "I . . . I have more fur also. I get bread? More apples?"

She peeked inside the bag and spotted the downy fur. "Sure. Of course."

They made the exchange, but this time he didn't seem in a hurry to go, and Grace was happy to keep the conversation going.

"You still living in the woods?"

"*Ja.* I trap."

"I noticed. Are you bored out there?"

He seemed puzzled.

"Bored. Um, you have nothing to do?"

"Is okay. I have comic and newspaper. I read."

"Oh!" She grabbed the *Chronicle*. "My uncle Mick writes for this newspaper." She opened it to his latest article and pointed at his name, then at herself. "My uncle."

"I understand, *Onkel,*" he said, and she thought how nice the language sounded coming from him. Nothing like the staccato bursts of German words she'd heard on the radio. "He is making this story?"

"Yes. He's the senior editor. Very important."

He leaned over the page, scrutinizing the words, his lips moving slightly. He was so different from anyone she'd ever met. Grace couldn't look away. She followed the broad slope of his shoulders, imagined him relaxing in a cabin, reading by a stove—

"What you are thinking?"

"Oh, nothing," she sputtered.

"I wonder is okay I come to here, Grace?" he asked. "Talk to you?"

"Of course! You can come anytime."

"Is okay I come and buy nothing? Just come to talk?"

She dared herself to be brave. After all, he'd started it. "Well, sure, but I don't even know your name."

"Rudi. I am Rudi." He stuck out a hand, which she shook.

"Nice to meet you, Rudi."

"I like to say . . ." He paused, concentrating. "I like to say I am sorry I not dance again with you. I like that one dance."

"Oh, well," she said. She could almost feel his hand on her waist, her fingers resting on the solid curve of his shoulder. When had her palms gotten so sweaty? "Me too."

"Maybe will be another dance."

"I would like that very much, Rudi."

The doorbell rang, interrupting them yet again.

"Is good to see you, Grace," he said, stepping away from the counter.

"Yes. I'm glad you came back, Rudi. Happy New Year!"

She was disappointed to see him retreat out the door, but excited, too. He'd said he wanted to come back—even asked her permission—which made her heart sing.

"Rudi," she said to herself after the next customer left. She liked the way his name felt on her lips.

Then she laughed out loud. "What on earth have I gotten myself into?"

Just a few weeks back she'd danced with a stranger who could barely speak a word of English, and now she was having all sorts of romantic thoughts about him. Her family would tease her if they knew, given her tirade the other night. And what would Harry say if he found out how easily she'd been swayed by a pair of blue eyes and a winning smile? Then again, her family was always encouraging her to look for Mr. Right. Maybe they wouldn't laugh. Maybe they'd understand what she was feeling even better than she did. It might just be that he was exactly what she'd been waiting for all along: a stranger from far away who walked in from the cold and swept her off her feet.

Except she couldn't ignore the sense of unease pulsing through her. Rudi might be the most handsome man in the world, and he was undeniably charming, but he was still German. And while she certainly didn't know every German living along the Eastern Shore, she couldn't help thinking she would have remembered him if she'd seen him before.

Rudi

TWELVE

Being with Grace, talking with her, made Rudi happier than he'd been in a long time. There was something about the way her eyes danced when he said the right thing, the way she watched him so closely . . . There was a glow about her that made him feel warm all the way through.

It was a new year, as she'd reminded him: 1943. The number meant nothing, but he liked the idea of a fresh start. As if the world had just opened a book and revealed a crisp, untouched page. What would he write on that page? He walked faster, unnerved by the thought. The longer he stayed at the camp, the greater the chance that he would be caught by either the Canadians or his own navy. Did his being stranded here make him AWOL? Would the navy classify him as missing or charge him with desertion? Or would they simply presume he was dead along with the rest of U-69's crew?

A menacing bank of clouds was building ahead, coming in quickly, and before long the first twisting, wandering snowflakes began spiralling down like timid children. Beyond them floated millions more, and they gained confidence and strength in numbers, blurring the landscape. Fortunately, the camp was only about twenty minutes away, as long as the path didn't get much worse.

But it did. The wind picked up, pelting him with stinging

ice crystals. He had to lean against the storm as he walked, squinting through it every so often to check for landmarks. By the time he reached the camp, the blizzard had gotten much worse. He shut himself in, struck up a lamp, then lit the fire before taking off his coat. When the next gust came, the camp shook and the trees outside creaked with strain. If any of the larger trees broke and crashed onto the roof, the camp would be crushed to splinters, a thought Rudi tried to ignore as he prepared a pot of soup.

It was going to be a long night.

Minutes later the terrible sound he'd feared cut through the wind: the ominous crackling and groaning crescendo of snapping branches. He pressed his face to the window, searching for the source, but could see nothing through the frozen pane and wild blizzard. A noise like machine-gun fire rang out as the roots of a tree were ripped from the ground, but he realized with great relief that it wasn't close enough to affect him. Not this time, anyway.

He turned back to the stove, then stopped. What was that new sound? Was it just the moaning of the wind? An animal? No, the creatures of the forest would have sought shelter long before the storm hit. A sick sensation hardened in his gut. He'd been out here a month and hadn't seen another soul, but this had sounded like . . . The noise came again, and Rudi hastily pulled on his coat and boots. Whatever was out there, stuck in this storm, was plainly desperate. He tore out into the ferocious blizzard, listening hard against the screaming gale. When he heard the voice again, he had no doubt. The weakening calls were coming downwind, from the direction of the water, and they were human. He ran as fast as he could towards the sound.

What might have usually been a ten-minute walk took at

least double, and by then the panicked voice he'd heard had stopped. Still, Rudi pressed on. Though the trail ahead was an unrelenting wall of white, he followed the path he had marked weeks earlier by making visible cuts high in the trees. Near the edge of the frozen lake he stopped and peered across its surface. Despite the blinding snow, he could see that a tree had fallen and crashed onto the lake's surface, smashing everything in its path; the ice around it was black with shredded bark.

Then Rudi spotted something beyond the tree. It could have been a thick branch tossed there by the storm, but it wasn't the right shape. Moving carefully, he edged onto the ice and realized most of the dark shape was hidden under the water. For just an instant the wind paused, taking a breath, and Rudi made out the body of a man.

The ice wasn't broken all the way through to where Rudi stood, but the area near the body was dark with exposed water, and more nearby trees wailed with the effort of standing upright. Nothing about this situation was stable. He couldn't simply walk out there, but he couldn't leave the man, either. He'd heard the screams only a half hour before; there was a chance he could still be alive.

"Hello! Hello!" he called.

No response. Rudi lowered himself to all fours, then started crawling towards the man, yelling against the wind the whole way.

"I come! You are okay?"

As he got closer, he dropped lower still, then finally wormed towards the hole in the ice. Both of the man's stiff wool mittens were frozen to the surface, anchoring almost half his body out of the water, and his frosted, unconscious face rested on one arm. Rudi reached for one of the mittens, but it resisted. He didn't pull again, not wanting to disturb the ice further.

Not until he could figure out what to do. A sudden Arctic gust roared through the forest, swept icy shrapnel into his face, and Rudi squinted against it. He scanned the ice, searching for ideas on how to proceed, then he spotted a heavy-looking backpack lying a few feet away and snaked towards it.

"*Gott sei Dank*," he exclaimed, pulling out a coil of rope.

He slid back to the unconscious man and dropped the rope over his head, sweating despite the cold. Before drawing it tight, he tied the loop under the man's soaked elbows and used his own hands as a lever to pry the frozen mitts and sleeves loose. Then he backed up ten feet and began to tug. The body was covered in a thin coating of ice, like an opaque white sheath, and though it was heavy and stuck hard to the broken surface at first, it broke free and came as he pulled. When he could, Rudi reached out and grabbed under the man's arms, dragging him the rest of the way to safety. At the shore, he heaved the body and backpack over his shoulders, then carried both back to the camp.

Once inside the cabin, Rudi laid the man on the bottom bunk and took a closer look. It was a boy, maybe five years younger than himself. Rudi pressed his fingers to the boy's cold neck, just beneath the jaw, then he closed his eyes, concentrating. A slow but promising pulse met his fingertips, and he immediately got to work. He removed all the frozen, sodden clothing, and by the time he had gotten down to the boy's bare chest, he felt a glimmer of hope; the clammy skin was pink, not blue. Rudi replaced the wet clothes with a blanket and laid his own still-warm coat on top.

He'd done all he could for now. The boy would either wake or he would not. His own fingers were still numb from the cold, so he turned to tend the fire and held his hands up to the heat.

The boy groaned.

Rudi jumped to his feet, and this time when he pressed his fingers to the boy's neck, the heartbeat was much stronger. He was still unconscious, but he would live.

Satisfied for now, Rudi investigated the backpack. It was a windfall, heavy with tools and food. The boy moaned once more and Rudi looked up. Something stirred in the boy's consciousness, for his brow creased briefly before relaxing back into sleep. He looked relatively strong, considering everything. Having survived an icy death, Rudi thought, he would want to tell his family a tale of his adventure. What would he say? How could he explain his deliverance?

Rudi suddenly felt sick. What the hell had he just done?

THIRTEEN

After about a half hour, the boy on the bunk began to shiver so violently the whole bed shook, and the coat keeping him warm slid onto the floor. The boy's eyes were still closed, his cheeks were a vivid red, but at least the frightening shade of blue had faded from his lips. When he moaned, his face contorted with pain, but Rudi was glad to hear signs of life. He'd frozen his own hands and feet many times and knew that the burning pain meant the boy was thawing. His limbs would feel as if tiny fires flared Inside them everywhere at once, consuming his muscles, but it was only blood pumping through them again.

When Rudi stood and laid the coat back over him, the boy's eyes popped open.

"Hello," Rudi said, startled. "You are safe." He spoke in English but received no reply, just a dull stare. "You can talk?"

"Who are you?" The boy's voice was hoarse and unsteady.

"Rudi."

The boy grimaced with pain, sucking air through his teeth.

"I pull you from water."

A shudder travelled violently through the boy. "I d-d-don't know you. Why are you here?"

"Trapping."

Thinking it might help to warm the patient from the inside,

Rudi filled a cup halfway with boiling water, then added snow to neutralize the temperature.

"Tea?"

The boy peered into the cup. "That isn't t-tea. It's hot water."

"Sorry. I have only this."

"M-might be coffee in my pack. P-pot's under the bunk."

The aroma that filled the cabin over the next few minutes made the whole terrible ice rescue worthwhile. Rudi took a grateful gulp, and though the coffee was weak it still tasted like heaven.

With effort, the boy moved, trying to sit, then he cried out and hugged his torso. After he'd caught his breath, he slowly straightened, not meeting Rudi's eyes. When he finally sat, slightly hunched but upright, and some of the colour had returned to his cheeks, he curled his pale fingers around the cup and sipped. Then he glared directly at Rudi.

"Who are you?"

Rudi shook his head. "No. I ask. Who are you?"

"T-Tommy. Tommy Baker. This camp belongs to my family. I came out to do some hunting."

"Where is gun?"

Tommy scanned the room. "If you didn't find it, I guess it's at the bottom of the lake. Your turn. What are you doing here?"

He shrugged. "I find camp."

"You 'find' it?" Tommy scowled at him. "What's that supposed to mean? You mean you *found* it?"

This was disappointing. Rudi had been practising his English by reading every night, and he'd been hoping to avoid obvious mistakes when he had to speak to a stranger. He knew he sounded somewhat stilted, but he had thought he was improving.

"You feel okay?" he asked, buying himself some time.

"I feel . . . not very good. I feel odd."

"I understand. I think this . . ." He patted his own torso and waited with his eyebrows raised.

"What, ribs?"

"Yes. Ribs is break. A tree is falling on ice and you. You are to death close."

" 'To death close?' " You mean 'close to dead?' "

"You remember?"

"I remember trying to get out, but I must have passed out." Tommy paused. "Thanks." Then his eyes narrowed. "Wait. Do I know you?"

"No."

"From the Christmas dance!"

That damn dance. Rudi never should have gone. He didn't remember this boy, but apparently he had made an impression. "Yes. I am at dance."

"What about the others? Your friends? Where are they?"

"Gone. I do not know. I am alone."

A pause, then, "You're *German*," Tommy whispered.

Rudi sighed. "*Ja*. German."

Tommy's gaze went to Rudi's heavy, black wool coat, the one he'd used as a blanket. No one could deny it was a military-style coat.

"Are you a Nazi?"

If Rudi admitted he was a Nazi, he would practically be offering himself up to the authorities. He had no idea how a prisoner of war would be treated here, but he couldn't risk anyone discovering his secret. On the other hand, the coat had given him away.

"No. I am no more Nazi," he declared.

"What do you mean, 'no more?' You *were* a Nazi?"

Maybe he shouldn't have said that, but it was too late now. "*Ja*, was Nazi. No more."

Interest began to replace wariness. "Why not?"

"I . . . I like here. In Canada."

"Not sure I buy that. Everybody knows Nazis want to take over the world and kill us all."

Apparently the Nazi propaganda machine had reached these remote shores. "This is not true."

"Sure it is. I've seen newsreels at the movie theatre, and I've heard speeches on the radio."

"Well, is not true for me," he clarified. "I am not fight again."

"You saying you're a deserter?"

Deserteur. The word hung in the air between them, the same in German as it was in English. Never in his life would Rudi have imagined he'd be calling himself that, not even in jest. Back in Germany, if they believed he was a deserter, he would stand before a firing squad. But here . . .

It was a challenge for him to agree, but he had no other choice.

His admission seemed to amaze the boy. "Wow. What kind of man deserts?"

"This is not your problem."

"I say it is. This is my family's camp. I want to know who is trespassing."

"What is that? Tress . . . ?"

Tommy raised one arm, then dropped it, reacting with a gasp to the strain on his ribs. Using the other hand he gestured around the room. "Trespassing is you living here when you aren't invited. You don't belong here, German."

Rudi needed to change the course of the conversation before it got too one-sided, so he dragged his chair over until he and Tommy were face to face. "You think is bad I pull you from water? Okay. But if I not here, you are dead."

The boy's eyes lowered. "Well, that's true."

"Drink coffee."

They settled into an uneasy truce, then Rudi got up to start more water boiling. He'd worked up a hunger, so he prepared two bowls of oatmeal and brought one to Tommy.

"How you are feeling?" he asked as he tucked into his food.

"I'll live." He took a bite. "I could fall asleep, but I'm afraid you'll kill me in my sleep."

Rudi waved his spoon. "I am not killing you," he said. "I am making you to live."

The boy finished his oatmeal and watched Rudi warily until he fell asleep from exhaustion. At last he laid back down and closed his eyes. He was snoring quietly within seconds.

Rudi observed the weak rise and fall of Tommy's chest under the blanket, and he thought terrible thoughts.

Until that night, he had kept his secret hidden. Now Tommy knew. Who might he tell? It would make life so much easier if Tommy . . . wasn't here, and it would be a simple thing to make that happen. The military had taught Rudi many techniques for how to kill a man quickly and easily, and this enemy was alone, injured, and sound asleep. From across the room Rudi could almost sense how easily his new knife would cut through the boy's pale white throat. No different from gutting an animal, though a lot messier. He could deposit the body in the snow and be gone before the spring thaw. If the roles had been reversed, he didn't doubt his enemy would kill him. He had been trained with that understanding for years. But training was different from the real thing. He had never had to kill anyone. Not with his own hands, anyway.

Troubled, Rudi climbed onto the top bunk and doused

the lantern. The walls flickered with firelight from the stove, a comfort against the relentless snow and wind outside. Already his tracks to the lake would be buried. Without Rudi's intervention, Tommy would not have survived. Would that have been a bad thing in the long run?

He stared at the ceiling, marvelling at how this day had changed everything. He'd awoken to a sunny, almost warm day, and he'd had a real conversation with Grace. Then winter had roared in and he'd rescued Tommy from drowning. Now he was sleeping under the same roof as the enemy. If he ever saw Grace again, he could honestly tell her that he was no longer bored.

FOURTEEN

At first light, Rudi rolled off the bunk and tried to land softly.

"I'm already awake," Tommy informed him. "Been awake for hours. Just can't move."

"Good. You are not dead. I make coffee."

Rudi put the pot on, then excused himself to go outside. Sunlight sparkled through the trees and danced on fresh drifts like fallen stars, and he cursed the sight. All his traps were buried; he'd have to dig them up and scout better sites to set them. At least the splintered trunks of broken trees had created deadfalls everywhere. Those were ideal locations for setting traps.

When he got back inside, Tommy was sitting up, one arm across his chest. "My feet feel weird. Kinda numb. Not sure if I can walk on them."

"Do you . . ." He made a motion like he was rolling dough between his hands.

"Rub them? Yeah. I can kind of feel one, but the other I can't feel at all. Help me up?"

Mindful of Tommy's sore chest, Rudi pulled him to his feet, helped him get to the table. While he settled, Rudi took bread from Tommy's pack and cut a few slices to make toast. The camp suddenly smelled divine.

"I think there might be eggs . . ." Tommy suggested, indicating the pack with his chin. "There's a box in there. Go ahead. Just dig through it. Nothing secret in there. Nothing you can kill me with, anyway."

"Again you think I am saving your life, then I am killing you?"

"You're a Nazi."

Rudi shook his head, trying to look disappointed rather than concerned. "You say this again?" He tapped his head. "Maybe ice make you forget. I am not Nazi."

He could tell from Tommy's face that he wasn't about to let Rudi off the hook that easy, but he appeared willing to let the argument ride for now. Rudi found the box of eggs and a small block of cheese, then got to work making breakfast, all the while trying to think of a safe conversation he could start. One that wouldn't end in accusations he couldn't answer. Unfortunately, Tommy spoke first.

"You know," he said through a mouthful of eggs, "it doesn't matter if you're deserting or not: we generally hate Nazis around here."

"Sorry to hear this." Rudi gestured towards the window with his toast. "You not see for long time persons. Too much snow."

Tommy's eyes darted to the window then back again. He shifted on his chair, looking uncomfortable at the reminder. "Yeah. I guess I didn't expect that big a storm. I should have known better."

Rudi pointed to his head. "I know storm coming soon. My head is making big pain."

"You get headaches when the weather changes? So does my mother. She told me it was going to snow."

"Headache," Rudi echoed.

"What?"

"I am learn English."

"How do you say headache?"

"*Kopfschmerzen.*"

Tommy laughed. "Sounds like a sneeze." He acted out the motion just in case Rudi didn't understand.

Sneeze, Rudi repeated to himself.

"Well, I've got a bit of a cough-schmertzin," Tommy said. He paused. "Hell of a thing, breaking through that ice. I've been out here a hundred times but last night, I couldn't see a thing. How'd you find me?"

"Tree falling is loud. And screaming. You are making loud scream." He looked at Tommy's feet. "Did you take off . . . *Socke*? Is that right word?"

"Yep. Sock. No, I'm gonna leave it on, just in case my foot's still frozen. The sock will warm it up."

"Maybe." Rudi wasn't sure about that logic. Maybe it was a Canadian thing.

Tommy's scrutiny made Rudi uncomfortable, but he couldn't escape it, so he grabbed the newspaper he'd bought from Grace and settled back onto the chair.

"I think you guys are losing in Russia," Tommy said, eyeing the paper. "I read something about Stalingrad beating a whole lot of Nazis. Not sure if that's bad or good, though. I've heard Russians are just as awful as you fellas."

Rudi pretended not to hear, just handed Tommy a different section of the paper, then focused on his own. "Reds Seize Two More Nazi Bases," read the *Chronicle*. Above that was another headline: "Nazi Buildings in France Bombed; Purge Reported." Tommy was right. Things weren't looking all that good.

Rudi pointed at the paper. "It say 'Liquor Rationed in Nova Scotia.' News is not good for Nova Scotia too."

"Yeah, well, that's Germany's fault. Never should have started the war, should you?"

A pile of snow slid off the roof, tumbled past the window, reminding Rudi he had work to do outside.

"If you are okay, I go to fix traps."

"Can I read your paper?"

After handing it over, Rudi headed outside, grateful for the excuse to leave. Everything had gotten much more complicated with the arrival of Tommy, and he needed time to himself to consider his predicament. At least he knew one thing for certain: over the last twelve hours, he'd come to terms with the fact that he wasn't a killer; Tommy was safe around him. But the boy would start asking more difficult questions soon, and Rudi needed to be prepared with answers. He'd admitted to being a deserter, but that wouldn't be enough. What reason could he give for being here, in this place? What could have brought him here—besides a sunken U-boat, that is? Because he would never admit he'd been onboard U-69. If people found out he'd survived that explosion, they might go searching for others. The last thing Rudi wanted to do was inadvertently sabotage his crew's plans to set up a bunker on the island—if any of them had made it there in the first place.

As he pocketed a frozen rabbit and a marten from a couple of traps, he thought back to the stories Otto had told him on the U-boat. Some of his family, he'd said, had emigrated from Germany to Nova Scotia after the last war. He'd said there was a settlement of Germans near here, maybe more than one. Could Rudi bluff about that? The idea was unnerving; Tommy knew every detail about this shore, and Rudi knew absolutely nothing. If only he'd asked Otto more questions at the time. Then again, how could he have known those answers would someday be important?

By the time Rudi returned to the cabin, Tommy had managed to crawl over to the stove—at least Rudi assumed that's how he'd gotten there—to add logs. Now he was sitting in

Rudi's chair, whittling a stick to a point, his pack open on the floor beside him. That explained where he'd gotten the knife. Tommy hadn't had one on him before.

He watched Rudi's every move. "Traps okay?"

"*Ja.*"

Tommy held out a hand for the rabbit. "I'll skin, you gut. Do you trap a lot where you're from?" he asked, making a starting cut. "And hunt?"

"I do this before, *ja.*"

Tommy pointed his knife towards Rudi. "Now you just hunt people."

Rudi closed his eyes. "You and me are here for long time. We cannot go out. You want all the time fighting?"

The boy's lips tightened, and Rudi understood. If he had been trapped somewhere with an enemy, he would have felt antagonistic as well.

"I am sorry for war. I do not make war," Rudi added. "We can talk something not war?"

"Like what? How Nazis eat babies?"

"*What?*"

"That's what they say."

Apparently, this was going to be a long day. "We do not eat babies."

" 'We'! So you admit you're a Nazi! I knew it."

Rudi didn't even bother to answer.

Tommy finished and handed Rudi the naked rabbit. "Where are your buddies from the dance?"

For a brief moment Rudi imagined his crewmates again, enjoying themselves at the party. It had been a good night. A night to be themselves for a while. But in the next instant the memory vanished and Rudi's cheek was frozen to the ice, the murderous flames flicking through black, black smoke.

"I do not know," he said. "I think maybe dead."

Tommy grunted, unconvinced. "Where did you come from? I don't mean Germany—that's obvious. I mean how come you're out here in the middle of nowhere?"

Years ago, Rudi had lied to his mother. It had been a small, unimportant matter he couldn't even recall anymore, but she'd caught him at it. The one lesson Rudi had taken away from that experience was what his father had quietly said to him later.

If you must tell a lie, keep it as close to the truth as possible. That way you will have less to trip on as you navigate around the truth.

"My boat sink," Rudi said. "East of here."

"I haven't heard of any Nazi ships going down around here. Which ship?"

"*Hannover*," he said, praying Tommy knew nothing of German ships from the first war. "In November."

"Huh. I would have heard about that, wouldn't I?"

"Maybe you do not know everything. Maybe you do not know all about German boats."

Tommy pulled the fur over the stretcher board, then set it by the heat to dry, and Rudi was glad to see he was doing it the right way. They'd be easier to sell if they were dried properly from the start.

"I suppose. What about your crewmates?"

"I tell you before. I do not know. They are gone."

Tommy appeared skeptical, but at least he didn't question Rudi's vague answer. Not yet, anyway.

"So . . . what, you just wandered around and found this place?"

At least he could tell the truth about that part. "Yes."

"That's when you decided to desert?"

This boy had endless questions. Fortunately, Rudi had

compiled a short list of answers over the past twenty-four hours. "I do not want to go to Germany. I am no more fighting. I trap here. I hope to stay to spring."

"You might have been able to get away with that, but I needed some time away. Things around home are . . ." He scratched a spot behind his ear, seeming ill at ease with the topic. "My cousin was in the army, and he got killed a few months back. It's been really hard on my family."

He knew Tommy was waiting for a reaction, but Rudi didn't move, reminding himself that he was not responsible for everything that happened in this war. He'd certainly been a part of some devastating attacks that kept gnawing at him—like that ferry back in October—but Rudi was an officer in the German Navy. Going against his conscience was the price he paid.

"I guess you're right." Tommy said after a while. "I don't want to talk politics with you. We're living in pretty tight quarters." He absently tapped his fingertips together, and the movement gave Rudi an idea.

"You have *Spielkarten*?" He moved his hands to simulate dealing out cards.

"Playing cards? Sure. In the drawer. What do you play?"

"I teach you *Sechsundsechzig*. Simple game."

Tommy caught on quickly, then he insisted they play cribbage using the board Rudi had spotted in the drawer along with the cards.

"What's it like in Germany?" Tommy asked. "Does everyone wear a uniform?"

"Only in military, same like here."

"Isn't everyone in the military there?"

"Everyone? No. My mother was teacher. She teach at *Kirche*, too."

"Keershe?"

He put his palms together and rolled his eyes skywards. *"Mit Gott und Jesus, ja?"*

"Church! Okay. Your mom teaches Sunday school. That's interesting."

"Not only Sunday. Every day she teaches."

"But Sunday at church. I understand. So people still go to church in Germany, and kids still go to school. Do the stores still open? People still work?"

Rudi didn't want to think about home. Out there in the quiet wilderness, it all seemed so far away, almost as if it didn't exist. Tommy's questions made him apprehensive, as if he were being dragged out of a deep sleep and shoved into the cold.

"Most," he said vaguely. Without his bidding, the Steins came to mind. The family had owned a store by Rudi's home, and they had four children the same age as Rudi and his sisters. Then one day he'd seen the six of them wearing yellow badges, just like the other Jews. The last time Rudi had been home, the store was gone and so was the family.

"Is there lots of marching?"

"Yes. In big streets is marching many times," he replied. "Here?"

Tommy snorted. "Here? In East Jeddore? No, any marching is done far away from here. Besides, a lot of our men are gone now, off fighting. Like my cousins."

"Why you are not fighting?"

"I'm too young. Another year or so and I'll go, but my mother says the war'll be done by then. Of course they said that three years ago, and we're still fighting."

"You want to fight?"

"I guess I do." He chose a card, changed his mind, and picked another one. "If I didn't go people might call me a coward, wouldn't they?"

Rudi grunted. "You do not want to fight."

"Honestly? I don't know if I'd be any good." Tommy paused. "Are you? Good at fighting, I mean."

Rudi's jaw clenched. "Yes."

"How did you learn to fight?"

"Practise. Much. I am in Jungvolk when I am ten. Must always do practise."

" 'Yoongfoik?' " Tommy tried. "What's that?"

"We learn to fight and we are . . . children. When I am older I am Hitlerjugend."

"Those are training groups? For war?"

"More than this. We are *Mannschaft*—"

"Mun-Chuft?"

"We do all things together."

"A team?"

"*Ja*, okay. A team."

The Jungfolk had been so much more than a training group or team, though athletics were certainly a priority. It had been a world of education, and Rudi had excelled at practically every activity. He recalled the thrill of standing side by side with the others, firing at targets, and he'd been fascinated by the lessons on mechanics. Together he and the other boys played football, boxed, wrestled, even went to camp, where they hiked for miles and got bloody playing war games. Most of it was a lot of fun.

When he and the other boys turned fourteen, they were old enough to graduate to the Hitlerjugend and then take part in the parades that January. Their hearts had nearly exploded with pride when they'd heard they would not only be marching behind their flag with the other forces, but that they would actually pass in front of der Führer and President Hindenburg, their polished leather jackboots clipping along the cobblestones with so many others. That April he'd been with the squads assigned to storm the Berlin offices of the Reichs Committee of German Youth Associations, responsible for either shutting them down or integrating their members into the Hitler Youth.

It had been an exciting time, one filled with personal and national pride. They were young and strong, they were mad with power, they were determined to please Hitler. They had been such a force, with their youthful optimism and dedication, their dreams of glory! Wherever they marched, the police had to block off the roads. And everyone—from the youngest to the very oldest—stood by and saluted them. Saluted *him*. The sense of power Rudi got from that had been incredible.

"—into the woods?"

"What?"

Tommy huffed. From the annoyance on his face, he'd plainly been speaking the whole time. Rudi had been thousands of miles and quite a few years away.

"I was asking if you'd figured out what you'll do when I leave."

Rudi took a breath and hoped Otto had been telling the truth. "Other Germans live here. They come before me years ago. I am going to there."

"Sure. There's a settlement down the shore and more in the city." Tommy chuckled. "Oh, and there's the crazy German couple on Borgles Island, but they're not what I'd call a settlement."

Borgles Island? Rudi forced himself not to react despite his shock. Someone was already living on that island? Impossible! His crew had been told it was deserted, that it would be a safe vantage point. But if someone already lived there, could any of Rudi's men have managed to meet them?

"Who is this on island?"

"Oh, I don't think those are the Germans you're talking about. It's a couple who have been out there for about ten years. Nobody knows their name or anything about them, but my father said he believed they'd come straight from Germany. They come up for supplies once a year or so, but they never speak to anyone other than to get what they need. They're nuttier than a couple of squirrels."

"Oh." Most of the explanation had been lost on Rudi. His mind was stuck on the fact that Borgles Island was not empty after all.

"So you're hoping to find other Germans? Are they Nazis, too?"

Rudi could be just as determined as this boy. "If you cannot stop saying I am Nazi, I cannot talk to you."

"Okay, okay." Tommy groaned and rubbed his foot. Gently he placed both feet on the table. "Yeah. It's better when they're up." He adjusted, found a more comfortable position. "So you'll just keep living around here?"

"Maybe I am finding other Germans. Maybe crazy people on island." He wished he had a better idea. Every option seemed impossible.

"You might be safer with my family than them," Tommy said. "Maybe they wouldn't mind."

"No, Tommy. Family is not wanting me. You tell me before, and I understand," he replied, picking up the cards and shuffling again. "War means no person is trusting. All people are afraid."

"True. And nobody ever wants things to change." He wiggled one foot. "I guess I'm just as guilty as the next guy when it comes to that, because I'll admit I was a bit scared of you at first. I'm always hearing about Nazis being such cruel people, then you're all of a sudden in front of me, you know? You're a big man, you're strong, and you've killed people. And me, well, I was practically dead when you found me." He sorted the cards in his hand. "You could have just killed me and nobody would've known."

It was ironic, Rudi thought, how his own thoughts had gone along a similar path. Tommy was in rough shape, but whether he realized it or not, he held a lot of power over Rudi's immediate future.

"But now," Tommy continued, thinking out loud, "I actually think I might trust you. It's like you're just another fellow from back home, except you've been looking after me better than most of them would have. So thanks."

"You are welcome." He thought about it. "I might trust you, too."

Tommy gestured towards his feet. "Easy to trust me, I guess. Not much of a threat."

"You are hungry?" Rudi asked, changing the topic.

Tommy laid two royal pairs on the table, gave Rudi a smug grin. "If you want to ask me a question, you have to put the words in the other order. 'You are hungry' is like telling me I'm hungry. You should say, 'Are you hungry?' And yeah. I'm starving."

FIFTEEN

In the morning, Tommy woke up first. When he tried to stand he crumpled to the floor, sputtering what Rudi assumed were some very strong curse words.

"Would you look at that," Tommy said softly.

Rudi peered over the side of the bed, curious, then flinched at the awful smell rising to his bunk. Tommy had finally stripped off his heavy grey sock and was peering closely at his foot.

"I . . . I think I've got to get to a doctor."

Rudi dropped off the bunk and crouched beside him, and his stomach curdled at the sight. A couple of toes on one foot were badly swollen and had darkened to a mottled red. This wasn't the first time Rudi had seen something like that, and he knew it was more than just a minor problem. Tommy was right about the doctor, except Rudi had no idea how they were going to get him medical help. The snow lay under a warm, promising blanket of sunlight, but the drifts had piled too high for them to simply walk through.

After another check of the blisters bubbling between Tommy's toes, Rudi decided he had to do something. While the boy rested, he went out and shoveled hard, starting on a trail so he could bring him home. He peeled off his coat and hat when sweat rolled down his back, and his arms shook from exertion after an hour or so. He straightened, peering beyond the trees towards the open meadow, wondering. If he could carry the boy on his back . . . except Tommy was almost the same size as Rudi. He'd never manage. And he suspected Tommy had a couple of broken ribs. If he carried him, the pain would be too much.

When he got back inside, Tommy was asleep, but he was restless. The shadows under his eyes were alarmingly dark against his pale cheeks. Carefully, Rudi folded back the blanket at the base of the bed. When he saw the frostbitten toes up close, his stomach sank. It didn't matter how much snow blocked the way, he couldn't wait any longer. Tommy's blisters had doubled in size and the bedding under his foot was stained with discharge. If it got any worse, if it evolved into gangrene, Tommy could lose a lot more than a couple of toes.

He couldn't let Tommy die. And that changed everything for Rudi.

He stuffed as much as he could into Tommy's pack, then pushed the boy's shoulder, jarring him awake. "Wake up. We go today."

Tommy pried his eyes open and blinked. "You said we can't. It's okay. We can go tomorrow."

"We cannot stay. I am taking you." He held out his hands as if he carried a tray. "What is meaning this?"

"What are you talking about?"

"I am hold—"

That woke him up. "You're planning to *carry* me?" Tommy struggled up onto his elbows, managing to laugh despite his obvious pain. "No way. They'd call me a fathead for sure if you did that. We have a sled out back. You know, for carrying firewood or a deer or something. It's hanging on the wall."

Rudi waited, unsure. "You have a fat head? This means headache?"

"What? No, no. Means I'm a dummy. Stupid, you know?"

"Stupid, I know," Rudi said wryly. *"Beknackt. Dumm."*

"Yeah. Dumb. Anyhow, I was talking about the sled out back."

"Sled?"

He made a motion, as if to drag something along the floor. "Yeah. You pull it."

A huge weight lifted off Rudi's shoulders. "Ah. *Ein Schlitten.* Yes. I need this. Where?"

"Against the wall." Tommy jabbed his thumb towards the back. "Outside."

Throughout the morning the temperature had risen dramatically, and the recent snow sagged, heavy and wet. Tiny drifts melted off branches like rain, cutting rivers into the snow. Slogging through it would be hard going even without the added weight of pulling a man in a sled, but the sun on Rudi's face was welcome. He used pillows from the bunks to make a chair of sorts out of the sled, then he helped Tommy into it and covered him with blankets. The sled had a handle, but Rudi decided to tie a rope around his waist and attach that to the handle so he could walk straight ahead, pulling Tommy behind.

"Usually I'm the one driving the wagon for the family," Tommy said, his voice groggy. "I guess you're my horse today."

"Do not sleep, Tommy," Rudi warned, stepping into the harness. The sled had sunk into the granular snow and didn't seem inclined to budge. He grabbed the handle and yanked, knocking his passenger back. "I do not know where is house."

Shoveling had been a lot of work, but Rudi was glad he'd taken the time to clear a good portion of the path. Other than the occasional tricky spot, they moved along fairly smoothly.

"I guess you're stuck now," Tommy said as they went.

"I am not stuck. We are going good."

"No, I mean you're kind of in a bad spot. What we'd call a predicament. Before this happened, you could've left me at the camp. Now you have no choice but to take me home and meet my family."

"Yes. No choice. I am sorry, Tommy."

"Why do you say that?"

He looked straight ahead but kept his voice raised so Tommy could hear. "German man is making trouble for family. Maybe they call *Polizei*."

"Nah. Not if I tell them about you."

"Tommy, even I do nothing, I am still being your enemy."

Farther down the path, Tommy spoke up again. "If they did call the police, would you be scared?"

"Would you?"

"Huh. Sure. It's just odd to think of a German being scared."

"Odd?"

"Odd. Strange. Because we hear all the time about how Germans are monsters."

Rudi opened his mouth to object, then he heard his father's words, the last piece of wisdom he'd ever shared with his son. He'd spoken them on the night before Rudi headed out to sea with U-69.

"The rest of the world fears us," he'd told his only son. "Our military is powerful, and we have a good chance of winning the war. But what you need to remember, son, is that no matter how many people we conquer, we are not the 'master race.' That is because no matter what you might hear, *there is no master race*. You must never allow yourself to believe you are better than another person."

Rudi had been stunned at the declaration and by the conviction in his father's voice. Even more, he was astonished at the risk his father, a lieutenant commander in the German Navy, had taken by saying this to Rudi. It simply wasn't safe to say things like that out loud.

Rudi cleared his throat. "Some Germans are monsters," he confessed to Tommy. "Some Canadians are monsters."

"That's true enough. I guess it's all about what you know. The radio says things, and the newspaper. You hear it enough, you just believe it without question. I suppose that happens in your country just like it does in mine."

He was right about that. When he'd first seen Canadian newspapers, Rudi had been shocked by what he'd read. For the first time he'd learned about some of Germany's losses—as well as those of the enemy. No mentions of defeat ever made it into German newspapers or radio. Made him wonder how many of the German news stories about Hitler's unstoppable fighters were actually true.

"I think this is how begins war. People do not listen to people."

Tommy didn't answer, and when Rudi looked back he saw he'd fallen asleep, lulled by the sled's rocking motion and a possible fever. He woke up when the sled couldn't avoid a hole in the snow, but Rudi dug them out and kept on walking, apprehension growing by the minute. Step by step they were nearing a place where he would become even more of an outsider. Leaving the relative safety of the cabin exposed him to the real world. Even if these people didn't know his background, they would see him as hostile; they'd be suspicious of everything he said or did. And they'd be right to feel that way.

"I think maybe is better you not say 'Nazi' to family," he told Tommy after a while. "Maybe say only German."

"I know what you're saying, but that wouldn't be honest," Tommy replied, "and they'd figure it out after a while. I did. It probably doesn't really matter anyway, since you're not fighting anymore, right? Listen, I'll tell them all how you saved my life. They can't hate you when they know that."

Yes, they can.

"What do you think?"

"I know nothing."

Pathetic as that sounded, it was the truth. Ever since he'd woken up weeks ago with his face stuck to the ice, he had no idea what was going on.

"I'll tell my mother who you are. I'll explain."

"And *Vater?*"

"Oh, my dad died years ago. He was out fishing."

"Sorry."

"It happens," Tommy said, false bravado in his young voice. "Fishermen drown. That's the way it is. How about your father?"

Rudi didn't like to speak of his parents. Especially since he'd been given very disturbing news about them a few months back, and he'd been doing all he could not to think about that.

He knew how to end that conversation. "He is dead. And my *Mutter.*"

"I'm sorry."

For a while all Rudi heard was the shushing of snow under the sled's runners, the songs of birds celebrating sunshine, and his own heavy, wet steps. Tommy told him to keep to the path, then fell asleep once more.

Left alone with his thoughts, Rudi remembered his parents. The last time he had seen them they had hugged him briefly, stoic expressions pasted on their faces. They'd waved a sombre farewell from the docks as his U-boat coasted out to sea, and at the time Rudi thought he might burst with pride. He was sailing off to defend his country, and he was doing it as a part of the same navy in which his father had sailed twenty years before.

Then things had begun to change. Out of the forty-four men on board U-69, Rudi was one of only a dozen or so who had been part of the Hitlerjugend way of life. Their training was far superior to that of the other sailors, and that became obvious from the moment the crew stood at attention on the deck of the sub for the first time. The Hitlerjugend graduates were the ones with the stiffest backs, the fastest responses, and the fiercest loyalty on their faces. The others—well, they seemed more to be doing a job than serving der Führer. Those were the ones who laughed the most and complained even more.

Over weeks and months, Rudi watched those other men, curious. After all the rallies, all the drills in which he'd proudly participated, the dispassionate attitudes of these men seemed almost sacrilegious. And yet deep inside—far too deep for him ever to mention it out loud—he felt envious of their freedom. Had anyone else from the Hitlerjugend ever felt uncomfortable with some of the lessons they'd been taught? Because more than once Rudi had pulled his government-issued dagger from its sheath and stared at the inscribed words on the blade—BLOOD AND HONOUR—and wondered if those two things must always go together. Was one weak without the other? Did his reluctance to spill blood put his honour in question? He'd seen the violence, even been a part of it, and though he was good at getting the job done, that aspect of his duties had never felt natural to him. The pride the Hitlerjugend were supposed to feel as the builders of a new, rejuvenated Germany was fueled by a growing, self-righteous sense of hate, and while some of the others seemed to thrive on the power they were encouraged to wield, Rudi questioned it more and more. Was he the only one with doubts?

He still believed Germany would win the war, still staunchly opposed anyone who spoke out against the Führer, but he started to question the dogma and revisit the odd bits of advice his parents had given him, the opinions that had once made him question their loyalty to the party and to the country. *There is no master race*, his father had said. *You must learn English*, his mother insisted. He'd been angry at them, ashamed of their ignorance. Now that shame fell on his own stubborn shoulders. By the time he realized his parents had been right all along, they were gone.

Rudi became aware that the sheltering woods were becoming sparser. The frozen sea showed itself once in a while, its grey and black shadows drifted in stripes by the recent storm. He stopped walking and squatted beside Tommy, jostling him awake.

"Is time you not sleep. I am lost now."

Tommy took in their surroundings. "You're not lost, but we're almost there. Just keep going. I'll stay awake, I promise."

"Okay."

"When we get there, you let me do all the talking, right?"

"Ja."

"I should probably warn you that my mother gets nervous around strangers. I'm sure you understand. Her being a widow and all, well, seeing someone like you might scare her a bit."

"Someone like me?"

"Sure. You know. A big, strong stranger . . . and German, too. So I'll just do the talking. That'd be best." He thought more about that. "Actually, no. I've changed my mind. I think you should say hello to her. That'd be the polite thing to do. Try this. I'll tell her your name, then you say, 'Nice to meet you, Mrs. Baker.'"

"Nice meet you, Mrs. Baker."

"Nice *to*."

"Nice to meet you, Mrs. Baker."

"Then you can say, 'I am Tommy's friend.'"

A feeling of warmth spread through him. "I am Tommy's friend." He put a hand on his chest. "*Ja*, Tommy, *du bist mein Freund auch.*"

"'Mein Freund,'" Tommy echoed, then, "Okay. We're here. That house just ahead."

The small white house was an uncomplicated, two-story building with plain navy shutters. A slow stream of smoke twisted from the brick chimney, promising warmth and comfort, and small boot prints covered the yard, converging in a big cluster around a lopsided snowman. Despite the idyllic scene, apprehension roared through Rudi.

At the door, he leaned down to help Tommy stand. The boy gripped the sides of the sled and struggled to one foot, then he reached for the doorknob. The door swung open, and friendly voices called from inside. Rudi fought the urge to run the other way.

"Hey, don't worry," Tommy said. "I'll look out for you."

Rudi took a breath for courage. He had no choice. He'd leave it all up to Tommy.

SIXTEEN

"Tommy?"

A diminutive woman in a white apron rushed to the door, sweeping Tommy into her arms. Rudi saw him stiffen as the damaged ribs grabbed him, but the boy's smile was brave.

"Oh, Tommy! I was so worried about you! Oh heavens, I'm glad to have you home! Are you okay?"

"Yeah. Uh, Mom, I had a little trouble, but—"

She released him and stepped back. "Trouble? What happened?" Her hands went to his face. "Oh, you're pale, Tommy! Did you—" She stopped short, seeing Rudi. "Hello there. Tommy, are you going to introduce me to your friend?"

"Mom, this is—"

"Nice to meet you, Mrs. Baker."

He had done all he could to round out the vowels, to soften the accent, but he could see she'd heard it. Her eyes went from welcoming to wary in one blink. *Nobody ever wants things to change*, he remembered Tommy saying.

Hello, Mrs. Baker. I am change.

"Mom, this is Rudi. He, well, I don't want you to go bananas on me, but he saved my life. He truly did. And then he dragged me all the way home."

"What?" She paled, but before she could ask anything about that, Tommy set his foot down and grimaced. "Oh, sweetheart, you're limping! Let's get you comfortable and then you can explain."

Still leaning on Rudi, Tommy hopped past his mother on one foot. She stepped out of the way, and Rudi was well aware he was being inspected the entire time. Was it his accent, or was it her fear of strangers he'd been warned about? Either way, he decided not to speak again unless he really had to.

In the living room, he watched them talk. Tommy spoke far too quickly for Rudi to understand everything that was being said, but he could tell from the horror on the woman's face that he was describing how he'd tried to get out of the ice.

Moments later she blinked at Rudi. "You saved my boy," she said gratefully.

"There's more to the story, Mom. After the storm, Rudi and I were stuck in the camp, and I think I broke a rib or two, but my toes, they—"

"Let me see. What's the trouble?"

She knelt by her son's feet, slipped off Tommy's boots, then rolled down his socks. His toes were much darker than before, and a couple of the blisters were actually bleeding. Both feet were a waxy kind of yellow.

"Oh, Tommy!" she gasped, her hands flying to her cheeks. "Frostbite! I'm going to call the doctor right now." She jumped to her feet and ran out the door without another word.

"My uncle has a telephone. We don't," Tommy explained.

Moments later she bustled back into the room. "The doctor's on his way." Her gaze went to Tommy's foot, and she clenched her hands. "Oh my. That looks terrible. I sure hope he can do something."

"Yeah. Me too." Then Tommy took a deep breath and blurted out, "Rudi doesn't have anywhere to stay. He was at the camp, but it's too far for him to head back now, so I said he could stay here a spell. Maybe help out while I get better."

Her mouth opened, but she seemed at a loss.

"I know he's a stranger to you, but he's not to me," Tommy said, filling the silence. "I wouldn't be here without him. I think we owe him a bed for a night."

She gave Rudi a tight smile. "Oh, I think we can do that, at least for tonight," she said. "He can bunk with you."

"Thanks, Mom. And don't worry. It'll be fine. Really."

Timidly, she asked, "So Rudi, where's home for you?"

Rudi had hoped this question could have waited. "I—"

"Mom, Rudi's German."

She hesitated just long enough for him to sense her shock. "So you . . . you don't live here in Nova Scotia?"

"No," he said. "I am living before in Germany, but I want living in Canada." He heard his mistake, rushed to fix it. "Sorry. I want *to live* in Canada."

"Rudi was with the German Navy," Tommy jumped in to explain. "But he doesn't want to fight anymore, so he was kind of hiding out at the camp."

Rudi winced. Somehow hearing the truth said out loud was worse than just thinking it.

"A deserter?" She covered her mouth as soon as she spoke the foul word. "I'm sorry. I didn't mean . . . that's a good thing, right? To want to desert from the German Navy, I mean."

Rudi found it easier to lie this time. "Yes. Is good thing."

She was considering his words when someone knocked on the door. "That must be the doctor." She gave Rudi an apologetic shrug. "Would you . . . I'm sorry to ask, Rudi, but I think it might be better if the doctor didn't know there was a stranger in the house. Fewer questions, you see. Maybe you could go to the shed for a little while? I will come and get you after."

Tommy agreed, though he sounded reluctant. "It's easier that way."

The shed was dark and musty, and the sweat from Rudi's long trek dried into a sticky, cold layer over his skin. He squatted in the corner, hugging himself and wishing none of this had happened. He should have let the boy drown. He should have walked away, let the rest of the ice crack and pull him under just as it had with Rudi's crewmates. Men died all the time. If Tommy had died, Rudi would still be living comfortably in the quiet camp.

Then he imagined Tommy dead, and he was ashamed. When had he become the kind of man who could think that way?

His instinct was to run, except a big part of him was tired of hiding. He was here now, and he had to believe this was for the best. As content as he had been at the camp, the uncertainty of his future had hung over his head like a rock. Here in the real world he still had no idea what might be in store for him, but at least he was no longer alone.

SEVENTEEN

"My mother wants you to meet Uncle Danny," Tommy said when Rudi came back inside. They'd just wolfed down some sandwiches, and Rudi was starting to feel more human. "He's kind of in charge around here."

"Now?"

"Yeah, I think so."

It was dark, but the house where they were headed was alight with electricity. Tommy had said his foot was already feeling better after the doctor cleaned it and wrapped it up, but he wasn't able to put any weight on it yet, so Rudi served as his crutch as they headed up the path.

"Uncle Danny's a good man, but he can be"—Tommy clenched his fist in illustration—"tough."

Tough. That was fine. Rudi knew tough.

The man who answered the door was tall, and Rudi estimated he was in his early forties. He was also wearing a wooden leg. Rudi stood tall but kept his face open, deferential, as he would while standing in front of his captain. He understood this kind of man, and he suspected strongly that what he said and did in this house would play a big part in determining his immediate future.

"Tommy!" Mr. Baker said. "I've been expecting you ever

since your mother said you were back." He eyed Tommy's bandaged foot. "You doing okay?"

"Yes, sir. I'm okay now." He gestured towards Rudi. "Uncle Danny, I want you to meet a friend of mine. He's kind of a stranger to these parts. His name's Rudi Weiss."

"Rudi Weiss." He held out a hand, and Rudi took it. Danny held on longer than Rudi expected, and his grip was tight. "So I'm to thank a Nazi for rescuing my nephew, am I?"

It felt a little like a slap. Rudi opened his mouth to respond, but Tommy spoke first.

"Rudi's not a Nazi anymore, sir."

"Oh really? Not anymore?" Danny slid his scrutiny to his nephew. "That sounds like an interesting story. Why don't you come in, and Rudi can explain how you two happened to meet."

Tommy gave Rudi one last warning. *Ready?* he mouthed.

Rudi smiled.

He entered the spacious living room, noticing the upscale but modest furniture. Paintings hung frame to frame on all four walls, some landscapes, but mostly portraits. He wanted to pause by each one, admire and appreciate the skill of the artist. He hoped he would get the opportunity.

"Audrey," Mr. Baker called down the hall, gesturing for the two men to sit on the couch.

"Yes?"

"Tommy and his friend are here. Would you bring us some tea, please?" He sank into an armchair, regarded Rudi coolly. "Too bad you've missed most of the family. My sons' wives have all turned in for the night. They work most of the day and have small children, so you understand they need to get their rest."

The only words Rudi caught were *family*, *children*, and *understand*, but he watched the man intently, wanting to comprehend everything. Mr. Baker was a soldier, he could tell, probably from the first war. His guarded countenance reminded Rudi of his own father; this man had a family to protect.

Tommy cleared his throat. "Rudi's working on his English, sir, but it's not very good yet."

"You been teaching him, have you?"

"Yes, sir. We were together a few days in the woods with nothing to do but play cards and talk, so we both learned some stuff."

"How interesting."

"You wanna hear how he saved my life?"

"I do love a good story."

Tommy relayed the story again, and Rudi had the distinct impression that Tommy was making him look better than he really was. Trying to get his uncle to think well of him, which Rudi appreciated.

"Well, that's quite an adventure."

Danny leaned back, his fingers steepled in front of his mouth. His gratitude seemed genuine, but Rudi knew it wasn't going to be that easy. It couldn't be.

"Thank you," Danny said, "for rescuing my nephew and bringing him back in one piece." He turned to Tommy. "How are your feet?"

"Just a couple of toes, sir. Doctor says he doesn't think I'll lose them. And I guess I broke a rib, which hurts like the dickens when I sneeze. I gather I'm pretty lucky—touch wood."

A flash of colour caught Rudi's attention, and he barely managed to contain his surprise. Standing in the doorway, gawking at him, was Grace.

"Grace, can you help your mother with the tea, please?"

"Uh . . . sure, Dad," she said, but as she turned away she shot Rudi a confused look.

Dad?! Rudi's palms were slick, his mouth dry. He did all

he could to look neutral, as if he hadn't recognized his host's daughter.

"And now Herr Weiss is living at your house?" Mr. Baker asked.

"Yes, sir. And he can help out since I can't do much."

"I'm sure." Mr. Baker studied Rudi thoughtfully. "He sure looks strong enough. Tell me, Tommy, did you find out what he was doing at our camp? A young, healthy German man all alone in the woods?"

"Of course. That was one of the first things I asked him."

"Because I must say, I never expected to have a Nazi in my living room." He squinted at Rudi. "Do I know you from somewhere?"

"He was at the dance," Tommy said.

"With his friends. That's right. And where are they now?"

"He doesn't know. He's been living on his own for weeks. His ship went down east of here and he says he was the only survivor, so like I said, he's been living on his own ever since. He was lucky to find the camp. And now he's decided he's staying here, not going back to Germany."

"I see," Danny said, tapping his fingers. "He deserted."

"Yes, well, I don't think he's proud of that part, but he says he doesn't want to fight anymore."

"Some might say that makes him a coward. Rudi, do you know that word?"

"No, sir. I don't think he knows it."

"I asked him, Tommy. Please let your friend speak."

"I understand, sir," Rudi replied.

"Good. So you understand that deserters are cowards."

"Yes, sir. Deserter is bad. But please understand. Nazi is more bad."

"Why do you want to stay here?"

"Is good, Canada. And people not killing."

"Sure we are. My boys are out there killing your boys right now."

Rudi stopped short, afraid he might accidentally say something he'd regret. He had to be smart, consider what this man was all about. What he'd done, what he'd lost.

"Yes, sir," he said. "Germany is starting war. I understand Canada must fight."

"He doesn't—"

"Tommy, don't you think your friend deserves a chance to speak for himself?"

Tommy slumped. "Yes, sir."

Grace and a woman Rudi presumed was her mother slid into the living room. He met Grace's eyes again when she stood between her father and him, offering tea from a tray, but he couldn't read her.

"So if you don't want to be a Nazi anymore, what's your plan?" Mr. Baker asked.

Grace almost spilled the tea in Rudi's lap. Wide-eyed, she turned towards her father, and Rudi wished he could disappear.

"Nazi?" her mother exclaimed. "What are you talking about, Danny?"

"Oh, it's nothing," Danny said, reassuring his wife. "We'll talk about this later. Thank you for the tea. Would you and Grace mind leaving us for a bit?"

Rudi saw Grace's reluctance in the way she stared at him, and once she and her mother left, he felt absolutely useless. She must have a million questions running through her mind. If only he could follow her out, try to explain. But Mr. Baker was waiting for an answer. All Rudi could do was try to convince this man to give him a chance. Maybe then he'd get the opportunity to speak with Grace again, to do what he could to ease the hurt from her eyes.

Grace

EIGHTEEN

Grace burst into her room and threw herself onto her bed, holding in a scream of frustration. A *Nazi? Really?* He couldn't just have been a shy trapper from somewhere "east of here"? But of *course* he was a Nazi! A damn murdering German most likely bent on killing them all. And he was a liar. He'd acted so quiet and sweet at the store, made her feel so special—how stupid she'd been! How utterly naive!

Then again, she should have expected something like this, she reminded herself. She should have known she couldn't get that lucky. After all this time, what right did she have to fall for a normal, attractive, interesting man? She squeezed the pillow, trying not to cry and failing miserably.

Her father knocked on her door. "Grace?"

She sat up, wiped her eyes. "Yes?"

"Can I come in?"

She didn't look too bad in the mirror. Maybe he wouldn't suspect the tears. "Sure, Dad."

He peered around the door. "You okay?"

"I'm fine. Just . . . oh, you know. Thinking about Norman."

"Well, I don't mean to intrude, but I wanted to tell you the same thing I just told everyone else. About the man downstairs. Rudi's his name."

"Oh?" Even hearing her father say his name made her feel

like sobbing again. "What was that you said about him being a Nazi?"

He stuck his thumbs through the base of his suspenders, leaned against her door frame. "We're in a bit of a spot right now. From what we've heard, he's a German deserter. But he did save Tommy's life, so—"

"What?!"

"Tommy fell through the ice. Rudi pulled him out and brought him home."

This was the strangest conversation she'd had with her father in a very long time. Maybe ever. How could he stand there, calmly calling Rudi a Nazi, then telling her Tommy almost died?

"Anyway," he was saying, "I've decided to let him stay with us for a while, since he doesn't have a place to live. He's been out at Abbecombec, at the camp." One eyebrow lifted. "But, Grace, I don't want any fuss about this. We're not going to mention to anyone that he's here until we get to know him better. If anyone sees him and asks who he is, we'll say he's a friend of a friend, freshly returned from war, and he's not in any condition to hold conversations. I want everyone to stay away from him, including you."

"Fine." She couldn't think of anyone she'd rather not see. "What's he gonna do out here? Work at the plant?"

"Tommy suggested that, but no. Whether he's deserting or not, he admits he was a Nazi. Not too many people around here would appreciate knowing we have one of them living here. I said he could stay and do some jobs around here until we figure out something else. That way he'll be out of sight."

She didn't know how to answer. So many emotions swirled through her, blocked her words. *Rudi's a Nazi. Rudi is a liar. Rudi's going to live right here!*

"All right then. You sure you're okay?"

"I will be." He started to close the door behind him, and she dared herself to say what she was thinking. "You're being awfully generous, hiding a Nazi here."

His mouth twisted to one side. "Well, we're not hiding a typical Nazi, I hope."

"Sounds like you are."

He sighed and drummed his fingers against the door frame. "We have to give him the benefit of the doubt. He saved Tommy's life. And he says he doesn't want to be a Nazi, which is something we should encourage, don't you think?"

"Yes, if you think he's telling the truth. I just don't know if he is."

"Of course. I'm unsure too, and I hope I made the right call. It's just that when I think about the predicament he's in, I can't help but think about your brothers. I'm doing what I hope someone would do for one of them, if it ever came to that." He shrugged. "We'll find out soon enough, I imagine."

She switched on the bedside lamp after he'd gone, sat back on the bed, and reached for *The Body in the Library*, thinking maybe Miss Marple could distract her. But the little wooden ladybug stared woefully down at her from its perch on top of her stack of books.

"You didn't tell me about him," she muttered, smoothing her finger over its back, "and I did ask."

For two days she followed orders and stayed away from Tommy's house, but she was aware of Rudi's presence every minute. She heard him hammering, occasionally saw him striding towards the shed, carrying supplies. When he paused mid-step and glanced up at the house one afternoon, she actually ducked behind her window.

And that's when she decided it was getting ridiculous. He might be the enemy, but he wasn't going to force her to hide in her own house. She had to face this problem head-on. On Sunday morning, as her family prepared for church, she excused herself, saying she felt unwell. Her mother came to check on her, but she waved her off.

"I'm not a child, Maman. And I'm not deathly ill. Thank you, but I'll be all right. I just need a little rest."

Then the bells on the wagon jingled, her family's voices faded, and Grace got to work.

Rudi

NINETEEN

The shed needed more than a new roof. The walls were rotting, as were some of the shelves—one had even collapsed, and everything was in disarray as a result. Once they had done an inspection, Mr. Baker arranged for a delivery of lumber so Rudi could fix the whole building. When he wasn't working on the construction, Rudi took care of Tommy's jobs, since his damaged foot made him just about useless around the house.

Tommy was contrite about Rudi's assignment in the barn, but Rudi waved him off. "Is good here, Tommy."

"Yeah, but he's not paying you. At the plant he'd pay a dollar and a quarter."

Rudi leaned against the wall. "This is good work, Tommy. I am not in *Gefängnis*—"

"Guh-fengus?"

He held both fists in front of his face as if he were holding bars.

"Prison?"

"*Ja.* I am not in prison."

"True enough."

Like everything else in his life, Rudi approached the work with determination, wanting to do the best he could possibly do. Mr. Baker kept an eye on him from a distance, came to examine his work every few hours, and he appeared generally pleased. He had given Rudi a chance to prove himself, which was all Rudi could ask for. And even though the guilt of abandoning his post and leaving the war still bothered him, a part of him felt freed, as if he could look around with open eyes for the first time in his life. He wondered what that said about him.

Under orders, Rudi never went farther than the house and barn. No one from outside the family saw him, so no one questioned the stranger in their midst. Of course, that included going to church—Tommy said Rudi's being there would "raise quite a ruckus," whatever that meant. It didn't much matter; Rudi hadn't been to church in years. So when the Baker family climbed into their sleigh and headed off to worship, Rudi went out to cut firewood from the load of cordwood that had been delivered the day before. He levered some of the long lengths onto a sawhorse, then cut them into a respectable pile of stove-length pieces using the bucksaw. Once they were split, he stacked them to dry where the sun could beat down on them.

It was a good, hard day's work, and it took his mind off everything, even Grace, of whom he'd caught only glimpses since he had stumbled into her house with Tommy that night. When he was done, he went inside the house and stripped down to his undershirt and trousers. He washed his face and hands, scrubbing off grime and sweat, then sat at the kitchen table with a newspaper to enjoy a few quiet minutes.

"Don't you look just like a regular Canadian guy, sitting there, reading the paper."

He nearly jumped out of the chair. He hadn't heard Grace's voice in days, and he had no idea what to say to her. He folded the newspaper neatly, set it aside.

"I brought you something."

She dropped a comic book on the table in front of him, her manner far less friendly than when she'd first sold him a can of tomatoes. Her eyes travelled over his undershirt, then she looked away. He was embarrassed that she saw him in this state of undress—especially since his shirt was still damp with sweat.

"It's an older one that I dug out of my cousin's collection," she said, indicating the comic.

The bright yellow cover was crowded with superheroes, all of them intent on foiling the Führer. Hitler himself gaped up at Rudi, his wide eyes uncharacteristically afraid.

"Ah," Rudi said, guilt landing like an anchor in his belly. He searched for the right words. "Thank you. I am not seeing this one before."

"Looks like a good one. 'Daredevil Deals the Ace of Death to the Mad Merchant of Hate.' I hope he really gave it to him."

What could he say? "I am not this," he tried, tapping his finger on Hitler's face.

"Maybe not today." The barb in her tone stung. "Listen, you may not be good at English, but you're a good storyteller, Rudi Weiss. You tell me one thing, then you tell my father and everyone else something entirely different. Which are you really, a trapper or a deserter? What would you do if I told my father that you're also a liar?"

He had wondered when she'd finally ask him that. "Why . . . you are not telling him before?"

"I wanted to see if you would."

Avoiding the accusation in her voice, he turned the page of the comic book, hoping to see something other than Hitler's panicked face. The next few pages weren't much better. The Führer was fat and ridiculous, bellowing orders which the allied superheroes swatted away like flies.

He shook his head. "I cannot say to him."

"Here's the problem," she said, setting one hand on her hip. "I have no idea who you are. I obviously can't trust you. Maybe you're something worse than either a trapper or a deserter."

"Worse?"

"Are you a Nazi spy?"

"Spy?"

"Don't lie to me!"

He held up his hands. "I do not know this word!"

She growled. "Are you telling other soldiers, other Nazis, about us? Are we in danger because of you?"

Spy . . . *ein Spion.*

"No! I am not."

She leaned towards him, her cheeks blazing. "I don't believe you!"

"It is truth! I am only me! I talk to this family is all."

"Another lie. I saw you at the dance. There were six of you there. Six." Her arms folded over her chest. "Tommy bought your deserter story, but I know you are *not* alone. You have five others with you. Where are they?"

"I think they are dead."

She shook her head, her lips tight with fury. Her eyes were shining.

He felt sick with guilt. "It is truth, Grace. I am alone." He closed his eyes, resigned. If any of his men were still alive, he sincerely hoped he wasn't about to betray them. "We come to dance from U-boat."

"What? You were on a *U-boat*? Here?"

"This is my work, U-boat. We are sailing many weeks. We want only to see people and have good time for one night. Is deep water near dance place. Is possible for us." He swallowed. "We have good time, then we leave. But U-boat is *kaputt gemacht. Zerstört.* Is *explodiert.*" He threw his hands up. "You understand? *Bombe?* U-boat is no more. My men . . . my men is no more."

She blinked. "That was *your* U-boat?"

"*Ja.* Is my U-boat. I am on ice, and I run. I am only me. I think others are dead."

She sank onto the chair behind her, two fingers pressed to her lips. "Oh, they're dead, all right. Linda called me and said a group of soldiers scouted out the island the day after the explosion. They came back empty-handed."

So it was true. He was alone. Everyone had died but him. He should have expected it, and yet grief gripped his throat. He dropped his head into his hands.

"You ran because you had nowhere to go." She spoke slowly, thinking it through. "You never planned to desert, did you? I mean, you only ended up here because your sub got blown up." Her tone was not sympathetic. "You and your Nazi U-boat came here to kill us, and now we have you."

He lifted his chin. "I am not here to kill you."

"You sailed in a boat that kills people. You've probably killed lots of people."

Memories of that October night threatened to return, but he swallowed his regret. None of this was his fault, and he was damned if he was just going to stand back and agree that it was. He was sorry the war was affecting people, hurting them, killing them, but he couldn't apologize for either the war or the past.

"I do my job," he replied. Annoyance rose quickly, like a bubble. "This is my job, and yes. I am German."

"You are a Nazi! You are the worst of the worst!"

He slammed his hands on the table. "What do you want, Grace? You want to kill me? Put me in prison?" He held his hands up, wrists together as if he were shackled. "Maybe I go to prison and *they* kill me."

She didn't back down. "Maybe. Why shouldn't they? My brothers are out there fighting men like you," she hissed. "Two of them are in ships, being hunted by U-boats. And my other brother's dead." She had to turn away, and Rudi remembered Tommy mentioning his cousin's death. "It's all because of Nazis like you."

He said nothing, stifled his anger. Everything she said was true. He hoped to God he hadn't killed her brother.

Sleigh bells rang outside, distant but drawing closer. The family was returning from church.

"You tell all this to father?" he asked.

It was a moment before she faced him again. Her anger had melted away, and her cheeks shone with tears. He had done that. He deserved whatever he got just for hurting her.

The bells were louder now; he heard a couple of voices as well.

"I tell to him tonight," Rudi told her, making up his mind.

Without a word she strode to the door, then paused with her hand on the knob. "You know," she said, her back to him, "I liked you. I wanted to believe you." Her voice had softened again, and he longed to reassure her. "I never really did, but I wanted to."

TWENTY

An hour later, he stood alone before Mr. Baker's chair, fulfilling his promise to Grace.

"Mr. Baker, sir. I have story."

"I'm listening."

Rudi let out a measured breath. "Is story of German U-boat sailor."

"Oh? Do you know this guy?"

"Yes, sir. I know this guy." He stood taller, dared himself to go on. He'd promised her. "This guy and friends win card game on boat. Prize is go to land for one night. They hear music, and are happy to find party. Lots of people dance, have good time."

Danny's frown was curious. "They got off the sub? Huh. Never heard of that before."

"Is maybe first time. I do not know. But is truth. Kapitän-leutnant say is okay."

"Wait," Danny said slowly. "Are you—"

"After dance men go back to U-boat. Next day comes airplane with *Bombe*. Boom! U-boat is gone. Only one sailor come out." He sat down, resigned. "End of story."

Danny was now staring openly at him. "What are you saying? That U-boat in the channel . . . Are you talking about that one?"

Rudi didn't need to answer.

"You were on *that* U-boat?" He shook his head. "But you told us . . ."

"I tell lie."

Danny's fingers curled around the arms of his chair. "So you're *not* a deserter."

"Sir, please, I must tell more story. When I come here, I am Nazi, yes. I am not deserter, not anything, just afraid. I go to camp and I am okay." He took a deep breath, finally saying out loud what he'd been contemplating for a while. "And now I feel myself happy for first time. I work hard, I hurt no one. I want to stay."

Danny was staring so intently at him that Rudi had to make a conscious effort not to look away. There was nothing more he could do to plead his case. He had given himself up to the inevitable conclusion, to the prison cell or firing squad or whatever the authorities decided to do with him, so he was taken completely off guard when Mr. Baker asked him to describe what it was like on the U-boat.

"Sir?"

"On a U-boat. Tell me about it."

"U-boat . . . it is hot, sir. Many people in small place for long time."

"Crowded."

"Yes, sir. Smells very bad." He tried desperately to remember what he'd tried so hard to forget. "We do not see many things, only U-boat."

"Of course. Because you're underwater. Did you enjoy being a sailor on a U-boat? A member of the Third Reich?"

He swallowed. "It is . . ." What was the word? "*Meine Pflicht*, what men do for country."

"Your duty, then."

Duty. He must remember that word.

"All right. I have another question. Were you proud to be on that ship? When your captain spotted enemy ships and ordered you to fire, was it exciting?"

How should he respond? Certainly being with the navy had been exciting at times, and he did indeed recall the thrill of firing a torpedo at last, after a long hunt. Was he proud of himself? Shouldn't he be? He had worked his whole life to be where he'd ended up. Yes, he was proud, but it wasn't like when he'd first started. The indistinct, abstract acts of distant violence they inflicted had begun to cut through his resolve when he thought about the men, like him, who lived on the ships they destroyed. U-69's intent was only to sink the ships and stop shipments, but men died along the way. Lives were lost. And with those lives went the photographs, the letters, the books, all the little things that proved those men had ever existed.

Rudi had spent many nights in his bunk, battling his conscience, trying to persuade himself that they were in the right, that he had nothing to regret. Only the notion of duty had calmed his tormented conscience.

"Rudi?"

He swallowed, tasting panic. "This is my duty, sir."

"That was not my question, sailor. Did you like being on board that submarine?"

He should have died weeks earlier. He should be forever trapped under the sea with the rest of them. Every day he lived was one he did not deserve, and he had no right to ask for more.

But this family had taken him in, hidden him, trusted him. The man seated before him had given him the benefit of the doubt despite his natural suspicions. And now Grace, beautiful Grace, suffered because of Rudi's lies. Because of him. He had to make it right, try to heal the hurt he'd inflicted, prove to her he was not the terrible man she now believed him to be. But how could he repair so much damage?

His sense of duty had been his light in the darkness before. What was he supposed to believe in now?

Danny Baker still waited for a response.

Listen to your heart, son. Do what is right.

Rudi lifted his chin. "Sir, you ask if I am proud being in navy. Navy is all I do as boy, as man, and I do best I can. So yes. I am proud. But I understand why you ask this question. You think U-boat is . . ." He reached deep into his brain, searching for a word Danny had once put there. "It is coward boat."

Perhaps it was. After all, Rudi and his crew had been responsible for the deaths of men they'd never seen. They could easily have been responsible for Norman's death, and he'd never have known. It had always seemed an odd, detached way to fight, but that's all he knew.

"Do I like U-boat? No, sir." He set his jaw as emotions threatened to intervene. "But I am good sailor. I do my job. But I do not like to kill. I do not want killing. I do not want war."

He was not included in the brief family meeting which followed. Tommy had taken him to the kitchen, ordered him to stay put, then turned back. Betrayal burned in his friend's eyes, and Rudi hated himself for it. He had set that fire, put that pain there.

After a while, Mr. Baker cracked open the door. "We'd like to talk to you," he said, and Rudi followed him back to the sitting room.

Mrs. Baker surprised him by speaking first. She was delicate and beautiful, a fairer version of her daughter, with softer features. A faded scar cut across one cheek, and it made him wonder.

"Rudi, you lied to us," she said.

Grace sat beside her mother, stiff as an officer on a firing squad. What had she said to the others?

"But we also understand," Audrey continued, "you were in a difficult position. What we want to know is what is going to happen now."

He waited, but no one said anything. Other than Grace and Tommy, they didn't seem angry, just curious.

"Are you planning to stay?" she asked.

"I . . . I can stay?"

"Is that what you want?"

"Yes, yes! I want to stay. I want to work." He looked at Danny, stunned. "You are not reporting me?"

"Frankly, I don't know who I would report you to," he admitted. "Our guys would lock you up in Halifax. I have a feeling the Germans—if I could actually figure out how to get you to them—would be a lot harder on you."

"I work hard, Mr. Baker, and I am not lying again."

Tommy was the only one still scowling. "We can't keep him hidden forever."

"We can for now." Mr. Baker folded his arms. "Rudi made mistakes, but I don't see what else he could have done, honestly. I could be wrong, but I say he stays."

How could it be so easy? Rudi wondered. How could all his wrongs have become all right?

Mrs. Baker said, "People deserve second chances."

Grace's parents shared a look Rudi couldn't read, then Danny said, "Rudi did what he'd been told to do, just like Harry and Eugene are doing now. If they got caught in a similar situation, I'd want to think they'd be treated fairly as well."

"Thank you, sir." Rudi breathed. This was more than he deserved.

Mr. Baker turned to Tommy's mother. "Now, Elizabeth, it's your house. If you're not comfortable with him staying there anymore, you just speak up. He can stay here."

Without a word, Grace rose and quickly left the room. Everyone watched her go. Rudi's stomach clenched; he wanted her to stay, to say something so he'd have an idea what she was thinking. Her father's decision meant Rudi could speak to her again, that he had a chance to persuade her that he was trustworthy, if that was possible.

"I think Grace has some thinking to do," Mr. Baker said. "Elizabeth, you let me know by the end of the day about him living at your house."

The look Tommy's mother gave Rudi was sad and forgiving at the same time. "He's welcome to stay if it's okay with Tommy."

Tommy's attention was on his feet, and one hand scrubbed roughly through his hair. "You lie to me again, I'm throwing you in prison with my own two hands. Then I'm dropping the key in the ocean."

"I will not lie again." God help him, he prayed that was true. Now that all his ugly truths were out, there should be nothing left to lie about.

They met each other's eyes, then Tommy faced his uncle. "Then it's okay with me."

PART THREE

Grace

TWENTY-ONE

She wished she could see it like they did. She wished she could accept his story, go back to how it had been before all this mess started. But try as she might, she couldn't. Rudi hadn't just lied to the family, he'd lied to her. She'd been gullible enough to believe the handsome trapper she'd dreamed about was a good man. *Fool me once,* she thought. She wasn't about to be stupid like that again.

He'd finished fixing the shed—she'd overheard her father commenting on what a fine worker he was—and started on the decrepit old barn. She still saw him once in a while, carrying things, speaking with her father, but she never spoke to him. At the same time, she no longer hid in her window. Now she made sure he saw her scowling down at him. The last thing she wanted was to forgive him and fall back into that naive trance she'd been in before.

Fortunately, the past two days she'd been too busy to worry much about him. All the men—except Rudi—had been harvesting ice, which they did every February. It was an exhausting job, and it had to be done efficiently. Grace and the other women cooked meals to bring the men throughout the day to keep their strength up. Working long hours, the men cut through two-foot-thick layers of ice using seven-foot saws, then they sliced it into hundreds of one-foot cubes. Using massive tongs, they hoisted the cubes onto a sleigh as quickly as possible. If they were too slow, the blocks could freeze back onto the surface of the water. When the fully loaded sleigh arrived at the ice house, every cube was added to create a house-high stack, then packed with sawdust to retain the cold temperature through the rest of the year. As long as the weather cooperated, ice harvesting was a fun, friendly event that most of them anticipated every year. It was also back-breaking work, and Grace imagined they could have used Rudi's strength, but her father insisted they had to keep him hidden from view. Until when, she had no idea.

"Here you go, Tommy," Grace said, handing him a bowl of chili with a biscuit on the side. "How you keeping?"

He wiped an arm across his brow, sheepish. "Some of those old fellas are still stronger than me. I have to work twice as hard to keep up."

A group of her father's friends stood round the wagon, laughing about something while they enjoyed their meals.

"I think it's all an act," she told Tommy. "I doubt we'll see any of them for the rest of the week. They'll all be laid up and crying for attention."

"Now you're just trying to make me feel better," he said, tasting the chili. "Oh, that's good. So good."

She stood beside him, scanning the ice, enjoying the sunshine and the view.

"Rudi's not here," he said, his mouth full.

"Of course he isn't. Why would you say that?"

One eyebrow lifted wryly. "You gonna tell me you weren't looking for him?"

"Why, I ought to slug you for that. What are you talking about?"

Tommy winked. "You and him."

"Oh, stop! I can't stand him. Who could fall for a liar like that?"

"Okay, if that's how you want to play it," he said, biting into the biscuit. "Did you bake these?"

"I'm not talking to you anymore." But she didn't leave.

Tommy mopped up the last of the chili with the bread. "How long are you gonna stay mad at him?"

"Be quiet."

"No, really. Because he's different now. He's not as intense anymore."

She didn't mean to seek out the barn, but it didn't matter anyway. He wasn't outside. "I don't know, Tommy. Why bother? I don't need him to be my friend."

Tommy handed her his bowl when her father whistled across the ice. "I gotta go." He gave her another wink. "Say hi to Rudi for me."

She rolled her eyes, then stacked the bowl on top of the others already piled in the wheelbarrow. Time to wash and dry everything, then start all over again.

"You can do that yourself," she tossed over her shoulder.

But something Tommy had said made her smile—the part about Rudi being less intense. He'd been that way at the store: kind of gentle and sweet, not close-lipped and military like he'd been around her father's house. She assumed that meant he was more comfortable, enjoying himself since the lies were all out in the open. At least she hoped they were. She couldn't imagine him hiding anything else.

As she got close to the shore a pair of chickadees swooped low in front of her, racing to a nearby berry bush. The sight of them took her away from the cold, to spring. Soon the snow would go—maybe even as early as mid-March. Winters seemed to alternate between being eternal and just popping in for a few wild months, and she thought maybe this year they were due for a nice, early spring.

Just then her heel slipped on the ice and the wheelbarrow wobbled, rattling the bowls. She did a frantic little dance trying to stay upright, but both her feet and the wheel slid out of control. *No, no, no, no! Don't break the dishes!* she thought madly as she fell. But she never hit the ground, and neither did the dishes. A strong arm wrapped around her waist, and another steadied the wheelbarrow, sparing them both.

"Rudi!" She dropped her voice to a whisper as he set her back on her feet. "What are you doing out here? Someone will see you!"

"You are okay?"

"I, uh, yes," she said, glancing back. "I'm fine. Thank you for helping me. But you'd better get going. My father will be angry if he sees you out here in plain view."

"Yes, I am going." Then he smiled, gave her that same twinkle that had hooked her before. "But I am sad because I not seeing you, Grace."

"Yes, well . . ." She scowled, cursing her heart for beating so fast. "I've been busy."

"But maybe you come to see me? Like I come to store?"

In a flash she was back at the dance, her hand on his shoulder, following him around the floor in a fluid *1-2-3, 1-2-3*, knowing nothing about him except that she wanted to know more. She shook her head, hoping to send the traitorous memories flying, but they held on.

"I don't know, Rudi. I don't think that's a good idea."

His shoulders sagged. "Is okay. I understand."

Then he turned back to the barn, and she watched him follow the snowy path. When he was out of sight she grabbed the wheelbarrow handles again and pushed it off the ice, up the bumpy trail towards the house. The bowls and cups jingled, the chickadees chirped, and the booming voices of the working men bounced over the ice, but Grace didn't hear a thing the whole way.

Rudi

TWENTY-TWO

Inside the barn's tired walls Rudi had found years of neglect, which made sense considering the fish plant was the major focus around there. To him, the long list of unfinished jobs was a golden opportunity to win Mr. Baker's approval, and maybe Grace's too. Everywhere he looked he saw well-intentioned projects that had been started but never finished. In every corner lay old lengths of siding and rusty tools just waiting to be put to use. He'd gotten to work right away, hammering four coffee cans' worth of nails on the anvil until they were straight, then he'd patched all the outside walls, including the holes chewed by squirrels and mice on the badly weathered south side.

This morning he'd decided it was time to take on the roof. When he peered up, daylight spilled through, and he thought most of the trouble had come from wind damage to a hip cap, which was an easy fix. He'd have the roof tight by sundown. He rifled through the bits and pieces scattered around the barn and found a length of tin, which he measured and snipped, then he went in search of a ladder tall enough to reach the top. After a half hour or so he paused to check his work.

"I brought coffee."

Grace's voice was the last thing in the world he'd expected to hear, but there she was, standing at the base of the ladder, holding a steaming cup meant for him.

He tucked his hammer into his belt and climbed down, then he sipped from the cup she'd given him. "Thank you. Is very good coffee."

She pursed her lips and turned away.

"You are still angry."

"Shed looks good," she said.

"Thank you."

Grudgingly, she faced him again. "The barn looks better already."

The coffee could have arrived with her mother as it usually did, but this one time Grace had chosen to come. She was giving him the opportunity he'd been hoping for.

"I am happy you are come to see me, Grace," he said. "I miss very much seeing you."

"Yes, well, I can't stay," she said, then practically sprinted to the door.

"Wait! Grace!" But the door closed behind her, and when Rudi peered out the window she was rushing back up the path. What had he said this time? What was that all about?

He kept mulling it over as he climbed back up the ladder. At least she'd come. That was a start. He'd be patient, he figured.

Rudi got back to work fixing the roof, and though Grace's unexpected exit bothered him, time flew by. Lulled by the repetitive manual labour, he began quietly humming tunes from his childhood, and an hour passed. He loved to sing, always had. He'd been in the church choir as a small boy, and when he grew up he'd become an audience member. He'd loved going to the opera with his parents, loved the beauty of the music, the spectacle of the performance.

"La donna è mobile
Qual piuma al vento—"

"What is that?"

Grace was staring up at him, wide-eyed, a basket in her hand.

"This is Verdi." He stayed in place on the ladder, not wanting to scare her off.

She tilted her head. "What's Verdi? Is that the German word for music?"

"No." He held his laughter in check. "Music is *Musik*. Verdi is a man. He is *Italienisch*."

Grace still seemed confused.

"You never hear *die Oper*?"

"'Dee Oper'?" she echoed, then comprehension brightened her face. "Oh! You mean opera? No, I haven't."

"I am sad for you." He cleared his throat. "Now you hearing more. '*La donna è mobile*,'" he resumed, throwing his voice to the heavens. "'*Qual piuma al vento*'. . ."

When he finished the verse he looked down. She hadn't moved a muscle.

"I've never heard anything like that in my whole life."

He started slowly down the ladder. "You like it?"

"It was . . ."

He loved that she couldn't come up with a word and decided to give her some of his own. "*Die Oper ist kraftvoll, mächtig, emotional*—"

"Emotional! Yes! That's the same in English. You're right. That was very emotional. Gave me goosebumps." She didn't step back when he reached the ground, and he took that as a good sign. "You said it was Italian, right? Can you speak Italian?"

"No. I sing Italian, I am not talking it."

"You mean, 'I sing Italian, but I don't speak it.'"

"I sing Italian, but I don't speak it," he repeated carefully.

"That's right." She held up the basket of food. "Hungry?"

"Yes." He gestured towards an old chest set against the wall. "You will stay for lunch?"

"I already ate."

He gave her his best pleading look. "You will stay for *my* lunch?"

At first he feared she might bolt again, but she tightened her lips with resolve, sat on the crate, and primly adjusted her coat around her. Rudi sat at her side, making sure to leave space between them. Instantly, his feet and back thanked him; standing on ladder rungs was hard on a man's body after a while.

"Is there a lot of that kind of singing in Germany?"

"Yes. Much music and *Gemälde*." Seeing her blank expression, he began to mime, dipping an imaginary paintbrush into an imaginary pot, then thoughtfully stroking it over an imaginary canvas.

"Oh! Art! Painting and stuff."

"*Ja*. Painting and stuff."

"My mother is an artist—a painter, I mean."

"Yes? I am seeing—"

"I saw."

"Pardon. I *saw* paintings in the house. Very good. Beautiful, like you."

When she blushed like that he knew she was pleased, but he did worry he'd gone too far when she didn't answer at once.

Then she offered a careful smile. "Where did you live in Germany?"

He unwrapped the food, pulled out a sandwich. He hadn't realized he was so hungry. "Düsseldorf. We make good beer."

"Beer!" She laughed at that. "What else happens there?"

"*Karnevals*. We have many." He took a bite of the most delicious sandwich he'd ever had, then held it out for inspection. "What is this?"

"What, that? Well, it's corned beef. You know. From a can. You've never had it before?"

He shook his head and took another bite.

"You do good work," she said, admiring the barn. "I've never seen it so clean and organized in here before. Kind of reminds me of how the store was when I first started working there. Everything was all over the place, so I sorted it out."

"You are happy at store," he replied.

"It's just a store, but it keeps me busy, and yes, I guess it makes me happy. Some of my friends are helping in the war, but I stayed here."

He caught a note of regret in her voice and instinctively wanted to reassure her, to bring back her smile—especially since it had taken so long for her to find it—but he didn't think that was what she needed.

"You think war is better work for you?" he asked.

"I wonder about that."

He didn't agree. "I think store work is better than war work."

She tilted her head, watching him intently, and he could tell she was really listening. When a shiny black curl tumbled out from under her kerchief, she tucked it absently behind her ear, and the subtle movement brought Rudi back to the dance hall. He'd touched his cheek to the top of her head when they'd been dancing; he'd felt how soft her hair was. He wanted very badly to feel that again.

She was waiting for an explanation, so he cleared his throat. "On boat there is captain and there is cook," he said, holding out one hand at a time. He lifted one. "Captain in charge." He dropped his other hand. "But if is no cook, captain is not eating. Or, there is captain and there is engineer. Without engineer, captain is going nowhere."

"That's an interesting way to put it," she said. "My father says people out here still need the store, that I am doing something useful."

"Your father is smart man. War is big, but war is not all things. War is not life. This . . ." He gestured around the barn. "This is life. Is living."

"I like that." She let out a satisfied breath. "My father's happy with your work out here."

"That is important, to keep father happy."

"What was yours like? Your father, I mean. I hope you don't mind my asking."

He loved that she was asking. "*Mein Vater* is—was—navy man. Always navy. I grow up with marching and drill and—" He lifted his hand to his brow in a mock salute. "Always *Jawohl*, 'yes, sir.' Is not sit and talk. When I am boy, maybe yes. Not when I am man."

She was watching him closely, her lips slightly open. "You've always been a soldier, then. We heard that: Germans train their armies as soon as their children can walk."

"Not this young."

"What about other things? Did you go to parties? Did you have friends?"

"Of course. But these are not like your dance. My friends and me dance with pretty girls, and we laugh, but we always talk of war. Men say, 'When can I go? I cannot wait.' And I say these things too, but I . . . I am not knowing what I talk about. Now, *ja*, now I know."

Her face fell, and he was sorry for saying anything.

"I'm glad we're talking like this," she said.

"You are? But I make you sad."

She worried one of her nails. "I am sad, but it's not your fault. I'm sad that there's a war, and I'm angry that so many boys

have to be out there, getting hurt or killed. It's such a waste."
She took a deep breath and let it all out. "Like my brother,
Norman. Gosh, I miss him. I hate that I—"

She was on the verge of crying, Rudi realized helplessly.

"I hate that I can't accept the fact that he is dead," she
finished. "I just can't seem to forget about him." She plucked
a handkerchief out of her apron pocket and dabbed at her
eyes. "I'm sorry. You don't know anything about me or him. I
shouldn't come crying to you."

"I like listen to you."

Gratitude swam in her eyes.

"No person can tell you to say goodbye, Grace. You love
your brother."

"I do. And I miss him so much. I miss my other brothers
too, but at least we hear from them most of the time. Those
letters are all I have to keep me going these days." She sniffed.
"Did you write a lot of letters to your family?"

"I have only sisters, but we do not write." Wouldn't that
have been nice, Rudi thought, to unfold a piece of paper and
know he hadn't been forgotten.

"Did you have a girlfriend?"

"No," he said, pushing any past dalliances from his mind.
They didn't matter at all; Grace mattered.

They both sat up straight when they heard her name being
called.

"Guess I'd better go," she said, rising.

He hung on to the reluctance in her voice and stood with
her. "Grace, your mother talk of second chance. I hope for second chance with you."

The corner of her mouth curled slightly, but she sighed.
"Rudi," she said. "I'll tell you the truth. I wasn't sure I wanted to
talk with you ever again. When I met you at the store you told

me you were German, and I guess because you were so nice, and the ladybug was such a sweet gift, I never even thought you might be a Nazi, of all things. Then you showed up here with Tommy, and well, everything got all mixed up. First you're a quiet trapper, then you're a hero, then you're a German spy—"

"I was never spy, Grace." She lifted a skeptical eyebrow, but he shook his head. "Never. But tell me, if I say in store that I am coming from U-boat, what you are doing?"

"I don't know. Probably wouldn't have spoken with you." She grimaced. "Reported you, maybe."

"I am . . . still nice."

"Yeah, but . . ." She didn't go on.

"So answer is no?"

"What answer?"

"You give me second chance?"

"You are determined, aren't you?" From the laughter in her voice, he could tell he was winning her over. "Stubborn, I mean. You don't give up."

"No, I don't give up."

She reached out, touched his hand. "Rudi, I want to trust you, but it's confusing."

She was right about that. "I know, Grace. But I am not giving up."

Rudi could feel the warmth of her hand on his even after she left, and her touch energized him. He inspected the building, deciding which project he might tackle after he finished with the roof. He noticed that one of the vacant stalls was being used for storage, and when he pulled back a tarp he uncovered a generator that had been sitting there a long time, unused. He couldn't see anything indicating what it had been used for or why it had been put away, but he thought he could probably figure out a way it could be put to use once more. The instructions on the label were in English, but that didn't matter. As a submariner, he knew machinery like the back of his hand, and this one piqued his interest. He'd shown Danny Baker he could handle a hammer. Maybe he'd be interested in Rudi's other abilities.

Grace

TWENTY-THREE

One of the hardest things about having Rudi around was not being able to tell Linda about him. She'd told her before about his visits to the store, but after Rudi had shown up at her house with Tommy that day, Grace waved off Linda's persistent questions by saying the trapper had disappeared. After all, her father had made it very clear she wasn't allowed to speak with anyone about him, and she understood the reasons. But the two girls had always shared secrets, and Grace was dying to tell her about Rudi and her confusing feelings for him.

When the telephone started ringing she immediately thought of her friend. How long would Grace be able to keep the secret?

"Hello?"

"Hey, Gracie."

It was Harry. She nearly dropped the phone. "Are you all right?"

He took a breath, and all the worst thoughts filled her head. Linda would have barged in on the conversation if she was still on the line, but she didn't. Maybe someone else was working the switchboard for a change.

"I'm fine, but—"

"Is Eugene all right?"

"Yeah, yeah. He's fine. We're both in Halifax. We wanted

to surprise you all by taking our leave at the same time. But something's happened . . ." One more tiny breath, then, "We found Norman."

The room vanished. The paintings and the ceiling and the walls disappeared and she couldn't find air to breathe. *Norman's alive! How was that possible?*

"Grace? You there?"

"But . . . is . . ." Her voice shook. So did the hand holding the phone. "Is he okay?"

Again he hesitated, and she wanted to scream.

"Harry! Is he okay?"

"He's alive, but no, Gracie. No, he's not okay. We're bringing him home. Can you find Maman and Dad right now? There's . . . a little explaining I need to do."

"Yes, hold on."

"I'll be right here."

In a blur, Grace raced through the house, calling out for her parents.

"What is it?" her mother asked, wiping damp hands on her apron. "For goodness' sake. One might think you—" She blanched, seeing Grace's face. "What is it? What's wrong?"

Her father came around the corner. "What's going on?"

"Dad, it's Harry. He wants to talk to all of us. Hurry, please!" Grace hustled them to the phone and held it between them.

"Son? Are you all right?" Danny leaned forwards, straining to hear.

"I'm fine. But I need to tell you and Maman something. It's good and bad, but it's going to be real hard for you to hear it."

Audrey shook her head. "You tell me, Danny." She left Grace and her father to share the phone, then sat down, hands clenched.

"We're ready, son. What is it?"

"Dad, we . . . Eugene and I found Norman."

"What?" Her father's voice practically sang with joy. "Audrey! They found Norman!"

She gasped, then melted into sobs, making it harder to hear. Grace squeezed close to the phone. What else did Harry need to tell them?

"That's wonderful news!" Danny cried. "Well now, I just knew they were wrong about him! I just knew. Well, when—"

"Dad, there's more. There's a lot more. He . . ." Harry's voice was tight with restraint. "We found him in Halifax. In an alley. He's messed up bad and down about thirty pounds. Barely recognized him. I'm not sure he knows where he is. Eugene's with him right now."

Tears of confusion blinded Grace. *What does this mean? How can Norman be in Halifax and not know where he is? What's wrong with him?*

Her mother stopped crying and the room fell silent. "What is it? What's the matter?" Audrey whispered.

When Danny spoke next, he sounded subdued. "Bring him home," he told Harry. "I want all three of my boys home tonight."

TWENTY-FOUR

On the drive to the train station, her father spoke with them at length about what they might expect to see with Norman. "In my day they called it 'shell shock,'" he said, jaw tight. "It's . . . it's different for everyone. It's because of the damn war. How can you not lose your mind when your job is to kill as many people as you can?"

I do not want killing, Rudi had said to her father. And he'd actually seemed afraid as he'd said it. At the time Grace had assumed he was simply concerned about being turned in. Now she wondered if that fear went deeper.

The night was cold and miserable, the road slick with freezing rain. No one cared. All that mattered was getting Norman home. At the station, they went inside to wait for the train to arrive, but though they huddled by the stove, the cold ran bone-deep. When the train pulled into the station, the family went out onto the platform to greet the boys, but Grace didn't recognize Norman. He was hunched over with Eugene and Harry on either side, and his head seemed to have been swallowed up by a massive red beard.

Her father was the first to speak. "My boys," he said, opening his arms. "All three of my boys. My God, I've missed you."

At the greeting, Norman jumped back, the whites of his eyes glowing in the station's lights.

"It's Dad," Eugene said gently. "He's excited to see you is all. Nobody's gonna hurt you now. The whole family's here, Norman. You're safe."

Everyone stood still as stone, waiting for some kind of signal, but no one knew what to do. Grace stared at Norman, a strange numbness closing over her. She knew she was supposed to be strong, supposed to welcome her beloved brother back as if nothing had happened, but she couldn't make herself go to him. Couldn't stop the tears that trickled down her cheeks and dripped onto her coat to mingle with the freezing rain. Her brother was a stranger to her. She was a stranger to him.

Audrey spoke gently, as if he were a little boy. "Oh, Norman. You don't know how happy we are that you're home, my precious son."

But when she reached for him, he shrank away, staying nestled between his brothers like a timid child in a schoolyard.

Audrey stepped back, and Danny put a comforting arm around her. He held a hand towards the truck. "Come on home, boys."

"Here we go. Almost there," Eugene said, easing Norman towards the vehicle.

Tommy drove, and Norman sat in the back seat with his parents, curled up into himself. Grace rode in the truck bed between the twins, feeling very cold, very wet, and very small.

When they got home, her parents seemed to know exactly what to do. It was like they pulled the cord on a lamp, Grace thought, the way they went from their enthusiastic welcome to a calm and reassured caretaking. After filling Norman with cookies and cocoa, he was shuttled to the bathroom, where he was cleaned, shaved, and his teeth brushed, then he was wrapped in blankets by the fireplace. He remained mute throughout, and everyone else spoke in hushed voices.

"Better?" Eugene asked, one dark brow raised. "You sure do smell a hell of a lot better."

The anguish filling Norman's eyes broke Grace's heart. He was afraid, he was grateful, he was humiliated, he was lost . . . He took a shaky breath, but his lips closed before he could speak.

"You're gonna get better," Harry assured him. "We're with you now. It's all gonna get better."

It was Grace's job to inform Gail that she was no longer a widow. Earlier that evening, the decision had been made that Gail would not be informed of her husband's presence until he was cleaned up. They hadn't known what they'd see at the station, but they knew Gail wouldn't be strong enough to face whatever it was.

Grace stood in the doorway, fist over her mouth. At a nod from her mother, she left the family and hurried outside. She couldn't wait to get out of the house. It felt like it was closing in on her. The family's anguish felt hot and sticky on the walls. Outside, the freezing rain continued, pelting her cheeks as she crossed the yard. But even outside of the house she couldn't escape; with every step she saw Norman's tormented expression. He was back from the dead, but at what cost? She stumbled off the path, feeling dizzy, then stopped, afraid to take another step in case she fell.

Someone was walking up the path, coming towards the house. Rudi. She awoke from her stupor and rushed towards him, grabbing his arm. He looked confused but let her lead him to the side of the house, out of hearing.

"You are okay?"

She shook her head, not knowing where to start. "It's my . . . My brothers are home."

Rudi's eyes widened with alarm. "Oh. I am—"

"No, it's not about you, Rudi." She swallowed hard. The

words she had to say should have been so wonderful. How had it all gone so terribly wrong? "You see, all *three* of my brothers are home."

He shook his head slightly. "I do not understand. Your brother Norman? He is alive?"

Her chin betrayed her first, wobbling with emotion. "They found him in Halifax and brought him home, but he's not right. He doesn't know where he is. He's . . . he's . . ."

His arms were around her before she knew what was happening, and she grabbed a hold of his coat as if it were a lifeline. The dark, wet wool against her cheek felt safe, smelled familiar, and he held her steady. She sobbed into it, vaguely aware of his whispers, of his soothing hand on her hair, and she let the comfort he offered carry her away. He was warm, he was strong, and in that moment he was everything she needed.

But the moment couldn't last forever. She backed out of his embrace and scrambled for a handkerchief, but he already held one for her. She took it and covered her face, too embarrassed to look at him. She knew how she must appear: her eyes red and swollen, her nose running.

"You are not happy he is home?" he asked quietly.

She dropped her hands, shocked he should ask such a thing, and terrified she didn't know the answer. "Of course I'm happy!" she exclaimed. "I mean, I . . . He's alive! That's what matters, right?"

"Right."

"But he just sits there. He won't say anything. It's like he's a different person. I don't even know if he sees me there. I just . . . I don't know what to do! Will he ever get better?"

"Grace, he is maybe afraid."

How dare he say such stupid things at a time like this? "Of course he is," she snapped, angry and miserable all at once. "We know that. We know he's had a terrible experience. But now he's home, and we're going to keep him safe. It's just that—"

His hand curled gently around her arm. "No, I'm sorry. I mean he is afraid maybe family do not want him anymore."

"What?" That made her pause. "Why wouldn't we want him?"

"Your brother is army, *ja*?"

She nodded.

"Army is . . ." She could see he was battling for words. "Army is difficult for any man. Your brother, he sees many, many terrible things in army, and he must kill men. This is . . . this is not Norman's . . ." He pressed his fingertips to his chest. "His *Herz*?"

It took her a second. "His heart? You mean it's against his nature to kill men? Of course it is."

"But, Grace, the heart, it can break from this. He is good man doing bad things. He is different now. If he is not the same as before, maybe he is afraid family will not like different him."

He might have stumbled over his words, but she understood. She was stunned by the awful thought, and guilt rushed in. "Oh."

Seeing Norman the way he was now had been so shocking, so real, so *unfair*, that she'd thought only of herself. Of how his change affected her. But of course he was hurting! He needed her—even more than she needed him. All of a sudden she couldn't wait to get back to the house.

"Rudi," she whispered, "thank you."

"I do not need thank you, Grace," he said tenderly, his hands in his pockets.

Somewhere a door creaked shut, and she remembered she had a job to do. "I have to get Gail, his wife. She hasn't seen him yet. We all need to be there for Norman." She stopped. "I meant the family. That was thoughtless of me."

He was so sincere, so sweet, such a contrast to the man they'd assumed he would be. Despite everything he'd done and said, she felt safe around him, and when they were apart, her mind dwelled on memories of his voice and his smile. On impulse, she put one hand on his shoulder and lifted onto her toes so she could kiss his cheek.

It was supposed to be nothing more than a thank-you gesture, but as her heels sank back down she couldn't stop thinking about the warmth of his skin against her lips. Tears surged to her eyes again, but they were different this time.

"Thank you, Rudi. For taking care of me."

The rain clouds had passed, and moonlight picked up the pale white of his smile. "If you need me, I am here."

Then he stepped out of her way, and she ran to Gail's, her mind a whirlwind of emotions. Her aching sympathy for her brother chased the thrill of Rudi until she could hardly see straight. Feeling slightly out of breath, she burst into Gail's house and delivered Norman's incredible news as clearly as she could, telling Gail he was back, he was *alive!* but she also warned her about that term her father had shared. About shell shock.

Gail gaped at Grace, not moving. "What's that mean?"

"He's . . . he's different, Gail, but he's going to be fine. You just need to be prepared."

Gail grabbed her coat from the hook by the door and together they sprinted back to the house. As soon as they were inside, Gail rushed to her husband's side. When he didn't show any sign of recognition, Gail looked at Grace, questioning.

"Is he deaf or something?"

"We've been talking to him in a normal way," she said. "I think he hears us, but he doesn't say anything. Just move slowly and he's okay."

Gail squatted by the arm of his chair, and though he didn't move his head, his eyes rolled up so he could see her.

"Norman?" she said quietly, tears rolling down both cheeks. "Sweetheart?"

Grace stood by the fire with Harry, watching in silence.

"Can you say something, sweetheart? Say hello? I've missed you so much. I thought you . . ." Gail's hands gripped the arm of his chair, and she swallowed hard to control her voice. "Little Joyce . . . she's walking and everything. You wouldn't know her, but she looks so much like you. She's so pretty." Gail was breathing fast, near panic, but Grace noticed she hadn't touched him once. "Please, Norman. Say something. Please? Tell me a joke? Make me laugh?"

No one spoke. The clock hit the hour and chimed nine times.

"Why won't he talk to me?" Her voice was shrill with hysteria. "Why does he look this way? What's wrong with him?"

"He just needs some time," Harry said.

"He's been on his own for a while," Eugene replied. "Dieppe happened more than six months ago, and we only found him today. He's real confused."

"What am I supposed to do?"

Grace's mother lowered herself to the floor beside Gail. "You just have to be there for him. Things will get better, but it might take a long time. His family is the one thing he needs."

Gail shook her head vigorously and started to rise. "I can't just *wait*. He needs to come home to me *now* and take care of us. His daughter needs him just like I do."

From the corner of the room, Danny finally spoke. "You don't think he needs you too, Gail? He needs you more than anything."

But her voice was thick with sobs. "I don't even know who he is anymore! He looks like Norman, but he's obviously not Norman!"

Grace felt helpless. Her poor brother's eyes were glistening. What was he thinking?

"That's enough, Gail," Danny said gently. "Norman is Norman. He's just having a rough time. The family's here for both of you, and we'll get through this together."

"Come with me," Audrey put her arm around Gail. "Seeing him after all this time has come as a great shock to everyone, that's all. I think you need to get some sleep, try to adjust. You will be fine, though. Just like Norman. And don't worry. We'll keep him here tonight."

Gail left with Audrey, looking pale and shaken.

Norman curled up in the chair, his shoulders rounded so his head hung low. His posture reminded Grace of a dog who had been caught doing something bad and now expected punishment, but what could Norman ever have done that might call for penance?

Rudi was right. Who knew what her brother had been through? It didn't matter to Grace, but the important thing was that it mattered to Norman. Maybe he thought whatever he had done was so terrible they couldn't love him anymore. Maybe that's why he'd never made it home from Halifax. Maybe the punishment he feared was rejection.

"She's just scared. We're all scared," Grace said, crouching by his side. "She loves you, Norman. She'll be back tomorrow."

Grace tentatively wrapped her arms around his neck. She was so relieved when he didn't pull away. He had lost too much weight; she could feel the bones of his shoulders. But he still smelled like Norman. He still *was* Norman.

"We love you," she whispered into his ear. Tears came

again, and she let them flow. "I've missed you so much, Norman. Every single day. You're my best friend," she reminded him. "No more going away for you. I know you don't feel right, but we're going to help you. No matter how long it takes, we're going to take care of you."

TWENTY-FIVE

Audrey put Norman to bed in his childhood room and stayed a while to help him adjust. While she was gone, Eugene put more logs in the fire and Grace made tea for everyone. They all settled in and waited for Audrey to return.

Danny said, "Damn, it's good to have all three of you home."

His voice cracked on the last word, and no one answered him. Then Audrey came into the room, her eyes rimmed with red. "I think he'll sleep. He didn't move when I tucked him in, but he was looking at me, you know—" she caught her breath "—with those sad eyes, and I—" She stopped short, and Danny reached for her hand.

Grace turned to her brothers, took a deep breath. "Please tell us what happened." When Harry and Eugene looked at each other, she stopped them. "No, no, no. Don't do that twin thing. Just tell us."

Eugene stood near the fireplace, hands in his pockets. "Today was supposed to be a great day," he said. "Harry and I planned it way ahead, coordinating leave time. We wanted to surprise you."

"Well, that happened." She gave him a wry smile. "Sorry. Go on. I won't interrupt."

"That'll be a first," Harry teased, taking a seat next to her.

She gave him a dirty look, then leaned against him. He put

an arm around her shoulder and gave it a squeeze. It felt good to share a joke after everything.

"We met at the navy building," Eugene said, "and we were on the way to a tavern for lunch when we spotted a man slumped in the alley. That in itself was nothing new. Men like that are all over the place. They don't eat, they don't talk to anyone, they just . . . exist, I guess."

That's what Norman seemed like to Grace. Like a starving stranger barely hanging on.

"Even on the ships," Harry agreed. "A lot of them live like that. Like shadows."

"But there was something about this guy."

"The beard."

"Yeah. The beard. Can you grow a beard like that?"

Harry shook his head. "You know I can't."

Grace had seen them try a few times when they were younger, but the bright copper scruff never managed to get past a certain point, and Harry's scar cut his into pieces. Norman had grown short beards before, but he'd always shaved them off, claiming they made him itchy.

"Anyway," Eugene went on, "maybe it was the way his head was angled, maybe the way he moved his hand . . . I really don't know. But we knew him."

"We went over and . . ." Harry dropped his eyes.

"We hardly recognized him through the filth on his face. But then we did, and we asked him to come with us. He kept staring at us, kind of blank, and then, well . . ." Eugene cleared his throat. "His mouth moved a little. He was saying my name. And that's when he cried. That's when we all cried."

Grace reached for Harry's hand, still resting on her shoulder, and their fingers locked together.

"I ran to the tavern and called you," Harry said. "When I

came back, I told Norman how warm it was in there, about the soup on the menu and all that, trying to say something that would help him think clearly again. God, it was so sad. He just stared up at me, those big eyes pleading like a baby's."

"He was helpless as a lamb," Eugene agreed. "He poked Harry's cheek—his scar—then he touched his own cheek, and we didn't know what to say. So we told him his face was okay. He just needed a razor. And soap. He stunk so bad."

"He wasn't scared of us, but everything else?" Harry shook his head. "His body shook like a leaf on a windy day. We had to hold him up, and the tavern owner didn't look too happy to see him, but that didn't matter." Harry sighed. "I saw some guys like this when we transported troops back. One of them had his jaw clenched so tight from nerves he couldn't speak. He couldn't do anything but moan. Another fellow I saw just cried all the time."

"You ever feel like that?" Eugene asked Harry. "Like you're losing your mind?"

"I don't think so. I mean, I've been so scared I couldn't think, but it seems to go away for the most part. Sometimes I can't really tell what's real and what's a nightmare. I don't sleep much, though. You?"

Grace had heard the brothers carry on these kinds of conversations between themselves before. It was like one was checking to make sure he was okay based on the other. It was comforting to hear them together, even if what they were talking about was unnerving.

"Yeah, I don't sleep either. Even when I'm on dry land I can hear the alarm bells, and I'm ready to leap out of bed at the slightest noise." Eugene turned to Danny. "Does it get better, Dad?"

Their father shrugged, squeezed their mother's hand. "Some nights are better than others, but I don't sleep much. Still."

Audrey looked across the room, met Grace's eyes, and she knew they were thinking the same thing. While they had worked hard at home, scrimped and saved, done all they could to survive this terrible war, none of it compared to what the men in their family had gone through. Her heart went out to each one of them, and another piece of it went to Rudi. Who had taken care of him when he got lost in the war?

"How did Norman get here?" Grace asked. "To Halifax, I mean. How did we not know he was still alive?"

Her father rubbed his chin. "I've been asking myself that same question. We'll just have to wait until he tells us, I guess."

TWENTY-SIX

Eugene and Harry's visit flew by. They were set to leave in a few days, so when a rare, almost warm winter afternoon arrived, Grace suggested they all enjoy a bonfire out by the dock.

"This'll be nice," she said to Harry as they guided Norman down to the shoreline. "Spend some happy time together before you have to go back."

At that, Norman's eyes snapped to Harry's and the shaking in his hands intensified. The arm Grace held tightened to steel cable.

"Not you, Norman! Oh, I'm so sorry," she said quickly. "No, you're not going back. You're never going back out there. Just Harry and Eugene."

"And we'll be just fine," Harry assured them both. "We made each other a promise, and he and I don't break those kinds of promises. We'll both be back before you know it." He leaned close to Norman's ear. "And just to get your mind off that I'll let you in on a little secret, since you don't seem to be in the mood to go spilling the beans about it. Promise to keep it to yourself?"

The corner of Norman's mouth twitched.

"All right, then. Here it is. Before I leave here, I'm gonna ask Linda to marry me." He wiggled his eyebrows. "It's about time, right?"

"What?" Grace squealed. This was news.

Harry scrunched up his nose, but his eyes were laughing. "Oops! Did you hear that? Darn. You weren't supposed to know, Miss Gracie. Now you just keep your pretty mouth shut about that."

"Over here, boys," Audrey called, waving. Eugene had set up a few chairs, and one seat was draped in a blanket. "Bring Norman over here. We'll keep him warm. That all right with you, Norman? And Harry, you sit over there by your father."

Harry whispered to Grace, "I am almost thirty years old. How does she always manage to make me feel like I'm five again?"

"All my boys," Audrey said as they sat, almost to herself.

Grace couldn't stop smiling. Sure, things were different, but they were together, and that's what mattered. Norman, she was certain, would wake up out of this awful state soon, and the best part was that he wouldn't have to go back to war after this. He was one brother she could keep an eye on for now. And when the war was finally over, Harry and Linda would get married. Nothing like love in the air to make people happy again.

And that made her think of Rudi. He was up at the barn, and she knew he could see the family gathering around the bonfire. He'd stayed away since her brothers had come home, not wanting to cause trouble, but every so often she found herself thinking of him, remembering the kiss she'd placed on his cheek the night Norman returned. She had meant it to be a small thing: a sign of gratitude, nothing more, but the memory wouldn't fade. Sometimes she almost wished she'd never done it, because that kiss had intensified everything about the way she was feeling, and she wasn't really sure what to do about it. Right then, though, she felt like Rudi should be there by the bonfire, among the family.

"Maman," she said, pulling her from Norman, "can I ask you a question?"

Audrey patted Norman's hand. "I'll be right back, dear. Grace and I will bring cocoa and tea."

Back in the house, Grace brought a pot of milk to a boil while her mother got cocoa from the cupboard.

"I want to introduce Rudi to the boys," Grace said quietly.

"Today?"

She kept her eyes on the pot. "They'll be going back soon."

"True. And I suppose they will probably need to know about him—if he stays, that is," Audrey reasoned.

Grace stirred the milk, taking care not to scald it while she worked up the nerve to say what she was thinking.

"Maman, I need to tell you something, and I'm not sure how to say it."

Her mother said nothing, merely added a steaming teapot to a tray.

"I feel like . . . It's . . . There's something about Rudi that I . . ." How did one put feelings like this into words? It came to her how difficult that must be for Rudi, with his rudimentary understanding of the language. "I wish I could explain it. When I talk with him I feel more . . . oh, I don't know."

"More what?"

"Alive."

The word came to her unexpectedly, and in that moment she knew she was right about it. She'd never met anyone like Rudi. He intrigued her, he challenged her, and she appeared to affect him the same way. She wanted to be with him, to understand him, to laugh with him. To hold his hand and kiss his mouth.

She was relieved to see not one shred of judgment in her mother's face. "We can never choose who we're going to love," Audrey said. Her voice was rich with a kind of nostalgia Grace could only guess at.

"I didn't say I loved him."

"I know you didn't." Audrey took the cooking pot from the stove and started pouring cocoa into her special white pot, with its pretty pink rose pattern and gold trim. "But if you do, I want you to know that it's all right with me, and with your father. We all know what Rudi came from, but his life is changing rapidly. We don't know where his choices will lead him." When the cocoa was poured, she turned to Grace. "If you are one of those choices, then he is changing his life for the better."

That wasn't the question she'd asked. How had her mother switched the words around so they changed everything? Had Grace ever mentioned love? Not even once. And yet here they were, practically discussing whether Rudi would be a good husband for her.

Except it did make Grace stop. And think of him again.

"You're a brave girl," her mother said. "Bring him out and introduce him if you want. Your brothers are good men. There may be some opposition at first—that's only natural these days—but they will understand. They only want you to be happy, after all."

"What about Norman?"

It was a question that had been bothering her ever since her brother had come home. His life had been ruined by the Nazis. How would he react to having one in their midst?

"Norman has a lot of battles ahead of him," her mother said, more subdued, "but they aren't because of Rudi." She moved to the door. "Come on. Before the tea gets cold."

Grace picked up the tray and followed her mother outside, intrigued. Ever since Norman had come home, Audrey seemed stronger, ready to go to battle for her son. In the past, her reluctance to discuss the war and other difficult issues had frustrated Grace so much she'd judged her, labelled her as weak. Now she saw that her mother's avoidance had never been a weakness, just an attempt to block out the horrors she and her husband had both survived. She'd chosen to suffer in silence. Just like Norman.

"If Rudi makes you feel alive," her mother said, "then bring him down."

TWENTY-SEVEN

When Grace walked into the barn, she didn't see him, but she heard his cheery whistling coming from the far stall. The sound made her smile; he was happy today.

She peered over the half wall, but his back was to her; all his attention was on her father's old generator. He'd removed the spark plug and filed the point. Protected by the plug's rubber cap, his fingers held the threads against the machine, then he gave the cord a good pull. She was as surprised as he was to see a strong spark.

"*Ja. Der Vergaser,*" he muttered to himself. "*Das ist gut.*"

She hadn't heard him speak in pure German before. Something about how comfortable, how natural, he sounded uttering those words gave her an unexpected thrill. She kept quiet, admiring the broad shape of his back, then the line of his shoulder as he reached backwards, towards the door. Still focused on the machine, he groped along the flat top of the half wall with one grease-smeared hand, his fingers inches away from a wrench. Grace placed the tool in his hand, startling him.

"I didn't know you were a mechanic, too," she said. His golden hair was growing out; she liked the way it curled a little over his ears.

He grinned at her. "Yes," he said. "We learn *Mechanik* in navy."

The last time they'd seen each other, she'd been crying in his arms. He'd held her, soothed her, and she'd kissed his cheek. Now the memory of his touch sent adrenaline roaring through her. Did he remember it as she did?

He was watching her, waiting for some kind of response.

"Uh, so is it going to work?" she stammered.

He rubbed one cheek, leaving behind a patch of shiny black grease. "Engine is working. I think is only dirty carburetor. What is it for?"

"It used to power the fish plant before my father put in electricity. I guess it's not for anything anymore. Are you going to fix it?"

"Is not broken." He scratched the side of his nose, turning it black as well, and she tried not to laugh at the mess he was creating. "But I need things."

Whether he'd meant to or not, his simple comment brought her into his project. She liked that. "If we have it at the store, I can get it."

"Einige Schrauben, Benzin, eine Drahtbürste . . ." He saw her blank stare, then he held up an old bolt. *"Einige Schrauben."*

"Bolts?"

"Ja. Bolzen." He mimed something, as if he was scrubbing something hard. *"Eine Drahtbürste."* He gestured towards the generator. "Is dirty."

"A scrub brush? For cleaning?"

"Ja."

"Ah. I'll bring you a wire brush. And you said Benzine?"

"Gasoline?"

"Okay. I'll ask Tommy to get me some gas."

"Und das Papier for the—" He held up two pieces of metal,

then showed her how the paper would fit between the two. "I do not know what is this. In German is *Dichtung*. Is making gas not come out . . ."

"Gasket paper!" she cried. How ridiculous did she sound? As if gasket paper was something truly exciting. "I know what that is. I've seen it on the shelves. Yes, I can get you that."

His eyes seemed even brighter over the blackness on his cheek. "Good. I make it work for your father. Is thank you for him."

"He'll like that." She pointed at the machine. "Are you finished for now?"

He stooped and grabbed a rag off the floor. "If you want talk to me, I am finished."

She'd thought it over on the short walk here, wondering how she should approach him with the idea of meeting her brothers. She didn't want him scared off by the fact that he would soon be surrounded by Canadian military men, so she figured she'd explain that the introduction was unavoidable. Especially now that Norman was home to stay.

"Um, I told you before that my brothers are all home."

He closed the stall door behind him, listening while he wiped his hands relatively clean with the rag.

"I want you to meet them."

The spell was broken. "Is not good idea. Your brothers not want me here."

The way he said it was so matter-of-fact, she was taken aback. Of course he would assume they would hate him. Yes, he was German. Yes, he had been part of Hitler's navy. But circumstances had brought him here, to her. He was a person, just like she was, and he deserved to be happy. She searched for the right words, wishing she could reassure him.

"My brothers are good men, Rudi, and they'll listen to me.

I want them to know you." He opened his mouth as if to speak, but she stopped him. "I want them to know that I like you."

The ice in his expression melted. "Okay." Turning back, he laid the tarp over the machine, and she understood the generator was a secret. "We go say hello now."

She loved how he trusted her. "One second." She pulled a handkerchief from her pocket. "You've got a little something here," she said, reaching for his cheek. He didn't flinch when she wiped off the grease, simply watched her, the corners of his eyes crinkled. In a single, fleeting impulse she was tempted to lift onto her toes and kiss the spot she'd cleaned.

"I hope they not hating me, Grace, because I like you, too."

Flustered, she drew away, but he pulled her gently back, wanting her full attention.

"Do not be afraid." He softly touched her cheek, his calloused fingers warm against her skin. The strangest tingle spread through her, a warmth she'd never felt before. "Be happy, Grace," he said. "When you smile, everything in my life is good."

He made it so easy. So she did.

"All is good now," he said, satisfied. "We can go."

Nerves skittered along Grace's neck as she stepped down the path with Rudi beside her. Was he as nervous as she was?

Harry and Eugene stood when they approached, questions written all over their faces.

"Ah, here he is," their father said, rising as well. "Boys, this is the man I've been talking about. Rudi Weiss, these are my three sons: Harry, Eugene, and Norman. I'm sure Grace has talked your ear off about them."

Grace knew Rudi wouldn't understand that her father was joking, and she was tempted to translate, but Rudi stepped forwards and held out his hand.

"Is very good meeting you," he said, clasping Eugene's hand.

"Same," Eugene said, watching him closely.

"I hear you're good with a hammer." Harry was always the gentler of the two, and Grace was so thankful for that.

Rudi relaxed a bit. "I like to work."

Norman followed the activity, but he did not offer a smile or a hand, so Rudi went to him and gave a small bow.

"I am happy you are home, Norman. Grace is very happy."

The Norman she knew would be the first to greet someone; he was the charmer, the instigator. But not now. She practically heard the scream trapped within him.

"Come and sit down," her mother said. "Cocoa or tea?"

"Thank you, Mrs. Baker. Tea, please."

"Rudi's English has really improved since he first came here," Audrey said, pouring for him.

"He reads too," Grace interjected. "A lot. He likes—"

Her father eyed her.

"Sorry. Rudi, tell them yourself."

Haltingly, Rudi admitted he'd been reluctant to learn English from his mother as a boy. "I am always busy with my father and other boys." He told them how she'd won him over by introducing English newspapers, comics, even books to his studies. Ever since then he'd pushed himself to learn, using whatever he could find. "I do not understand most, but I learn a little every day."

Eugene's expression hadn't softened throughout Rudi's explanation. "I hear you like Canada."

"Very much."

"Except you were going to attack us."

Grace's heart sank. She had hoped this would go smoothly, but perhaps that had been too much to expect.

"You've never had to do that, Eugene?" her father asked,

surprising her. "Attack on command? I'd say we've all had to do that at one point or another, wouldn't you?"

"True enough," Eugene allowed. "I apologize."

Rudi shook his head. "I am not need apologize. I understand. I am enemy." He looked at Danny, then at Grace. "But I am lucky. Your family is good to me."

"You understand we are curious," Harry said.

"Curious?"

"They have a lot of questions," Grace explained.

"Of course."

The same questions were asked, the same answers given, and Grace watched helplessly as Rudi was accused and judged. Norman hadn't moved a muscle but seemed to be following the conversation. If only he could speak.

When Eugene had finished the interrogation, he faced their father. "What's your plan, Dad? He's a likable fellow, and I imagine he's been a help around here—but you can't keep him a secret forever."

"He sticks out like a sore thumb," Harry agreed, stating the obvious.

Everyone stared at Rudi.

"It doesn't matter what you think," Grace heard herself say. "We're not going to turn Rudi in. He's our friend now, whether you like it or not."

Eugene held up his hands. "Hey, little sister, I'm not trying to upset the apple cart. It's just the truth."

Her father opened his mouth to say something, but her mother spoke first. "Rudi is welcome to stay with us as long as he wants." She gave them the sweet but resolute smile they'd all seen so many times as children, and everyone understood this was simply how it was going to be. "We'll figure it out along the way. We always have."

TWENTY-EIGHT

March had come in like a lion, and Grace bowed her head to plow through the miserable wet wind. Against her chest she clutched a heavy sack. The items within were not the sort of things she'd normally think to buy, but Rudi was clearly excited about surprising her father with the generator, and she loved being in on his secret. She'd paid for everything herself.

As far as secrets were concerned, keeping Rudi from Linda was becoming increasingly difficult. Now that she was engaged to Harry, Linda phoned Grace frequently to discuss wedding plans and gush about how excited she was. Grace longed to reciprocate, to tell her friend how happy she was lately, how she felt truly attracted to a man for the first time, but that was out of the question.

Meanwhile, news about the war worsened by the day. Since Rudi had come along, Grace had begun to track its progress more diligently, but what she read in the papers seemed more fiction than fact. Under their leader's command, the Nazis, she learned, were rounding up Jewish families and sending thousands of them to camps of some kind, where they were forced to work. Some of these poor, innocent people were even being killed. Everyone knew Hitler was evil, but this kind of thing made no sense. Could no one put a stop to it?

She'd asked Rudi about it. At first he was reluctant to discuss it, but she told him what she'd said to Harry at Christmas: she just wanted to understand.

"It is war, Grace," he said. "No one is doing good thing in war. You know this."

"But what about these camps, Rudi? What are they? Is it true?"

As soon as she asked she knew it was true.

"I am not seeing these camps, but I know them. Yes. Is true."

"They're killing people because they're Jewish?" Her voice rose with outrage. "But why? Why would—"

"Because he is madman," Rudi said calmly.

"Can't *someone* stop him?"

"Is not only him anymore. Nazi machine is *unerbittlich*. It is not stopping." He swallowed hard, and she wondered what he was thinking, what he might be remembering. "If some person tries to stop this, they go away."

"Go away?"

"Killed. Or they take to camps." His grief was unmistakable now. "No one ever sees those people again."

Alarmed by his pain, she didn't ask him again. And he didn't say anything more about it. But the long-ago Christmas conversation with the family came back to her, and she remembered how she couldn't bear to imagine the enemy as regular men, just the same as her brothers. She'd been right. It hurt too much to think that way.

Closer to home, everyone was on edge. The St. Lawrence was teeming with wolf packs, groups of German U-boats hunting along the coastline. The radio reported that U-boats had sunk almost two dozen Allied merchant ships in the Gulf of St. Lawrence in just four days, killing hundreds of merchant sailors and destroying 150,000 tonnes of war supplies. Her only consolation was that she knew her brothers had not been involved in the fighting. They had both completed recent journeys and were in port somewhere relatively safe.

It was impossible for Grace not to associate Rudi with U-boats. The very idea that he'd both lived and worked on one of those lethal machines made her feel sick. She could picture him, tall and efficient, following orders without argument, firing torpedoes . . . and yet she was starting to think she knew him well enough now to see another side to that view. Rudi wasn't a machine. He wasn't a killer, either. How might it have been for him, existing in a metal tube with no assignment but to seek out and destroy? What did that do to a man? He'd helped her understand Norman's pain, and by doing so he'd shed light on his own. Whenever her mind went to the U-boats she thought how Rudi's heart—his *Herz*—must constantly ache with guilt.

At least he was here now. Like Norman, he was safe, and he was surrounded by people who cared about him. He was right where he was supposed to be.

Not wanting her family to notice the parcel she carried, Grace took the path past the house, went directly to the barn, and slipped inside. Rudi helped her out of her coat, then unpacked the items one by one. The look on his face was like that of a child at Christmas.

"This is everything," he said. "Thank you."

"I got you something else as well. To help with your English." She pulled a small, blank book and a pencil from her pocket. "Keep this with you and write down new words."

His happiness was contagious. "This is *wunderbar*! Very, very good."

"I'm glad you like it."

"It is excellent." He bit his lip. "It is right way to say this?"

"How about, 'Thanks, Grace. It's perfect.'"

He repeated what she'd said, then added, "So are you. Perfect."

She squatted beside him, pretending to inspect the wire brush. "And you are a flatterer."

"What is 'flatterer'?"

"A man who says nice things to girls."

He pulled out his book and she watched him sound out *flatterer*, then print the German equivalent. Feeling a bit silly, she made her first attempt at his language.

"*Schmeichler?*"

"You speak good German, Grace." He tapped the book with his pencil. "Tell me, this flatterer. Saying nice things is bad to do in Canada?"

"Of course not, but a lot of the time men say them just for fun. Words don't mean anything unless they're the truth."

He watched her with a sort of bemusement. "These words are truth. You not believe I say truth?"

"Nobody is perfect," she replied, rising.

"Maybe not perfect," he allowed. "But you are . . . *besonders.*"

"Beyzonders?"

"Not like anyone."

He stole her heart when he said things like that. For someone with limited English, he sure knew how to use the words he did know.

"I see Tommy brought you the gasoline," she said, resisting the temptation to return the compliment.

He didn't look away from her. He was so intense. Sometimes it made her slightly uncomfortable. Most of the time it thrilled her.

"Wait," he said, and he opened his book. " 'Besonders' is?"

"I guess you mean special."

He held out the book. "Please, you can write?"

His eyes were on the tip of the pencil as she wrote what he asked. "That 'c' sounds like 'sh,'" she told him. "'Special.'"

His lips formed the word. "Yes. You are special."

She slipped past him and stopped by the generator. "Show me what you're doing."

Following her lead, he showed how he'd removed the carburetor and explained that he would soak the pieces in a bath of gasoline for a couple of days, then use the brush to clean it entirely.

"This is going to make my father real happy." She peered out the window. The rain wasn't letting up, but she was out of time. Every time she was with Rudi she wanted to stay longer. "I'd better go to supper. I'm working tomorrow, but maybe I'll see you after?"

He helped her into her coat, then leaned forwards and spoke softly into her ear. "I hope so, Grace. I am not going anywhere."

TWENTY-NINE

Grace sat by the fireplace after supper, trying to focus on her book, but it was a lost cause. Her mind kept skipping back to Rudi, recalling his delight with the book she'd given him, hearing again the word he'd used to describe her. *Besonders*. She'd never forget that. Norman sat in the armchair across from her, watching the fire. His fingers picked relentlessly at themselves, cleaning the long-gone dirt from his nails. Everything in the room was quiet except for the snapping of the fire and the soft pattering of rain falling outside, and the tranquillity was hypnotic. She sighed and flipped back to the beginning of the chapter, determined to follow the story this time.

"Does it make you a coward if you hide under a dead body?"

Grace nearly jumped out of her skin at the sound of Norman's voice. "What did you say?"

"Does it make you a coward if you hide under a dead body?" he repeated calmly.

She tried to make sense of what she'd heard, then realized with a slow, dawning horror that he wasn't asking for an answer. His simple words had been spoken matter-of-factly, like he was wondering if it might rain tomorrow. But anyone could hear they veiled a complicated world of misery. Bracing herself, Grace sat back and willed herself to be strong. If he was brave enough to say it out loud, she must summon the courage to listen.

"Because I remember my friend Bob—Lieutenant Clarkson—I remember running behind him in the pouring rain." Norman spoke softly, as if he were telling a bedtime story. He was staring at her, but she didn't think he was seeing anything at all. At least nothing in the room. "And bullets were coming down around us like hail. The mud kept slipping under my feet, and we were trying to run uphill, but we kept stumbling, then getting back up. It was like we were stuck in place. All the time the Germans kept shooting."

Grace didn't move. She barely breathed.

"Don't know how I didn't get hit," he continued, "but Bob did. He didn't yell or anything—or maybe he did, but I couldn't hear a thing. All those bullets kind of made me deaf. Then he fell backwards and knocked me down with him. I must have hit my head on something because I know I blacked out for a couple of seconds. When I woke up I couldn't move. I thought I was drowning, then I realized it was just Bob on top of me. He was a big guy, and his pack was about seventy pounds, so I wasn't going nowhere. The Germans were still bearing down on us—I was so scared I couldn't tell you if that mud under us was ice or fire. I kept yelling, 'Bob! Bob! Get the hell off me!'"

He closed his eyes. "But he never got off. Not until a German rolled him off."

"Oh, Norman," Grace whispered. "What did you do?"

He held his hands up as if to surrender, and they shook with effort. "Then, well, there I was, lying on the ground, staring up at the soldier. I had thought about playing dead, you know? But I didn't because I knew he'd check with his bayonet, and I sure as hell didn't want to die that way. So I just stared at him. He was about my age and I think he was just as confused as me, but, well, he was on the winning side. I'd been there before. I knew how easy it would have been for him to put that blade through me. But he didn't. He kind of jerked his head to the side and said '*Komm, komm, mein Freund.*'"

Mein Freund. Rudi had called Tommy that, Grace recalled.

" 'Come, come, my friend.' " For the first time Norman really looked at her, really saw her there. He curled his fingers over the arms of his chair and leaned to one side. "Can you imagine him saying that? Like it was a game of tag or something. Maybe hide and seek." He shook his head and lost his focus again. "I didn't fight him at all. I gave up my gun and started walking in front of him, hands up. The firing had pretty much stopped by then, other than the occasional *pop! pop!* but then someone shot from behind, I guess, because this time I fell forward—stuck under the German's body." He let out a snort. "Craziest thing, landing under guys like that, twice in a row. Some might call that lucky, I guess. I'm . . . I'm still . . ."

He rubbed his eyes violently, pressing hard against them, and when he lowered his hands again his skin was blotched with red. "I landed in the muck," he went on, "face to face with another dead guy. Looked right into his wide open, dead eyes. I couldn't make out his uniform, didn't know if he was a good guy or a bad guy, but he was surely dead. And so was the German on my back."

One of the logs in the fireplace cracked, shooting bright orange sparks into the dark cavity of the chimney, but Grace barely noticed. She was in the mud with her brother, paralyzed with fear.

"And that, well . . ." He took a deep breath. "That's where it got real confusing for me. I just lay there. I could feel the cold mud on my face, and after a bit the last of the man's warmth seeped through both our uniforms. I could have gotten up. I wasn't hurt or nothing. I wasn't screaming. Not on the outside.

But on the inside, sweet Jesus . . ." He swallowed, then whispered, "I couldn't stop. My heart was in my head, and it was roaring at me to get the hell out, to go home. But I couldn't move. I thought if I could hide under that dead German forever I'd be okay.

"And I kind of wonder if that's when my heart decided to leave without me, because the rest of me just lay there, not even knowing if I was breathing. I stopped caring." His gaze went to the fireplace again. "Someone came to get me at some point. It was one of us, but I don't remember who. I don't remember what they said; I was numb from the inside out. Took me days to feel anything again. And still I . . ."

He swallowed again. "I don't know who the hell I am anymore, Gracie. Gail's right. I'm not the same. So who the hell am I?"

Now she understood how he'd lost himself, and the agony of it tore her apart. She could see the vivid, awful truth, the *open, dead eyes*, and she wondered how he could ever escape the abyss. Was this what war was like? Did Harry and Eugene see the same unspeakable horrors? Had Rudi? She'd said she wanted to know, but now, oh, now she wished she'd never heard any of it. How could she not break into a million pieces for all of them?

"You're you, Norman," she said quietly. "You're my dearest brother, my best friend, and the person I missed more than anything on earth."

"I . . . I don't know," he whispered.

"Grace is right. You're you." Their mother had appeared in the doorway, their father at her side. From the compassion on their faces, they'd been listening.

Audrey's voice was gentle but determined. "You've survived things that threatened to tear you apart, and you've got scars."

She paused, and Danny took her hand. "But no matter what happened, no matter what you did, you are loved."

Her father cleared his throat. How difficult this must be for him, Grace thought. All her life he had battled his own torturous memories. Even two decades later he lost himself on occasion.

"Son, I know what it's like when the memories and nightmares pull you under. Sometimes you can't fight them. They get so strong—" Danny's voice caught, but he kept on. "Over time it'll get easier. It will; I promise."

Brushing tears from her cheeks, Grace got up and knelt by Norman's side. His hand was cool despite the warmth of the room, so she pressed it between both of hers. "You're a good brother and a good man, Norman. And we're proud of you. And we will always, *always* love you."

He stared at her, his eyes shining, and she wondered if she might lose her own mind while trying to save his. The source of his pain was invisible, but it was so impossibly real she could feel it with him. He sat close, but she knew he was still thousands of miles away. How could she keep him safe if he couldn't get home?

Then Norman smiled. It wasn't the smile of old, flashing with challenge, seeing humour in everything, but it was a beginning. Grace held in a sob, but it rose from her heart, swelled in her throat. At last, at last she could see him: her brave, stubborn brother, fighting his way back to them.

THIRTY

In spite of the war, things were looking up in Grace's world. Norman was talking a bit more every day, and Rudi had devised a plan for the generator. During his rummaging, he had found another discarded piece of machinery—a large fan—and that had given him an idea. The next time she went to see him in the barn, he enthusiastically pointed out an old shack near the plant that wasn't being used. After a few broken sentences, Grace realized he was saying the shack would be a perfect overflow space for salting and storing fish.

"When generator is working, I take it to there and build fan. I am fixing shed to make tables and what he is needing." Energized by the possibilities, he gestured to the various old pulleys and ropes hanging on the walls of the barn. "These *rolle*—"

"Pulleys?"

"Yes." He grabbed his little English book and handed it to Grace. "Please? *Pulley?*" then he spelled the German word for her. "Yes. Thank you." He rolled a small rope in his fingers. "This *Seil . . .*"

"Rope?"

"*Ja, ja.* Rope—" He wiggled a finger at the book and she wrote it down. "Rope is for putting together pulleys and making to turn."

"How can I help?"

He waved a hand towards the other buildings. "You can make people not see?"

While she ran interference, he spent the next day in the shed, and the work was done by supper. Early the next morning, before the sun had risen and any of the workers arrived, Grace and Rudi had gone together and started up the fan. The blades made their first few tentative rotations then sped up, lifting the air and humming with determination, tickling her face.

"You did it!"

She took an impulsive step towards him but stopped just before she could throw her arms around his neck. He saw her hesitation and reluctantly took a step back.

"I'll go get my dad," she said.

All the way up the dark path to the house she thought about Rudi, about how proud she was of his accomplishments, about how important he had become to her, and about how completely happy she was when she was with him. She allowed herself to imagine what might have happened had she embraced him just then—would he have kissed her? Would she have kissed him back?

Muttering something vague about surprises, Grace dragged her father from the breakfast table, insisting he come and see something. Once he was at the shack, he stared in wonder at the fan, then the generator.

A broad smile lit his face. "I can't believe you did this."

"It was all Rudi's idea. It's for drying the fish."

"I can see that," he replied. "How'd you get the old thing going again?"

"Is not broken," Rudi said, showing him.

"Huh. Gummed up needle valve." Danny gave Rudi a warm, almost paternal look of appreciation, and Grace wondered if it affected Rudi as it always did her. Yes—she saw him stand taller, bolstered by Danny's recognition.

"This cool air sure will be welcome come summertime," her father said, raising his face to better feel it. "The workers will thank you."

"I am happy to help."

"Well, that's good, because you sure seem to know what you're doing." He shook Rudi's hand. "You know, I'm real glad things worked out like they did, Rudi. You were in a pretty rough spot for a while, and a lesser man might have abandoned ship. I, for one, am glad you stayed. Not only that, you've been doing great work around here." He took a step towards the door, then looked back. "And when this damn war is all over, well, we'll find a way to work this out so you won't have to hide away all the time."

After he left, Rudi shot Grace a grin, which she returned.

"Come on," she said, "Let's go for a walk."

The curtain of night had begun to lift, revealing the soft promise of daybreak. She grabbed a blanket from the house and led Rudi up a nearby hill, then she spread the wool plaid over the brittle winter grass. From here the view of trees, ice, and endless, indecisive layers of grey seemed to go on forever.

"Is good place here. Very quiet," Rudi said, settling onto the blanket beside her. He tilted his head to the side, towards the old house. "What house is this?"

"My great-grandparents built it, but it's falling apart. No one's lived there for a long time."

He took in the view around them. "Good place for house."

Grace had always thought that. She'd lived here her whole life and never got tired of sitting here. Sharing it with him made it even better. In the distance she saw the haunting grey profile of a navy ship, then saw Rudi was watching it too. What was he thinking? Did he see friend or foe, or was he able to see it simply as a ship?

"Must have been scary, living underwater."

It took a few seconds before he responded. "I do not like live underwater. All is same." His fair eyebrows lifted. "Is more good here. I see beautiful things."

He certainly knew how to twist a phrase to his advantage, she thought for the hundredth time. "Do you really think you should be flirting with me?"

"What is flirting?"

"Like flattering. Trying to make me like you."

"I do not understand. You do not like this?" His eyes were like magnets. "You do not like me?"

She hugged her knees to her chest, letting her head fall back so the sun warmed her face. "I do. I like you a lot. It's just complicated." Maybe she was being too tough on him. She lowered her chin, started again. "Let's talk about something else. Tell me what you were like before. When you were little, I mean. Living in Germany."

"When I was boy?" He shrugged. "I was good boy. I am playing *Fußball—*"

"Football?"

"Yes, and *Eishockey*, and also I like *Boxen*." He held up his fist, jabbed it at an imaginary opponent. "You know this? *Boxen?*"

"Were you good at it? At boxing?"

"I am very good. On U-boat—" He stopped. "Is okay I tell boxing story if is on U-boat?"

She nodded.

"Sometimes we are *Boxen* when we come to surface," he explained. "Men are in sub long time and we need moving, so we are fighting. We say 'he win' or 'he win,' and some men win money."

"You were betting on fights?"

"Yes. Betting. And I," he said proudly, allowing himself to boast, "I win every time."

She smirked. "You're that good, huh?"

In illustration, he drew his fists together, held them in front of his chin, then twisted his right shoulder forwards. His punch shot straight out, followed by a left roundhouse, then a sharp right upper cut. He was showing off, and she loved it.

"You're pretty fast." She tried to sound unimpressed. "Norman was a boxer too."

He leaned back on his hands, looked towards the sunrise. They sat quietly, listening to the cries from the early birds as they circled overhead.

"Is your name short for something?"

"Means what?"

"Rudi. Is that from a different name? A longer name?"

"Ah. Yes. Rudolph. *Mein Großvaters* name."

"'Gos Fata'?"

"*Ja*, uh, my *Vater* has *Vater* . . . ?"

"Grandfather! Oh, I like that," she said. "I like when a child is named after someone. My name is just mine. Nothing special about it."

"Is pretty name. What means 'grace'?"

"My parents say it means 'forgiveness.'"

He waited for her to explain.

"Forgiveness is when one person says they're sorry, and the other person says okay."

"Ah," he said, considering that. "So I am ask for grace, Grace."

The quiet simplicity of his request won her over. "Nicely done," she replied. "Well, I . . . I think I will give it to you."

Satisfaction shone in his grin, and she couldn't help giggling.

"You are cold?" Rudi asked a moment later when she shivered. "Sun is coming but maybe we go inside."

The horizon was painted a vivid purple and pink, and it would bloom into scarlet before too long. She wanted to share it with him, but he was right. Besides, the workers would be arriving soon.

"A little cold," she admitted.

Rudi got to his feet and held out a hand to help her up. When she stood beside him he kept her fingers entwined in his, and his touch felt both new and natural. She never wanted to let go. Seeking permission with his eyes, he raised her hands to his lips and gently kissed the back of one. She couldn't look away, didn't want to.

"The best way to warm up is with a hug," she suggested shyly, opening her arms.

When he drew her to him, she inhaled the familiar wool of his coat, felt the warmth of his breath, and she remembered the last time he'd held her. They'd stood in the rain and she'd clung to him, sobbing for her dear brother and all the pain she couldn't escape, and he'd kept her safe, helped her breathe again. Now she was there for something else.

"*Umarmung,*" he said, and her breath caught at the sweet intimacy in his voice. "This is hug."

The wind whistled around them but never between, not until Rudi let go and brought his hands to her face. His mouth was inches from hers, and Grace closed her eyes, wanting so badly to feel his kiss.

"Hey, Grace!"

They jerked apart as if they'd felt an electric shock, and an awful sense of dread pooled in Grace's stomach.

"Oh, hey Linda," she said, stepping even farther from him. "What are you doing up here?"

Her friend had stopped short. "Well, well, well! I can't believe what I'm seeing." She walked towards them, intrigued. "Remember you told me to come over this morning? You said you got a new skirt, and I wanted to see it."

Grace could have kicked herself.

"But you weren't at the house. I didn't realize . . ." She studied Rudi. "Do I know you?"

Grace moved to lead her friend away from him. "Linda, sometimes you have the worst manners in the world."

"Hold on a second. I remember you," Linda said, sidestepping her. "From the dance. It was dark, but I'd remember you anywhere. What did you say your name was?"

He opened his mouth to answer, and Grace interrupted. "He didn't."

Linda blinked, shocked. "Why, Grace! I'm surprised! You're carrying on with a strange man? What's gotten into you?"

This was going too far. "He's not a strange man. He's my friend. We got to know each other at the store."

"Got to *know* each other?" Linda propped one hand on her hip. "I'll say you did! You told me he'd come by the store a couple of times, but from what I just saw, this is a lot more than just a visit!"

"Oh, never you mind. We were just saying goodbye before I went to work."

Then Rudi did what she'd been hoping he wouldn't do: he spoke. "Yes," he said. "I go to work now also. Have nice day, Grace."

A pause. "Is that a *German* accent?"

Grace did everything she could to appear as if nothing was out of the ordinary. "Yeah, he's from that settlement west of here, you remember them? He's up this way trapping."

Linda wasn't going to give up as long as Rudi was around.

"Well, have a good day." Grace shot him a warning look. "Maybe I'll see you another time."

"Yes." He gave Linda a small bow. "Is good to see you again."

After he left, Linda bubbled over with questions, but Grace couldn't afford to get caught up in any lies. She waved a hand, dismissing the interrogation entirely.

"Mind your own business," she said. "If I wanted the world to know what I was doing I'd have taken out an advertisement in the newspaper, wouldn't I?"

"Well, he certainly is handsome," Linda replied, watching Rudi head down the hill. "He's really German?"

"Yes, he is. Now I've already said I don't want to talk about it. And I don't want you to talk about it either. With anyone. It's my own business, not yours. Come on. Let's go see that skirt I bought. Maybe you'll want to borrow it sometime."

They passed Tommy as they got close to the house. "Hey, Linda. I guess you met our secret house guest, huh?"

Linda swivelled towards Grace. "Oh, he's a guest *and* he's secret, huh? I can't believe it! Were you *lying* to me?"

Tommy paled. *I'm sorry*, he mouthed to Grace.

"What are you up to, hiding a German?"

Grace's heart was going a mile a minute. "Oh, Linda. I told you. He's just a trapper. We're friends is all. Nothing to get in a flap about."

"Is that right? So why's he a secret?"

"To avoid exactly this kind of thing."

Tommy stepped up. "He's a good fellow. We're just giving him a little help."

"Sure, except you're not telling anyone about him. In my books that means you're hiding him." Her eyes narrowed. "You know, we're supposed to report people for doing that kind of thing."

Grace did the only thing she could think of. "It's not just me, Linda. We all decided it was the right thing to do—including Harry," she blurted.

It worked. Linda cooled noticeably at mention of her fiancé. "Really? Harry approved of this scheme?"

"We all agreed. So you have to keep the secret too. He'd be so disappointed if it got out."

"Well," Linda said, sweet as cherries. "If Harry wants it to be a secret, I'll be the best secret keeper there is."

Rudi

THIRTY-ONE

Rudi started walking before he knew where he was going. He had to get out of there. He wasn't supposed to have overheard that last conversation, but he'd been standing just behind the barn when Tommy accidentally said the wrong thing. Grace wouldn't tell Rudi about it; she wouldn't want him to know that his presence was putting her family in a precarious position.

Hadn't he'd always known this could happen? That the Bakers were putting themselves in danger with him there? But he'd allowed it to go on because he was so happy. That kind of selfish mistake wouldn't happen again.

It didn't matter what he did, how many times he rejected his former life, he would always be Rudi the Nazi to these people. He could save a dozen Canadians from drowning, build a hundred sheds, fix a thousand generators, and he would still be the German spy. He should have escaped into the wilderness after he saved Tommy, found a way back home, but then Grace had come along, challenging him, thrilling him, and he'd just about decided he could live there after all. If she could ever love him—did he dare think that way?—maybe the others might someday be able to see beyond his past.

But that was wishful thinking. He should save himself the effort of hoping for anything. No matter how Hitler's forces were doing, now that he was in Canada, Rudi was on the wrong side of a war. He would be forever labeled a German, a Nazi. It was a tattoo that would mark him until the day he died. A year ago, that wouldn't have mattered. He had been proud to serve his country. But so much had happened since January. His world had been turned upside down. In his heart he knew he had changed, but the others couldn't understand.

He couldn't offer himself up to the authorities now that Linda knew he was there. The Bakers could be called traitors for helping him, the men's military reputations would be destroyed, and Grace would be humiliated. That simply wasn't an option. What Rudi needed was to disappear. Could he live in hiding the rest of his life? If that was a possibility, where could he—

Borgles Island. Grace had said the army had already checked it; no one had survived the explosion. The only people supposedly over there were the strange German couple from years before, and Rudi would leave them alone if he found them. Encouraged by the idea, he stepped up his pace, keen to get moving.

Then he paused. It felt wrong, leaving Grace without a goodbye.

She wouldn't be at work for another hour or so, but he couldn't wait for her. He was out of time. He pulled out the little book she'd given him, wondering how to write what he felt. How could he make her understand how difficult it was for him to leave her, how much it hurt to do it? He needed her to know that he'd kept his promise to her: he'd never told another lie. And he had to make sure she knew his feelings for her were true as well.

Would she understand this was all for her? That he'd throw himself on a grenade before letting her be harmed in any way? He stared at his book, at a loss. Where were the words he needed? Even if he knew them, would they be right? How could he say so much in a letter? When he finally figured out what to say, the words that came to him were in his mother tongue, but he translated to English as best as he could. After signing his name, he folded the paper a few times and wrote her name on the outside, then he slipped the note under the shop's door. When it was done, he peered through the window. It had spun across the floor and landed in an ideal spot; she couldn't miss it.

But he couldn't drag himself away. Not yet. The little piece of paper held him there, and he wished he could take back what he'd written. If only this wasn't so *complicated*, as she'd said. But it was, and no one could change that. Everything was different now. He had to leave because he had to protect her. Love did that to a man.

His intent had never been to hurt her. In truth, he'd never meant to love her, either. But this morning, when they'd stood together before the sunrise, he'd cradled her face in his hands and he'd known. He'd made mistakes, and they'd both paid for them. She'd given him so many opportunities to prove himself worthy of her, and if he wasn't who he was, he might have succeeded. This letter would hurt her again, but it was the only way to keep her safe. Just like before, he had no choice. At least this would be the last time he would cause her any pain.

He turned and left the note behind, heading into the woods towards Borgles Island. Well fed and without any fresh snow to battle, he found the journey much quicker than his initial one had been. That night he moved by the light of a nearly full moon and stopped only once to catch a few hours' sleep in the broken-down camp he'd discovered the first time. He arrived at the island late the next night, having crossed the thick ice in complete darkness. Once he was on land he saw no lights, smelled no smoke.

But that didn't mean he was alone. A fairly recent, silver-grey outline of boot prints met him by the shore. From what he could tell there was only one pair, and they appeared to be about the same size as his own. He squatted by the dents in the snow, his heart hammering. Could they belong to one of the crew? Despite the odds, he began to believe it might be possible. Could any of them have survived out here in the middle of nowhere? Or were these prints from one of the other people Tommy had mentioned? He followed a meandering, well-tracked trail, ducking under snow-laden branches and avoiding fallen trees. The boot prints led him to a cabin hunched under a sagging roof piled high with heavy snow. Icicles hung like teeth from its edge.

Someone lived here; the frozen, recently cut hindquarters of a deer hung in a nearby tree. Rudi paused at the entrance to the cabin, listening, but still heard nothing. He gave the door a tentative shove and found it wasn't locked—who would think of locking anything out here?—and he poked his head into the dark room.

"Anyone here?"

An arm wrapped around his neck so quickly he hadn't felt it coming. A blade pressed against his throat, and a foul, unwashed odour rose from the sleeve's rough fibres.

"*Nicht bewegen.*" The voice was unfamiliar; the language was not.

"I'm not moving," Rudi calmly assured the man in German.

"Who are you?" the stranger demanded, still speaking German.

Something wasn't right. This man was definitely not from the crew, but he didn't sound old enough to be one of the two Tommy had told him about.

"I'm Rudi. I'm not here to fight."

"Why are you here?" the man yelled into Rudi's ear. "Why are you in my house? My house! My house! Why?"

His shouts were furious, but the syllables were laboured, as if the man's tongue was too big for his mouth. Was he drunk? Rudi couldn't smell alcohol.

"No one comes to my home! Mine, mine, mine!" The yelling dropped from a near howl to an urgent whisper. "This is my home. Adam's home. You are not welcome here!"

Rudi knew better than to antagonize an unstable attacker. "I am not here to cause any harm, Adam."

The pressure on his neck eased slightly. It was gone entirely when Adam stepped away, knife still clutched in one hand. Rudi turned towards him, tried to read the scruffy man, but couldn't. Adam was a couple of inches shorter than Rudi, and a long, matted beard reached halfway down his chest. He wore nothing besides a set of long johns that might once have been white, and he lifted up and down, up and down on his toes.

With the back of his knife hand Adam pushed a tangled fall of hair off his brow. His bulging eyes darted all over the room, never directly meeting Rudi's. "I . . . I want— Go away!"

Rudi scanned the room and noticed a small table with three rickety chairs standing by the old stove. *Why three?* "Are you alone out here?"

"Why do you want to know that?"

Tommy had specifically said two people had come to the island about ten years before: a husband and wife. It was difficult to determine Adam's age through the grime on his face, but he was definitely not that old. Ten years ago this man would have been a child.

"Come, come," Rudi said cordially. "We do not have to be strangers. I am alone myself."

The man shook his head and held his hands towards the open door. The knife blade glowed dully in the moonlight. "No, no, no. You . . . you . . . you must go."

Rudi wanted very much to do exactly that, but Adam was too unpredictable to trust. The knife might just plunge between Rudi's shoulder blades if he turned to leave.

"Mother said never let people in here. Adam never goes off the island, and nobody ever comes here. Mother would be angry. You can't be in here."

He spoke like a child with a man's voice, and Rudi realized he was most likely *verzögert*—mad or simple, whether from an injury or from birth. That might explain why he'd never been seen by Tommy or anyone else. Maybe his parents had hidden him on the island to keep him safe from any danger. But this place was not dangerous. Why would they have been afraid?

"How long have you lived here?"

"Don't know, don't know, don't know. Adam is always here. Always on Adam's island." He shook his head, muttering to himself. "I was a boy, then I was a man. Adam the boy, Adam the man."

"Is your mother here?"

"No." The man's cheeks inflated beneath his beard, as if he were holding his breath. "It is my island, not yours. You cannot have it."

Rudi had grown accustomed to the darkness. He followed the lines of the room, noting the sparse, primitive furnishings. The place was in a terrible state, but strangely, it was homey. A single plate and cup sat on the table near the stove, and the man's disheveled bed was piled high with worn blankets. From the lived-in condition of the cabin, he had been there a while. And he was most definitely alone.

"I don't want the island, Adam," Rudi said.

Adam didn't believe him. His head started shaking again, as did the hand holding the knife. "People always want to take the island. But they can't stay here. Mother says no. Mother says they can't. Make them go away."

Them? "Who? Did someone come here?"

Adam turned towards the only window, gaped up at the moon. "Mother says no," he whispered, then he moaned, a sound of terrible grief, and his hands flapped wildly beside his head. "Go away, I told them. Go away! You can't have my home!" He spun back and stared straight at Rudi. "They tried to blow up my island!"

There it was. Rudi needed to know more, but he had to be careful with his questions. "Who tried to do that, Adam?"

"The boat under the water! They came with guns and uniforms. Father said no guns. No uniforms. No war. No soldiers. Mother said *never let anyone in!* Only bad boys talk to strangers!" He spun away again, then lunged for a framed photograph at his bedside and held it to his chest. "Mother and Father say, 'Who is in that boat?' Mother says *run, Adam, run!* So I run but . . . but . . . but I saw what happened. Mother and Father went to the boat, then—" He flung his hands into the air. "Boom! The plane came and the boat was on fire, the ice was on fire, and Mother and Father . . ." His voice dwindled. "They fell under the ice, and they never came back!"

Rudi could imagine the scene, the confusion, but most of his memories of the event were lost to him. He remembered the first plane, the one strafing the ice with bullets, but not the second plane. He had been right there, but the explosion had thrown him so far he'd never seen anything beyond the aftermath.

"What happened next?"

Adam replaced the photograph, handling it as if it were a precious, fragile thing instead of a rough wood frame.

"Two soldiers went in my house."

They *had* made it! Which ones? he wondered. And where were they now? "Yes, and then?"

"I waited and waited until it was dark, then I came back," Adam said. "Two soldiers were sleeping *in my parents' bed*, snoring and being loud. Too loud." He stalked over to the table and slammed his hands flat on its surface. "They put a machine on the table and it made *too much noise.*"

The radio. It had survived. But where—

"So I threw it in the sea when they were sleeping. And then I put the soldiers there, too."

Rudi stared at him, his jaw hanging open. "You killed them?"

Laughter bubbled up Adam's chest, rising quickly to a hysterical giggle. "The boat killed Mother and Father, so I killed the machine and I killed the soldiers. I did that all by myself. It was just like killing a deer only the soldiers were slower." His face fell. "But then I was *really* all alone."

Rudi's stomach rolled. The only survivors of his crew were dead, killed by the man standing before him. "I think it's time for me to go," he said.

Adam watched him warily as he moved towards the door, then he leaped in front and stood face to face with Rudi. His eyes were too bright. "Maybe we can play cards. I can't play by myself."

"You can play solitaire," Rudi suggested, sidestepping him. "I don't know how. Stay with me."

"I'll come back another time. I can teach you solitaire then." Adam's fury returned in a rush. With both hands he shoved Rudi's chest, slamming him hard into the wall behind him. "No, now! Stay here right now or never come back."

"Whoa," Rudi said, holding up his hands. He needed to

catch his breath after the impact. Adam was stronger than he appeared. "I will come tomorrow, maybe." He headed for the door, careful to give Adam space.

"No!"

Adam's knife appeared out of nowhere, cold and brutally sharp as it sliced through Rudi's right sleeve and arm. He spun out of the way, clutching his injury, but Adam was in a full tantrum now. He ran straight at Rudi, knife in front, and Rudi responded automatically by shoving his arm away. His round-house punch smashed into the side of Adam's face, knocking him off balance, but it wouldn't be enough to stop him. Ignoring the agony shooting up his wounded arm, Rudi put his weight into a solid left, launching Adam off his feet.

But the cabin was much smaller than the boxing ring had been. The blow carried Adam too far, and the back of his skull smashed against the solid cast iron stove. Rudi watched helplessly as Adam's body crumpled to the floor and lay perfectly still.

THIRTY-TWO

Adam had no pulse. When Rudi drew his hand away from his neck, it was wet with blood. More pooled at the base of the stove, seeped into the uneven cracks of the floor.

Sliding off his knee and shaking with adrenaline, Rudi sat beside Adam's body. None of this felt real. How could he have just . . . How could it be possible that he had come to this empty place with no intent other than to disappear, and he'd ended up killing a man? He went over the fight a million times in his head, trying to think if he could have done anything differently. Could there have been another outcome if he'd thrown a gentler punch?

It didn't matter now. Adam was dead.

He became aware that his back ached, and his injured arm throbbed. When he got to his feet, he left a dark, speckled trail of blood on the floor. He dug around the cabin until he found an apron, its flowered pattern long faded, then ripped off one of the ties and knotted it around his arm, hoping to stop the blood flow. It was the best he could do.

But what about Adam?

His instinct was to flee. No one in the world knew either one of them was there, and now, even more than before, Rudi needed to escape detection. Not only was he a German, he had officially become a killer. Fighting panic, he forced his breathing to slow; he needed to think clearly. As long as Adam had useful tools or weapons hidden away in the cabin, he might at least be better equipped for running this time. He scanned the cabin, not sure what he was looking for, then paused on the picture frame Adam had been holding minutes before. From what he could tell, the photograph was similar to one he'd seen of his own parents, taken about thirty years earlier, just before the start of the first war. He picked up the frame, wondering at the couple staring blankly back at him, their faces shadowed in black and white.

His boat had killed the parents, then he'd killed the son. "I'm sorry."

The corners of the old frame were loose and appeared to have been repaired more than once; a number of tiny nail holes punctured the wood. Curious, he unlatched the small door in the back of the frame, wondering if other photos might be tucked inside. Instead he found a yellowed paper—a birth certificate—and things became clearer. The son of Wendel and Isolde Neumann, Adam had been born in Berlin in June 1918, two years before Rudi's own birth. That meant Adam had been brought to Canada as a child.

A terrible thought occurred. If, as Tommy had said, Adam and his parents had left Germany a decade before, that would have been somewhere around 1933. Rudi had been only fourteen in 1934, but he clearly remembered the new subject they were taught that year. He recalled feeling more disturbed with every word the teacher said, but he hadn't seen the same kind of doubt on his classmates' faces. Still, he was sure he couldn't have been the only one to see the new "Sterilization Law" as barbaric. Under this law, the German government had begun to forcibly sterilize handicapped people to prevent them from ever having children.

Yet another horrific path taken towards Hitler's dream of the perfect Germany.

In 1934, Adam would have been sixteen, almost of the age at which the sterilizations were enforced. Had his parents brought him to Canada to protect him?

He studied Adam's body, this time with pity. He'd never left the island, he'd said, and no one ever came. Knowing what he now knew, Rudi realized it was possible—no, it was *probable*—that Rudi was the only person Adam had ever met, other than his parents and any long-lost childhood contacts. No wonder he'd been afraid when strangers invaded his home.

With Adam's parents gone, no one had any idea the boy existed. How remarkable, to live twenty-five years and leave no sign behind to mark your life. Where was Rudi's own birth certificate? His mother had kept all their important documents in a jewellery box, he recalled, along with ancient silver baubles she'd inherited along the way. Where were they now?

He doubted very much that he'd ever see any of those things again, just as he doubted he'd ever see his parents. For so long he'd avoided thinking about them; it had almost been a blessing that out of necessity he'd been too concerned with his own survival to dwell on his loss. But now, holding the birth certificate of the man he'd just killed, Rudi gave in to his grief.

Months ago, when he was still on U-69, he'd been informed that his parents had been reported to the Gestapo for criticizing the government. He knew the story was most likely true, and the worst of it was he was fairly sure he knew how it had happened. There was nothing he could do, so Rudi had filed the information away in a dark corner of his mind where he hoped to forget about it. But it was always there.

As a boy, he'd been trained to listen in and report, and he was proud of how quiet he could be. Like a cat creeping into a room. No one even knew he was there. One night, in the quiet of his parents' house, he had overheard his mother and father whispering about Rudi's education. He wasn't overly surprised that his mother had concerns—after all, the Hitler Youth regularly barged in on church meetings and Bible studies, looking sharp and intimidating in their brown shirts and swastika armbands. But his father's objections were unexpected. Hearing them, Rudi had stormed into the sitting room without a second thought, his head held high, and it struck him that, upon seeing him, his parents seemed . . . afraid, and a whole different kind of power filled him.

"You should not talk about the Hitlerjugend like this," he declared brashly, bolstered by years of lessons. "We are learning very important things that you do not understand. *We* are the future of Germany, not you. I can report you for speaking like this, you know."

His mother's eyes were glassy with tears. "Rudi," she said, then she covered her mouth with a trembling hand.

Why should she cry? Rudi was the model soldier-in-training, the first in the group to salute, the first to complete the assigned push-ups, chin-ups, sit-ups. His teachers said only good things about him, and he had been accepted into the Kriegsmarine, the German Navy. His mother should celebrate his successes, not be sad.

His father cleared his throat. "Rudi, you are a good soldier, and you are a strong, brave young man. But son, you are also intelligent. We want you to use common sense as well as the lessons."

"I always use common sense," he blustered. "What do you mean?"

His father rubbed his forehead hard, something he did when he was troubled. "I mean that they teach you many things nowadays, and a great deal of it is new, created by the Third Reich. And some is . . ."

Rudi's mother put her hand over her husband's, worry plain in her expression. "What your father is trying to say is that it is all right for you to question what you are being taught. Yes, you are the future of Germany, because when we are gone, you will grow up and take our place. But some of the things you are being told are simply not true. Listen to your heart, son. Do what is right."

Werde der du bist. Become who you are.

He knew what was expected of him by his superiors, but how could he turn in his parents for loving him? They had given him everything—them and the Hitler Youth, of course. If he did his duty, he would be lauded by his leaders for making such a bold move. He would be an inspiration to all the other boys. But Rudi did not have the heart for it. Angry at himself and his parents, he turned away and almost bumped into his sisters, who he discovered were even quieter than he.

"Will you report them?" Helga demanded.

Marta finished the accusation. "Don't be so weak, Rudi. It is your duty."

He brushed past them, saying nothing.

"Maybe I will," Helga said smugly as he headed down the hall. "Then we'll see who is the most loyal to the Vaterland."

Werde der du bist, his mother had told him. *Become who you are.* Except he'd had no idea who he was. Not like his sisters. Helga and Marta had been outstanding members of the Jung-mädelbund, then the Bund Deutscher Mädel in the Hitler-jugend, and finally the Glaube und Schönheit, where they were groomed to become model wives who would produce model sons. They could hardly wait to prove themselves. Rudi had been proud of his role in the military, but his sisters had been more than that. Every cell in their bodies had been devoted to der Führer and his vision of the world. And when Rudi walked away from that long-ago conversation in the living room, he'd seen contempt on his sisters' faces.

Maybe he should have done something, spoken to them of love and family, of loyalty and understanding. But he had been no more than a boy. Years later, as he coasted out to sea, he had no doubt Helga and Marta would have jostled for position to report their parents for being disloyal. And he knew how the authorities would have treated his sisters' report, because he'd seen it happen many times to other people. It wouldn't have mattered that his father's military record was exemplary; that would have been smashed to pieces by their twisted declaration. His father would most likely have died trying to protect his wife. Once he was gone, Rudi's mother would have been shipped to a bleak, hopeless camp with nothing but her memories and her devotion to God's word. Not enough by far.

Linda's words from that morning stuck in his head, meaning so much more than she could ever know. *We're supposed to report people for doing that kind of thing,* she had said. He knew that rule so well. At least with him gone, she would not be able to report them. Wherever he went he would have to start over, change who he was yet again. He was almost getting used to this transient life. If he could live his life all over again, how would he do it?

An idea snuck in without his bidding, and though Adam's death filled him with guilt, his skin prickled with a suggestion of hope.

No one had any idea Adam even existed.

Grace

THIRTY-THREE

Grace was still steaming about Linda when she got to the store. She slid the key into the lock, and the cheery bell welcomed her inside. She couldn't entirely blame her friend, she reasoned, because if Grace had walked in on Linda in the arms of a stranger, she would have questioned it, too. Especially if those arms belonged to a German. But still. Linda was like a dog on a bone. If she wasn't so darn nosy there would be no problem at all.

A square of paper lay on the floor by the counter, neatly folded. She picked it up and turned it over, startled to see her name printed on the other side. She'd seen that handwriting before, she thought, and unease stirred as she unfolded the note. Grace never had been able to get past her terrible habit of flipping to the end of a book to see the ending first, so she couldn't stop her eyes from dropping to the name at the bottom. Her pulse quickened. *Rudi.*

Hello Grace

I am sorry. I must go away. I cannot make Trouble for Family. Grace, I am very sad to leave you. You are special to me. I am dreaming of you, and I keep you safe in my Heart. Thank

*you for Trust, for believing in me. I wish you Happiness in
Life.*

*Mit herzlichen Grüßen,
Rudi*

She leaned against the counter and read the note twice
more, blinking through tears, trying to convince herself it
wasn't real. But every time she read his letter the words said the
same thing.

He was gone.

A teardrop fell and smudged his writing, so she set the letter on the counter to keep the rest of it dry. She folded her
arms to stop herself from reaching for it again, but she couldn't
simply forget the carefully drawn letters. What had been going
through his head as he stumbled through the words? What did
he mean about causing trouble? Had he done something? The
thought that he might be hiding another secret made her feel a
bit queasy. Or was it something else? Had *she* done something?
Said something? Had the intimate moment they'd shared that
morning chased him away?

She pressed her hands against her cheeks, imagining she
could still feel the warmth of his coat against her skin, rough
and reassuring, smelling of wood and grease and Rudi. That
memory and this little piece of paper were all she had of him
now. All the happiness she'd felt, all the hope and light . . . it
was gone. How could he have left her? What could have made
him—

The truth hit her. Linda. He must have overheard her
threats. And though Grace knew her family was doing the right
thing, Linda's accusations had still made her feel ashamed somehow. What would that have felt like to Rudi, hearing that his

very presence endangered the Bakers? She knew how much he respected her father, how much he'd come to trust and love her family. He would have left without hesitation, needing to protect them. What would she have done in his shoes?

"I wouldn't have run," she informed the letter. "I would have stayed. I would have fought back."

The more she thought of his leaving, the tighter her jaw became. Why hadn't he come to her? Maybe they could have solved it together if only he'd trusted her. He was always so full of compliments, but what about commitment? What about sticking around when the going got tough? How could he just leave her like this?

Except she also had to admit that life here wasn't the same for Rudi as it was for her. She was in no danger of being thrown in jail—or worse—and nobody was about to get in trouble because of her. Rudi was probably right to go, she admitted, except . . . when she thought of him gone, she felt off balance, as if an empty space had just opened up beside her.

She teetered on the edge, fighting disbelief. How could this have happened? They were from different worlds in every sense of the word, and yet despite everything, they'd found each other. They'd found love . . . then he'd left it behind.

"Stop that," she said out loud, containing her emotions. She had no right to just stand here and feel sorry for herself. She had work to do. A life to live. She had it so much better than so many other people. If Rudi was gone, he was gone. She would have to accept that and move on. Stepping behind the counter, she reached for her apron and tied it around her waist. She needed to focus on inventory, since the store was running low on a few items. List in hand, she walked to the shelves and started marking things down.

But when she reached towards the higher shelves, her mind

flew right back to Rudi, to how he'd stood there for the longest time, reading labels with such determination. She thought of his first tentative efforts to barter food for fur, then his pride when he'd given her that sweet ladybug, still perched in a place of honour in her bedroom. She thought of the dance, of how her heart had pounded when his arm slipped around her waist. She'd followed his steps, trusted him to guide her. She couldn't recall anyone else being in the building, had no idea what song the band played, but she remembered with perfect clarity the sense of contentment that had filled her entire being during that one brief dance.

He'd approached her as a stranger, walking across that dance floor and offering his hand. It was true he'd come from a whole different world, but there was nothing foreign about Rudi anymore. Not to Grace. Being in his arms felt like home. Like she'd finally found what she hadn't known was missing. She wanted him. She loved him.

She'd survived loneliness before, knew its ache, but everything was different this time. With her brothers, she had felt as if everything she'd ever known in her past was gone. With Rudi, it was her future.

THIRTY-FOUR

Four days later Grace answered a knock on the door, and for a moment she couldn't speak. Rudi stood before her, hat in hand. It was almost like seeing Norman after being told he was dead.

"Grace, I—"

She cut him off by throwing her arms around his neck. "I thought you were gone," she cried. "I thought I would never see you again."

"I am sorry, Grace. I did not know what to do," he said, holding her tight. "I could not make your family being in danger. But now things are changed."

He drew away, his fingers curled around her arms. The intensity was back in his eyes, blazing over the dark circles beneath. She'd seen that beseeching look before from him, and her stomach sank. What now?

"Please," he said. "I need to speak with you and your family."

❧

He had gone to Borgles Island, he told them. There he was attacked by a crazy man named Adam, and Rudi had killed him in a fight. That's all Grace understood from his explanation, because her mind was stuck on the first part. *He had gone to*

Borgles Island, the place where the U-boat had gone down. *He'd gone back to find his crewmates.*

How could she have fallen for this man, even believed she could be in love with him? Every sentence he stumbled through reminded her that he was the enemy, and he was a liar. She could never trust a man like that with her heart. She'd be better off as a spinster.

Her father was watching Rudi closely, arms crossed. "You disappear from here without a word, and you kill a man."

Rudi turned to Grace, but she didn't help him. He was on his own. "It was accident. He has knife," he gestured to his bloodstained sleeve, "and I have only hands. I take you to see the man, yes? You are seeing is accident."

"Well, I guess I'll have to go, make sure he's buried right." Her father shook his head, clearly annoyed. "Why did you go to Borgles Island in the first place?"

"To look for his men," Grace said through her teeth.

"No, Grace. Not for men. In camp, Tommy is telling me other German people live on island. I think if I find them maybe they are helping me go to Germany."

"That's a lie," she hissed. She could see the hurt in his eyes, and she channeled her own into anger. "You knew the men from your submarine might be there, and you went to find them. You are a spy after all."

His nostrils flared slightly. "No, Grace. I say to you one more time only. It is last chance to believe me. I am not spy, and I am not lying." He held out his hands. "I put note under door. You find this?"

She didn't trust herself to speak. She had cried over that note for the last four nights. Now that he was here, her emotions were in turmoil. He had left her. He had broken her heart. How could she trust him to stay?

"What note?" her father asked.

Rudi took a deep breath. "I go to island because I need to go away from here. I do not want people to say Baker family hide Nazi. This means trouble for Bakers. I do not want to hurt this family. I say this in note for Grace."

"I'm confused. Why did you come back here to tell us this?" her mother asked. "You could have just kept going."

"Please understand, Mrs. Baker. I go to island because I not want your family in danger," he repeated. "That is truth. But I come back because is more to tell."

He began by informing them that Tommy had been right about the couple on Borgles Island. "But Tommy is not knowing people have son. He is man now, not boy. Parents keep him on island because he is not smart." He jabbed his thumb against his temple. "He cannot think like man, only boy. You understand?"

Danny looked sideways at him. "You saying he was an imbecile?"

"I think is right word. Please understand, in Germany they do not want people like this. Government is *sterilisieren*, means they not let them make babies. I am sorry. I do not know word."

Grace's mother did, though. "I read about that," Audrey said, surprising Grace. "They sterilize handicapped adults so they can purify the race. Hitler is obsessed with making Germany what he considers to be perfect."

"Yes! This is what Hitler wants. So parents come to Borgles Island and tell nobody about son. He never meets other people. Never." Then he explained how Adam's parents had died in the U-boat explosion and how Adam had killed the two German soldiers.

"So there *were* German soldiers over there!" Grace exclaimed. "The army just didn't see them."

"No," he told her firmly. "Adam kill navy men before army is coming. Adam has knife. He cut me, then he is coming again, so I hit, and he . . ." He grimaced. "It is accident."

Grace's eyes went to Rudi's bloody sleeve and her resolve softened slightly. How long since he'd last slept?

Then Rudi said, "What I say tonight, all of this is truth. And now I must tell one lie." He pulled a faded piece of paper from his pocket and handed it to her father. "But it is very big lie. And it is lie I am telling until I am dead."

She leaned over to read it, then sat up, regarding Rudi skeptically. "Adam's birth certificate?"

"Yes. No person knows this man. No one. If I am taking his paper, I am him."

Her father was studying Rudi with a kind of disbelief. He reread the certificate, then handed it back. "I don't know, Rudi. It's not easy to live a lie your whole life. Why would you want to do this?"

"Because I do not want to go to Germany, sir. I want to stay here. I want to work hard and be happy." Rudi looked directly at Grace, lowered his voice. "I want to be with you, Grace."

Grace covered her mouth, battling tears. She wanted so badly to understand him, to trust him, to go back to how things were four days earlier, but she was so tired of putting her heart out and then getting it stepped on.

Her father cleared his throat. "Rudi—"

"Please," he interrupted, exasperation in his voice. "I need to talk. I know you think I am telling lies all the time. I know this, and is difficult for me. Before I come here"—he lifted his chin with pride—"*I* am the man people trust. People come to *me* for help. I tell truth all my life, sir." A sad smile touched his mouth. "Only here, I do not know what to say. You ask who I am, and I say too many truths, maybe." He held up one finger.

"I see Grace at store, and I tell her my friends go but I stay. This is truth." A second finger joined the first. "I say yes when Tommy says I am deserter, and now I understand this also is truth." Looking resigned, he added his thumb. "Number three is I am afraid I make trouble for your family, so I go away. This is truth." He faced Grace, pleading for understanding. "If I find other Germans on island, maybe they are sending me back. If I am in Germany, I make no trouble for you."

He held out the piece of paper. "Now I know what to do, and this is my only lie. This man, Adam, is dead. But he is dead means *I can live*. This paper is telling people I am on island many years, so I am not Nazi. Yes, I lie about before, but if I am Adam I tell truth about who I am now."

The room fell silent, then an unexpected voice said, "I like it." Everyone's attention went to Norman, sitting across the room and nodding his approval. "I'm with you, Rudi."

THIRTY-FIVE

"*I want to speak for* Rudi," Norman said, his voice quiet but firm. His fingers tapped softly on the arms of his chair. "I think he's having a bit of trouble, and somebody's got to stick up for him. And, well, since we're all being so honest here, I gotta say I'm also pretty sure his plan'll work."

At first no one said anything; they were too shocked to hear Norman speak up like this. He'd been steadily improving, but this was unexpected.

Danny broke the silence. "You been sitting around for a while now, not quite yourself. You feel fit enough to get into this conversation?"

"You're a tough act to follow, Dad, but yeah. I think I can, if that's okay."

"Go ahead. We're listening."

"I've never been in a sub, and I never will, God willing." He grimaced at the thought. "But Rudi lived in one of those buckets of bolts, and he followed orders. That's the way it goes. Whatever branch of service you're in, you sign up and you swear you're gonna go where you're sent and do what you're told. Dad, you know what I'm talking about. I know you never planned on living in those trenches, eating rats and stuff."

Norman's eyes were bright and clear. Grace stared at him in wonder.

"I'm only saying that because it's the truth, Dad. I know you don't like to talk about it, and now I understand why. I truly wish I did not, and I'm sorry I ever questioned what you were going through."

Danny accepted the acknowledgement and the apology without a sound.

"The way I see it," Norman continued, "we're all in this boat together. Rudi's just another passenger." He cocked his head to one side. "It's like, well, it's like when I was being shipped into Dieppe. We were boxed together like matchsticks, all of us scared out of our minds, puking on each other's boots, praying, crying . . . and when they lowered the hatch we ran out like sheep. Shots were flying, and some of my friends dropped dead in the boat where they stood. I never got a chance to say anything to them. Like everyone else, I ran for my life. I was terrified. As you know, I ended up cowering in the rocks under a dead soldier," he said, chuckling to himself. "I can tell you, that was not how I'd planned to fight this war." He turned to Rudi. "And I doubt very much that being here with us is how Rudi thought it would go for him. Am I right?"

Rudi was watching him, gratitude plain on his face, and sympathy warred with Grace's doubts.

Norman let out a long, slow breath. "I haven't told you my whole story, and I'm sure you've been curious," he said. "I guess I've been too ashamed to say anything about it until now, but I'm watching Rudi, and I'm learning what it's like to stand up to your fears. He's doing a strong thing here, and it's gotta feel like the whole world's against him."

Norman seemed reluctant to go on, but everyone was waiting. "And I kinda know exactly what he's talking about. You see, the truth is," he said, "well, I'm a deserter."

Grace's mouth gaped, and she saw her parents sit up with alarm.

"Now son," Danny said, "I don't think—"

"And just like Rudi," Norman carried on, "I never meant to be. After they pulled me out of Dieppe, they laid us out in the medic tent. I heard the doctor saying he wasn't sure my head was messed up enough that I should go home, but that I needed some looking at. But that kind of mess meant they'd put me in a special hospital first, see if they could fix me, and I'd heard stories about the kinds of things they did to men like me. I was almost as scared of that as I was of the Germans."

Norman's eyes had lost their focus again, and Grace could only imagine what he saw.

"While the medics were figuring out what to do with us, me and the guy in the next cot were talking. Well, I guess that's what you could call it, anyway. He wasn't making much sense." He leaned towards Danny just a little. "He was worse off than me, but it was the same kind of problem. It was all in his head, you know? When he talked, it was like he was having trouble figuring out how, but I did understand him when he said he'd never had a headache like that one. Felt like it was right behind his eye. One of his eyelids drooped, so it was almost like I could see his headache in a way. Poor fellow kept getting sick. I heard one of the medics saying it was an aneurysm." He flinched slightly, as if he could see it all over again. "He was on his way home. God, I wished I was him. I'd have happily taken on that headache and given both my legs to get outta there. Anyway, there was a hell of a lot of confusion going on in the tent, so much yelling, and I guess they didn't get to him in time because he died an hour or so later. Never even made a sound. All I could think was that the poor sucker didn't get to go home after all, and then I guess . . . well, I saw an opening. When no one was looking, I switched dog tags with him. I had no idea if it'd work, and I was so scared they'd come back and charge me with something, but I guess maybe they thought they were the ones who had mixed things up, because they took his body away, and they sent me home." He threw his hands up. "I did it. I was out. I was free."

He paused, then he stared down at his fingers as they returned to their new habit of picking at invisible dirt. "Except when I got off the ship in Halifax, ready to come home, I couldn't do it. I . . . couldn't face my own family." His voice cracked. "I dropped the other guy's tags in the garbage and became a nobody."

Grace's heart broke for her poor, lost brother, and tears streamed down her mother's cheeks. The idea that he'd been afraid to come home was the worst of all. From across the room she noticed Rudi's stricken face, and everything came together for her. She knew her men. Norman, Harry, Eugene, her father, and yes, Rudi, were strong, courageous fighters, ready to stand up to the worst violence the war could hurl at them, to defend their country and freedom the only way they knew how. Out there, she thought, their bodies were constantly in danger, but the most terrible damage, the pain no one warned them about, was to their minds and souls. And no medicine could heal that.

"We're all put in this world for one lifetime," Norman said. "You taught me that, Dad. We do with it what we can. I guess the plan is to do something good, or at least to be happy." He inclined his head towards their mother. "You taught me that part, Maman. Then war comes along and makes that almost impossible. But Dad, you found Maman in the middle of it all. Then the Explosion happened and you found us, gave us boys a life we never would have had. None of these things were planned, but they happened.

"Rudi didn't plan to end up here, but he chose to do the right thing: he brought Tommy home even though he could've left him to die. Then he stayed here and worked hard." He turned to Grace, showing her the wonderfully honest smile she remembered. "And Grace, it sounds like he wants to take charge of his life and do whatever he can to be with you. You gotta admit, that's a pretty big thing."

When he'd finished speaking, he sat quietly, and his fingers still picked at themselves, but he seemed different now. Less like a snail in a shell. It was as if the family had witnessed the actual moment when he shed the weight of all that guilt and shame.

She could tell Rudi was watching her, waiting for some kind of reaction, but she couldn't look at him. Not yet. She understood everything Norman had said, and she knew he was right, but she was still afraid.

"Let me see that paper again," her father said.

Rudi leaned forwards and gave it to him.

"According to this," Danny said, "you want us to call you Adam."

"Adam. Yes. Adam Neumann."

"Adam Neumann," he mused, rereading the paper. He passed it to his wife, and she folded it carefully before handing it back to Rudi.

"Every family has its secrets," Audrey said. "I can accept that one."

Danny put a hand on hers and squeezed gently, watching Norman, then turned to Rudi. "All right, Adam Neumann," he said, groaning as he stood. "I guess you'd better take me to Borgles Island."

Adam, not Rudi. He was changing before her eyes, and the unexpected sense of loss that washed over Grace in that moment made her light-headed. Rudi was Rudi—even though he'd been so many different people in the short time she'd known him. Maybe it was easier for the others to accept this change because they saw him as a friend. But for Grace, that wasn't enough. The others hadn't fallen in love with him like she had. And now that he was changing, she had so many questions. Would Adam look at her the way Rudi had? What would he do now that he had a fresh chance at life? He could do anything he wanted. He might not even stay.

But before he stood, Rudi leaned towards Grace and searched her face. And something in her melted. Maybe, just maybe, he would stay. The thought swelled in her, grew more urgent—*Please stay. I want you to stay*—because every day she was around him she became more convinced that she needed him.

"I am good man, Grace. I will show you," he said.

For just an instant they were the only two in the room, and she wished she could cling to that feeling forever. But her family was waiting.

His honest, blue eyes returned to the others. "Thank you, Baker family. God bless you all."

PART FOUR

THIRTY-SIX

April 1943

Rudi—or rather, Adam—no longer hid. He worked as hard as any other man in the plant, and Grace's father paid him accordingly. There was more energy in his step, fresh confidence in his smile, and to Grace's delight, he often stopped by the store to visit her. He was polite and friendly to people he met, and the curious looks he received at first evolved into familiar greetings.

Two days of pea soup fog finally washed away under a miserable, shivering rain, so when Rudi arrived at the store that afternoon he brought with him the sweet, homey smell of wet wool. Raindrops beaded his cap and coat, and his cheeks were red from the chill. Old Mrs. Gardner was on her way out as he arrived, so he held the door open for her.

"Hello, Adam. Lovely to see you again," she said as she left.

"You have a nice day, Mrs. Gardner," he replied, then he turned back to Grace. "Nice lady."

"She certainly is," Grace replied, her mind still on the conversation she and Mrs. Gardner had just had. All of a sudden she had quite a lot to think about.

"I bring footstool."

She barely noticed it. "Oh, thank you. It's perfect. You can just leave it over here."

"You are having good day?"

"I am."

He tilted his head, studying her. "Something is different."

Surely he couldn't read her that well, could he? "What do you mean?"

"I know you, Grace. Something happened."

As ever, his intensity both charmed and intimidated her. He was always so interested in everything she said or did. He was right, though. Something had happened, and it was more than just a distraction.

She leaned against the counter. "Actually, I just had a really interesting conversation with Mrs. Gardner."

"Yes? You can tell me?"

"Sure. Maybe you can help me figure out what to do." She let out a breath. "Actually it's bad news and good news. The bad news is that Mrs. Gardner is sick. Very sick. She says she's dying."

"This is very bad news."

"And she has no family. No children, and her husband died a long time ago," she said, feeling guilty. Terrible news like this shouldn't bring her such joy. But how could she not want to celebrate? "She said she wants to leave the store to me in her will."

His fair eyebrows lifted. "Grace, this is *wunderbar!*"

"This would be my own store." Her thoughts were a jumble. "I still can't believe it. I don't even know if I can do something like that."

"You can. You already do this."

"Yes, but . . ."

"But, Grace, this is so good news. Our life will be so happy. When we are married, you will run store and I will make it bigger and better."

"You are incorrigible. And before you ask, that means I can't fix you. Why do you always say such crazy things?"

"Because is truth." One side of his mouth curled up in a

devilish way, and he walked right up to her, put his arms around her waist before she could object. "I mean what I say, Grace. I am good man, and you are wanting to marry me."

She put her hands on his shoulders, grateful the store was empty in that moment. "You have a rather high opinion of yourself, don't you?" She could tell he had no idea what she'd just said, so she made it easier. "Why would I want to marry you, Adam Neumann?"

He'd gotten used to his new name, she thought. She wasn't entirely comfortable with it yet, but she was getting there.

"Many, many things," he said. "I get money from working, I am strong, I am handsome—What? You tell me this before!"

How could she not laugh when he said things like that? He was adorable, and the twinkle in his eyes was contagious. But it was the way he kissed her cheek that stopped her heart.

"You are dream girl to me, Grace." He kissed her other cheek. "I am making you love me someday."

She already did, but she wasn't about to tell him that. Not yet.

Her family was thrilled with her news about the store, and she started thinking about Rudi's suggestions about improving it. Maybe she could build a cozy tea room off the side. In the summer maybe they could sell ice cream, maybe even get one of those milkshake machines. Oh, it could be so much fun, making the place her own.

When she was at work the next day, everything was exactly the same as it had been before—except it was all different. The shelves, the floor, the windows . . . they would one day be hers. When the phone rang at the end of the day, she sounded like she was singing when she answered.

"Good morning! Gardner's General Store."

"Hey, little sister."

"Eugene! What are you doing, calling me? You coming home?"

"Yes . . . and no. Grace, I couldn't reach Maman and Dad. There's been an accident—"

Every happy thought vanished. "What?"

"It's Harry. He's in the hospital."

They heard a gasp. Too late they both realized there was a third person on the line.

"What is it, Eugene?" Linda demanded. "What's wrong?"

"Don't worry, Linda, he's okay. We got in a bit of a tussle with a U-boat, and he took a little shrapnel to the head."

"His head!"

"Yes, but it didn't go deep. Just added another mark of honour to that scar he's already got. Don't worry. He's better looking than ever."

Grace turned her back to the store and leaned over the counter, head in her hand. Harry was hurt. How many of these telephone calls was she going to get? "You're sure he's okay, Eugene?"

"He will be. Still unconscious, but the doctor says everything went fine in surgery—"

"Surgery?!" Linda's voice was shrill as a chicken's.

"Linda, let Eugene speak."

"Those damn Germans shot my Harry in the head!"

"Linda, please. We need to be calm. What should we do, Eugene?"

"Tell Maman and Dad to come to Halifax and meet us at Ste. Anne's Hospital. And pack a bag. Uncle Mick says we can stay at his place for a few days while Harry recovers."

"I'm coming, too," Linda interjected.

That would make being calm impossible. "Linda, Uncle Mick doesn't have that much room."

"Oh no?" she snapped. "Does he have room for your Nazi boyfriend?"

Grace willed herself to stay cool. "Adam is not a Nazi, Linda. And I would prefer it if you didn't speak that way."

But Linda was like a dog on a bone. "I know what you are doing, pretending it's normal to have a German living there, but it's wrong. It should be reported."

So much heat rushed to Grace's head she felt light-headed. Linda hadn't said anything about Rudi for a while, and Grace had thought she was finished with her threats. "What are you saying?"

"You shouldn't be protecting the enemy!"

Eugene finally took control. "Linda, this is not the time. We need to think about Harry right now."

"Fine," Linda said. "But I am not happy about this. Somebody's going to pay for causing him pain." Her voice cracked with emotion on the last word. "I'm sorry. I just . . . I hate this. The war is bad enough, but him being shot is the most terrible thing. Please tell Harry I love him."

"Of course we will, Linda."

As she hung up, Grace looked blankly around the shelves she'd restocked that morning. What had been exciting minutes before now meant nothing.

She understood why Linda reacted the way she did—she loved Harry. If someone threatened Rudi, Grace would do anything to protect him, too. Now, once again, one of her brothers was hurt. Would these trials never end? Would none of them ever be able to move on from this horrible place in time? How crazy it was that she'd just been dreaming about the future, as if it could be happy! Rage pulsed from her heart to her throat until there was nothing she could do to hold it back.

When her sobs slowed, she lifted her head off the counter

and looked around, finding her anchor among the neat rows of canned vegetables and goods. Every item stood exactly where she'd put it, all lined up like soldiers. In the few minutes since Eugene had telephoned, nothing in the store had changed. She took a deep breath, appreciating that small fact. The place was untouched, unaffected by the world's troubles, and something about that was comforting.

Strange that such an unrelated thing could change her whole perspective, but it did. Life would go on in this village whether the war did or not, she realized. That's just how it was, and there was nothing anyone could do about it. All she was responsible for was making sure the life she lived was a good one, that she took care of the people she loved, and that she did everything she could to ensure they were happy.

"I can do that," she said out loud.

With fresh resolve, she wiped her eyes, closed the store, and headed home.

THIRTY-SEVEN

As arranged, Eugene and Uncle Mick met them at the hospital that evening. Grace and her mother rushed to embrace Eugene while her father shook Uncle Mick's hand.

"How's my boy doing?" Danny asked.

"He'll be okay," Eugene replied. "Doctor said the wound was superficial. Just needed a few stitches."

The door to Harry's room opened, and the nurse appeared.

"Are you all here to see Mr. Baker? He's had some medicine, and he's probably going to sleep the rest of the night. Would you like to see him anyway?"

At the sight of Harry all wrapped up and lying still as death, both Grace and her mother caught their breath. Most of his head was swathed in clean white bandages, though they'd left his good eye uncovered. The purple, crescent-shaped bruise underneath it was very dark, striking against his pale skin, but his chest rose and fell softly under the light blue hospital pyjamas. He was alive. *Thank God.*

"The doctor wasn't worried at all, and he's seen thousands of men wounded," Uncle Mick assured them, putting a companionable arm around Audrey. "I've seen much worse. Hell, Harry's *been* worse. Remember the little fella so long ago? He's a fighter if ever I've seen one."

"That's true," Audrey managed. "All my boys are fighters."

They were quiet, each to their own thoughts, and Harry continued to breathe, slow and easy. Grace took his hand and whispered, "We love you, Harry. And Linda does too. She's anxious to see you."

"I gave the doctor my telephone number," Mick said, "and I told my housekeeper to expect a crowd for dinner. How's about we head up that way when you're ready? You've probably forgotten how hungry you are."

Back at Uncle Mick's house, Grace called Linda. Eugene stood by, listening in as Grace assured her friend that Harry was doing well and receiving the best of care. Other than that, the conversation belonged to Linda, as usual. She was furious at the entire German race for Harry being injured, and she warned them she wasn't going to hold her tongue a minute longer. Grace winced at some of her words, tried to refute others, but there was no convincing Linda of anything. What bothered Grace the most was the way she kept talking about Rudi, as if he was the root of all the evil in the world.

"Please don't do anything crazy," Grace said when Linda paused for breath. "Harry's gonna be fine, and there's no need to do anything to involve Adam. Think about your actions— you could ruin his life."

"I don't care about his life, Grace."

"But I do. Don't do anything. Promise me."

"I'm sorry. I can't do that. I have to look out for me and Harry now."

"Oh, Eugene," Grace said when the conversation was done and they'd both hung up. "She's going to ruin everything."

Eugene put an arm around her as they headed back to the sitting room. "Maybe she'll behave."

"Has she ever?"

"How did that go?" Danny asked as they came back in the room.

From his expression, Grace figured he'd overheard some of the conversation. She pressed her lips together. "She's angry. She's not thinking straight and she's threatening to accuse . . . Adam of being a German spy."

"She seemed set on it, from what I heard," Eugene agreed. "Not sure a train could stop her."

"Maybe not a train, but I think I know what might." Danny faced his old friend Uncle Mick. "Hey, newspaperman, I have a story for you."

Grace's jaw dropped. "Dad!"

"I wondered if you might do this," Audrey said.

Uncle Mick settled into his chair, lit a cigar. "Is that so? Just like the old days, huh?"

"Yep, but you might have to fudge a couple of things," Danny said.

Mick's mouth twisted to the side. "Just a couple?"

Grace sat back, surprised to hear her father launch into Rudi's story, beginning with the explosion at Borgles Island and ending with Adam's resurrection.

"I see," Mick said, blowing smoke rings. "So . . . the way I see it, the story starts when *Adam* saves Tommy. Off the record, we're saying there never really was a Rudi, right?"

"That's right. The story's true. It's just that we need to reduce the two main characters to one."

"Okay, okay. Let's make sure I have all this straight," Mick said, setting his cigar in an ashtray. He leaned forwards, checked his notes. "Adam Neumann came to Borgles Island with his parents when he was just a kid. We know that's true because we have his birth certificate as proof. When the U-boat exploded in December, it killed Adam's parents and everyone on the ship. Right so far? But it all worked out, because after they died he decided he'd had enough of the island, and he went to the cabin at Abbecombec. There he rescued Tommy, and he's now joined your community as a hard worker. He may be a German, but he's also a hero. That's what you're saying, in a nutshell." He tilted his head towards the telephone. "And that?"

"Is the only person threatening to blow the story apart."

"It's not really her fault. She loves Harry," Grace explained. "And this war, I mean, it's so easy to just take sides and not think straight. For the longest time I believed all Germans were bad, and I'm ashamed of how I saw them as monsters instead of people. But I'm not the only one, am I? I mean, it's in all the newspapers and on the radio, isn't it? How they're the bad guys no matter what. Really, they're just men doing their duty like Harry was doing."

"True enough," Mick agreed.

"Oh, and off the record, Rudi—or rather, *Adam*," Danny corrected himself, "says he's done with fighting. He was right in there with the rest of them, but he's done now."

Uncle Mick tipped an imaginary hat at Grace. "All for the love of a pretty girl, sounds like."

Grace blushed, but she didn't deny it.

Her father shook his head. "No, I think it's because he enjoys working for me so much. I still can't understand why you didn't want to come up and work at the plant, Mick. I did offer you a job, as you recall."

Mick took a puff of his cigar and released its fragrant smoke. "I know you did. I just can't imagine why I wouldn't give all this up to live in fish stink."

"The offer stands."

"I'll let you know." Mick rolled the cigar thoughtfully

between his fingers. "So Danny, this Rudi guy. He's the real deal? You believe in him this much?"

"I do. We all do. Wouldn't ask you if we didn't."

Grace watched Mick intently. Her uncle was a well-respected man here in Halifax, and he had a reputation to protect, but Grace knew he and her father went way, way back. What had they survived together in those vile trenches? What would he do for a friend after all this time?

"I'm going to go put some more coffee on," Mick said, rising slowly from his seat. "Looks like I have a story to write. I might be up a few hours. Way past your bedtime, anyway. You all just tuck in and I'll see you at breakfast."

Rudi

THIRTY-EIGHT

Grace had left for Halifax a week ago, and in that time spring had arrived. The fishing boats were out in full force, and the plant was getting busier. Rudi was comfortable working there now, and just as he'd hoped, the other workers barely paid him any attention. He had told them a short story about growing up on Borgles Island, but other than that he didn't speak much. If they came up with too many questions, Rudi tended to conveniently forget English, which proved frustrating enough that they gave up.

From what Rudi knew, the trip to Halifax was going well. Grace had telephoned him to say that Harry was going to be all right, and the whole family hoped to be home soon.

It was almost closing time at the plant, and Rudi was cleaning up when Linda arrived. She strode into the building as if she belonged there and rooted herself in front of him. Before he could say anything, she started talking.

"I would like to speak with you," she said, her voice as cold as ice.

"I finish here, then—"

"Now." She peered over his shoulder at one of the others. "Can I take him?"

The other worker shrugged.

"Good. Come with me. Now."

She practically ran across the yard to the barn and he followed, unsure what to think. When she pointed at an old bench, indicating she wanted him to sit, he did.

She didn't. She stood before him, arms crossed. "I don't want you here."

"I am sorry. Why you are angry?"

"I have lived here my whole life, and I know everyone and everything that goes on here. This is where I will spend the rest of my life, this is where I will raise my family. Nothing is going to stop me from doing that."

He comprehended the words but not entirely the meaning or her tone. "I understand."

"I don't think you do. Let me explain. You are, no matter what you say, German. Your country is at war with my country. You may be pulling the wool over my friends' eyes, but you don't fool me. You and I are enemies. Do you understand that?"

"This . . . is not true," he said warily.

"Oh, yes it is. I don't know where you've been since 1939, but it's most definitely true. In case you missed it, we are at war, Mr. Nazi."

"Of course is war," he said, "but I am not enemy, and I am not Nazi."

She took a long step forwards so her face was right in his. "Stop lying to me. You're not some harmless come from away. A strong, healthy German man like you didn't just come from some island. I'd bet my last dollar you're a Nazi spy, and I do not want you here. If it weren't for men like you there would be no war. There would be no innocent young Canadians coming home with their head shot or their leg blown off. There would be no innocent young Canadians bundled up in blankets, afraid to go to sleep at night. You, *Adam*, are the enemy, and *I do not want you here.*"

Rudi had never heard a woman speak this way. She was more frightening than any commander he'd had to face before. He wasn't sure how to respond.

"Well?" She folded her arms. "Do you have anything to say?"

"I . . . I do not know how to answer. I tell you I am not Nazi. I am not making fight or hurting anyone."

"Maybe not right now, but I bet you've 'made fight' with lots of men before. Killed a bunch, too."

How was this happening? Everything had been going so well. "I do not—"

"I am warning you: I am going to report you. I will call the police and the navy and the newspaper, and I will personally speak with everyone on my switchboard, which includes practically the whole Eastern Shore. If you are smart, you will listen to what I am saying." She waved her hands at the ground as if she were scattering hens. "Go, German. Scram. Get lost."

He got to his feet. "No, Linda! I am not going. I am with Baker family, and we are friends. You cannot—"

"Yes, I can!" she shrieked. "And I will!"

The crackling sound of gravel under tires came from the road, and they both looked to the approaching car. When she turned back to Rudi, her cheeks were flushed.

"Good. Harry's finally back where he should be. Now's your chance to disappear." Her eyes narrowed dangerously. "Go away and stay away. And if you ever come back I will tell everyone who you really are, Nazi."

Then she turned and ran to the car, waving her arms in the air, leaving Rudi behind.

He let out a long breath. He was so tired of this. How many times did he have to excuse the man he had been? Beg forgiveness for things he'd been ordered to do, and even for things he hadn't done? Maybe he should just do what she said, follow through with what he'd considered doing before: lose himself in the woods, become just as much of a hermit as the real Adam had been.

He stood at the far end of the yard and watched as the black metal doors of the car creaked open and the small, cheering crowd parted as if they welcomed royalty. Harry's head was bandaged, but Rudi could see his happiness even from this far away. He wished he could go closer and welcome him home, but he knew he didn't belong in their excited circle. This was yet another son coming home, wounded while fighting a war against Rudi's country. Worse, this one had been hurt by the very machine in which Rudi had first arrived at this place.

Then Grace stepped from the car, and his heart soared. The longing he felt was something entirely new, and it hurt like nothing ever had. She was laughing about something, her black curls bouncing around her shoulders. If he was closer, would she smile for him? Reach out her hand so he might take it?

But he wasn't closer. And he wasn't welcome. Linda had made that perfectly clear. He turned away and started up the hill to where Grace's great-grandparents' abandoned house stood. The last time he'd been here, Linda had come, had spotted him with Grace. But before that, the place had felt almost magical.

"Rudi!"

He whirled around. "Grace! You are all right?"

Her cheeks were bright and she was out of breath. "Are *you* all right? I . . . I just saw Linda, and I . . ."

He looked away.

"That's what I thought," she said. She grabbed his hand and squeezed it. "Don't listen to her. Please. She had no right to even speak to you."

It felt good, hearing her defend him, but he didn't think what she was saying was true. "It is okay."

"No, it isn't." When they reached the top of the hill she sat on the grass, indicating that he should as well. As soon as he did, her face crumpled. "I'm so sorry she bothered you. None of this should be happening. Why can't everything just be easy? Why couldn't you just be a regular guy that I'm crazy about?"

Some of his old confidence returned at that. "Maybe if I am regular guy, you are not crazy about me."

That made her smile.

But Linda's words came back to him, and he shook his head. "I am who is sorry, Grace. You and your father are right when you tell me before. Is complicated," he reminded her sadly. "To be Adam is too much work."

"Not for long." She dug in the bag at her side and pulled out a folded newspaper. "I brought this for you."

"What is this?"

"Just read it. I can help if you need."

The bold headline grabbed him from the start: "A Hero of Different Stripes: Adam Neumann, the Mysterious German Recluse Who Saved a Local Man's Life."

He looked at her, stunned. "What is this?"

"My uncle Mick wrote it. Do you remember that time I showed you the article he'd written in the *Herald*? Well, this time he wrote a story about you." She put a hand on his forearm. "Soon everyone who reads this will know who you really are, Adam Neumann."

The newspaper type was small, the words mostly impossible to read, but he stumbled doggedly over them. And what he read was too wonderful to believe. When he went through it a second time, he pointed out specific words so Grace could translate for him.

"You see what I mean?" she asked when he'd finished. "After

this article, nobody's ever going to accuse you of being a Nazi, and they won't accuse us of breaking the law."

This changed everything. He took a deep breath. Took another because he couldn't seem to catch the first one.

"You are wrong before, Grace Baker. You say is complicated, you and me, but is not. It is easy." He set his palm against her cheek. "I like you very much, Grace. Very much."

She leaned against his hand. "I always wanted to trust you, Rudi. It just took me a while to figure out that you deserved that trust. I understand it now." She blinked through tears. "I'm sorry it took me so long."

The wind jostled her curls and he couldn't resist tucking one under her hat. "I am not lying to you. Never."

"Say, 'I will never lie to you, Grace.'"

Against her pure black eyebrows and the windburned red of her skin, her eyes were like blue crystals, sparkling in the late-day sunlight. He thought he would very much like to buy her a ring someday. One set with exactly that same coloured gem.

"I will never lie to you, Grace."

"I will never lie to you, either."

She leaned towards him, and he was there. Her lips were warm and soft, her breath fragile as a butterfly's wing, but the kiss they shared carried a strength that was like nothing he'd ever felt before. She was here, she was his, and he knew in that moment he wanted nothing more than to be with her for the rest of his life.

"In German," he said quietly, his thumb tracing little circles on the soft skin of her cheek, "this is *ein Kuss*."

"Ein Kuss," she repeated, and he felt the feathery touch of her breath on his lips. "I call it something else. I call it a promise."

She was the most wonderful girl in the world. "Come. I promise you again."

When they drew apart this time, her expression was serious. "You know what this newspaper article means?"

"Tell me."

"It means you don't have to go back to Germany."

He smiled against her lips. "I know this, yes."

"You can stay with me."

"Yes. Yes, I am staying with you, Grace." Why should he ever leave? He was home.

EPILOGUE
June 1945

"*Why are they building a* new house, Auntie Grace?"

The hammering had been going on all week, punctuated by men's voices and the *wub-wub* of an occasional saw. They were getting as much done as they could while the weather was good.

"You know why, Joyce. Can you please hand me your daddy's shirt?"

"This?"

"Thank you."

Grace clipped Norman's shirt to the line, then reached down for her niece's next offering.

"Put Benny's next, okay? Beside Daddy's."

"That's a good idea," Grace agreed, chuckling at the contrast between baby Benny's tiny shirt and her brother's. "What's the difference, Joyce?"

The little girl's freckly face lit up at the challenge. She looked so much like her father. A stubby finger pointed at one shirt, then the other. "That is big and blue. That is small and white."

"Good girl. How many shirts have we hung today?"

Joyce spun on her heel and scampered back to the beginning of the line. "Pants too, Auntie Grace? How many pants?"

Grace took a clothespin from her mouth, finishing up with the socks. "Nope. Just shirts. You can count the pants after."

"Okay! One . . . two . . . three—" She got to three before she remembered her initial question. "How come Uncle Adam's building a new house?"

"You know why," Grace repeated, smiling as she remembered.

Rudi's request that she meet him in the barn that night had been an odd one. They usually met there anyway. Ever since the generator's restoration, the barn had become "their" place, a spot where they went whenever they wanted to be alone. His expression had been both charming and difficult to read, and she'd been intrigued.

That night she'd stepped inside the barn and everything looked different. Rudi had brought two chairs from the house and set them around a crate, which had been covered with her mother's lace tablecloth. Two places were set for dinner, and a candle flickered between them. She turned to him, thrilled by the surprise, then realized he had dropped to one knee. She caught her breath, and her lips formed around his name, but she couldn't speak.

"*Heirate mich, Grace,*" he said, his voice deep and sincere. "*Ich liebe dich. Ich glaube, ich habe dich immer geliebt immer.*" He held up his hands, and she set her trembling fingers on top. The candlelight caught her tears, blurring her vision, but his face, open and honest and certain, was all she needed to see. "Marry me, Grace," he translated, his English confident. "I love you. I think I always have."

The memory was so perfect she hoped it would never fade, but it almost didn't matter. He constantly did things to please her in some way or another. Rudi was funny and romantic and determined to do his best at everything, including loving her.

Grace shaded her eyes and looked up the hill, admiring the day's progress. It was odd seeing the rough sawn lumber in the same place where her great-grandparents' ancient house had stood for so many years. It had been bittersweet to take the old place down, but everyone agreed it wasn't sturdy enough to fix. And since it stood in her favourite place, Rudi had decided he wanted to build their house there. They'd kept the foundation, but that was all. They'd put down new floor joists, insulation, planks, and walls, and now they were starting to work on wiring. Grace understood little about the process, but Rudi enjoyed every step of it.

From where she stood now she could see the construction crew, hear bits of their comfortable conversation. She knew her father had gone to the lumber mill with Tommy that day, and she was surprised to see they weren't back yet. She hoped that didn't mean they'd messed up the rafter order again.

"The big house is too crowded now, Joyce," she said. "We can't all fit anymore."

"But . . . Maybe you can stay in my room! We can play!"

"That's very kind of you," Grace said, watching the construction site. Rudi worked side by side with her brothers, his hair almost white in the sun. "But where would Uncle Adam sleep?"

Grace thought of that little complication and her heart leaped. Their own house. Their own room. Their own bed.

Just then, Harry said something that made Eugene guffaw, then Rudi and Norman joined in. The easy, uncomplicated sound squeezed her heart, almost brought tears to her eyes, and she realized what she'd missed most of all during the war was their laughter. Now she had nothing to miss.

The twins had arrived home for the final time just a month before. They'd stepped off the docks along with thousands of other servicemen and headed to the taverns to celebrate the end of the war. Not surprisingly, all the residents of Halifax had wanted to make merry alongside them. As a result, the tram service had shut down for the day, as had all restaurants, taverns, movie theatres, and shops. When faced with the prospect of a party without food or drink, some of the more determined servicemen decided they'd help themselves, and before long the situation had escalated into looting. The next day, Halifax's already overcrowded streets went mad in what people were now calling the Halifax Riot.

"It was fun for a while, but we'd had enough of most of those fellows," Harry said when they got home the next day. "Eugene and me dragged Uncle Mick out of the crowd and stayed at his place for the night."

The celebration carried on after they arrived home, and no one could claim to have had a dry eye that night. Whether the tears came from laughing or crying, they were cleansing.

Since then, every day had felt like a celebration to Grace.

"He can stay with Uncle Tommy," Joyce suggested, breaking into her reverie.

"I don't think so, Joyce. But don't you think it'll be fun, having a new house to visit? You can help me decorate. I can put your drawings up on the wall, just like Grandmère's paintings."

"I'm going to paint one for you tonight!"

"That would be lovely." She picked up the empty basket, rested it on her hip. "Let's go visit the new house. Your mom's up there, see?"

Norman had his arm around Gail's waist and was whispering something in her ear that made her gasp, then giggle.

"Oh, you are bad, big brother," Grace teased as she passed him.

He kissed his wife's cheek. "I do my best."

Norman had come a long way from two years before, though the memories still came and went. She saw the panic in his eyes sometimes, saw his hands shake uncontrollably when he heard a sudden sound, but he was learning how to fight back. Gail was stronger now as well, and she was helping him every step of the way.

"Even I know this meaning of bad is good," Rudi said with a smirk.

She arched an eyebrow. "Yes, and *you*, birthday boy," she said curtly, "are *very* bad."

He bowed, pleased.

"I have something I'd like to show you," she said. "Could you take a few minutes?"

Eugene pushed the brim of his hat up with his hammer and plucked a cigarette out of his mouth. "Lesson number one," he said, blowing out a stream of smoke. "If your fiancée wants you to take a few minutes out of building her house, you'd better go."

Laughing at Eugene's suggestion, Rudi took Grace's hand, and she led him to her parents' house. He was still living at Norman's place, but all that would soon change. For now she had to settle for goodnight kisses, but those were wonderful and always full of promise.

"What is this, my almost wife?"

"Oh, it's nothing, really," she said as they walked, though her heart sang with excitement. For his birthday she'd wanted to give him a gift that reflected how much she loved him, how much she respected his past as well as their future. "It's just a birthday present. I hope you like it."

Long before, Rudi had said music was his passion—at least until Grace had come along. He sang when he worked, hummed when they walked, and he had big plans of one day taking her to an opera. She'd started thinking how wonderful it would be for him to have more music in his life again, and just for fun she began perusing catalogues whenever they arrived at the store.

She'd taken the leap and special ordered a fancy Philco console, and now it stood in the middle of her parents' sitting room in a temporary place of honour, three feet wide and three feet tall, its dark wood finish polished to a shine. Even Linda—who had been forced to give Rudi the benefit of the doubt since he refused to go away—had grudgingly approved. The console was a bit dear, but Mrs. Gardner had left Grace the general store just as she'd promised, and being the owner of a small but successful shop made it easier for Grace to pay for things over time. She didn't regret a single cent of interest.

On the table beside the console she had set out Verdi's *Rigoletto* and some records her brothers had suggested. On top of the console sat the sweet ladybug he had carved for her so long ago.

She stood beside him, her hands clenched in anticipation while Rudi stared at the console, blinking but not speaking. Then he stepped closer and placed his hands on the smooth wood. Still he said nothing. He picked up the opera record, read the words printed on the case, and she waited in suspense.

"I hope that's the right record," she blurted. "The Philco, well, it . . . it plays records *and* the radio, so you can listen to whatever you want."

He put the record down and turned to her, and she saw tears in his eyes. "Grace, I . . . This is best—"

"Eesh leebe deesh," she exclaimed, her eyes brimming. She hoped she'd said it right and didn't sound as awkward as she felt. She'd practised in front of the mirror so many times.

"I love you too, Grace." He pulled her into his arms and held her tight against him, resting his cheek on top of her head. "You are my love. You are my music."

He had the turntable spinning in no time at all, and he selected the Bing Crosby record Norman had recommended. He held out a hand and she went to him as she had so long before, in that crowded hall shimmering with red and gold. His arm wrapped around her waist and her hand went to his shoulder, then a little past, so her fingertips brushed the smooth, warm skin of his neck. The violins played the opening notes, and Rudi led her around the room, his lips at her ear.

"Do you remember the first dance?" he asked.

She snuggled closer. "Of course."

"You are all I see that night," he murmured. "Everyone is dancing and talking, but I see only you. We have rules; U-boat men cannot talk to people at dance. But I cannot stay away." He kissed the side of her neck. "You were like a dream."

His warm hand was firm on the base of her spine, and when they whirled across the floor she felt like she was flying, careless and free. From somewhere on earth an orchestra serenaded them and a man crooned beautiful words.

"'I love you,'" Rudi sang, his voice sweeter than Bing's could ever be.

She closed her eyes, listened to every one of his syllables as if she'd never heard the song before. He didn't know all the words, but she liked his version better.

Afterword

U-69 was indeed the U-boat responsible for the heinous and tragic sinking of the SS *Caribou*, the doomed Newfoundland Railway passenger ferry. At 3:51 a.m. on October 14, 1942, U-69's Kapitänleutnant Gräf ordered the SS *Caribou* to be torpedoed approximately thirty-seven kilometres (twenty nautical miles) southwest of Channel-Port aux Basques, Newfoundland. Most of the 137 who died were women and children.

U-69 was later sunk in the North Atlantic, but it did not happen off Nova Scotia as I wrote in this story. On February 17, 1943, the U-boat attacked an Allied convoy, but depth charges forced her to the surface. Somewhere in the middle of the North Atlantic, the destroyer HMS *Fame* fatally rammed and sank U-69. None of her forty-six crewmembers survived.

Who were the men in that crew? Could they possibly have been the mysterious, but very real Germans who arrived at the dance that night? We will never know.

Acknowledgements

Every story has a starting point, and *Come from Away* came from my readers. After *Tides of Honour*, I received a lot of messages asking what happened to Danny and Audrey and the rest of the Baker family. It got me wondering, too.

My husband and I live on the Eastern Shore of Nova Scotia. It's a long, quiet stretch of coastline with rocky fingers of land reaching into the Atlantic. Houses are scattered; some have neighbours, some don't. Lobster traps pile up during the off-season, and when the ice is thick enough, stubborn fishermen will cut holes through it and try to tempt smelt. Our little town has a library, a gym, a post office, a bank, a bakery, a railway museum, a high school, and a couple of pizza joint– convenience stores that are right across the street from each other, competing for a really tiny customer base. This summer we got our first food truck down at the beach, so that was new.

Seventy-five-plus years ago, the Eastern Shore of Nova Scotia was a long, quiet stretch of coastline with rocky fingers of land reaching into the Atlantic. Houses were scattered, but family members tended to settle near one another. They had a railway station, lumber camps, a fish plant, a school, and general stores. Switchboards and post offices were operated out of homes. Electricity was new.

We moved here in 2008. We came here knowing no one,

but we were excited about the move. We made some great friends, we had a lot of fun, we learned a lot, and we are happy in our new home. (We even got chickens!) Not bad for a couple of "come from aways." That's the term traditionally used for anyone who wasn't born here. To some it's considered derogatory, but I don't see it that way. It's just a fact. We chose to come from away, we were welcomed, and we chose to stay. Rudi's situation was more complicated, but I knew all would end up well. Nova Scotians have warm, welcoming hearts.

Memory Lane Heritage Village, just up the highway from me, is host to the Eastern Shore Archives, which is full of prime examples of warm-hearted people. My friend Linda Fahie told me I'd be welcomed up there if I ever wanted to know about our area's history, and she was right. The last time I was there, I met her, along with her fellow volunteers Christine Mitchell, Pearl Turner, Bernadette Monk, Ruby Webber, and Memory Lane's executive director, Thea Wilson-Hammond. I settled in comfortably, archive-approved pencil in hand, while they told me stories they recalled from long ago. That's when the subject of skulking U-boats was raised, and that's when I heard the unlikely tale of a few U-boat sailors disembarking in one of our deep harbours and joining a community dance. The moment I heard that—after they convinced me it was true—I knew where the story would come from. Sweet Linda is always receiving unexpected messages from me, asking random questions about our history, and she's been so kind with her time and knowledge that I gave her a part in this book, but I need everyone to know that the real Linda isn't like this one. Rudi would have been safe with my friend.

Research opportunities surface—hang on and you'll see why I'm using that word—in the most incredible places. Just as I was researching U-boats, I discovered that my daughter's boyfriend's father, Petty Officer Second Class Ben Towns, had been a submariner. "Ah!" I thought, "I can ask him all about it!" but he went one step further. I would like to thank Ben for the once-in-a-lifetime opportunity to tour the HMCS *Windsor* (submarine) while it was docked at Halifax Harbour. The experience gave me great insight into what it might be like to live under the sea for months at a time . . . and it made me extremely grateful I've never had to do that!

And while we're on the subject of harvesting friends (does that work?), I met Birgit Peterson online while playing *Hay Day*! She's originally from Germany, and she said that if I ever needed help with German translations, I should ask her. So I did. I told her Rudi knew some English and was trying to learn as he went along, and I asked her to remember back twenty-five years to when she was just learning English. Would she have spoken in this way? Would she have used this word or that? She cheerfully took on the challenge, and now Rudi sounds like he knows what he's doing (in my opinion). Thanks, Birgit!

This year has been wonderful for me. *Tides of Honour* and *Promises to Keep* hit *The Globe and Mail*'s bestseller list, and Audible.com produced them both as audiobooks. I have been interviewed by newspapers, radio stations, and in the *Costco Connection*, I have spoken on panels and on my own at places like the Toronto Public Library, the Halifax Word on the Street festival, and many book clubs (in person and online). These opportunities might never have come if not for the wonderful team backing me up at Simon & Schuster Canada—in particular, Rita Silva, publicity manager. Rita keeps an experienced eye on everything that's happening, and has made sure my name is known among literary folks. She takes great care of me.

A while ago, I made a choice to focus my writing on Canadian history, to bring back our country's stories in a way that would not only educate but also compel readers to learn more about our past. My editors, Nita Pronovost and Sarah St. Pierre, and Simon & Schuster Canada's president, Kevin Hanson, have encouraged me to seek out these stories, and through their editorial expertise I have learned and grown a great deal as an author. My books would not be what they are without my team's insightful, generous guidance. My talented cover artist, Elizabeth Whitehead, has gone to great lengths to research and find exactly what my stories need for eye-catching and effective covers. I am extremely fortunate to enjoy a wonderful partnership with the beautiful Sarah St. Pierre, whose keen observations and intuition constantly show me new, amazing ways to look at what I'm doing. She inspires me to do better, and I am so lucky to be able to call her my friend. Sarah, I think you're gonna love the next adventure . . .

Jacques de Spoelberch, my literary agent extraordinaire, has been steadfast and determined with his support for me ever since we first joined forces back in 2010. I rely on him, I trust him wholeheartedly, and I thank him so much for everything he's done for me.

Most of all, I want to thank my readers. Of all the millions of books out there, you chose to pick up one (or more) of mine, and that means the world to me. If you've written me an email or a message or a letter, know that I was thrilled to hear from you. And if you've written a review on a site like Amazon, Chapters, or Goodreads, please know that I am extremely grateful. Those reviews really do help readers find new authors.

Of course, no book of mine would ever be written without the support of my family.

I want to thank my mother for always being there for me, and for being my biggest promoter no matter where she goes. I headed out to Calgary and the Crowsnest Pass to research my next novel, and as always she made sure I got everything I needed, including hugs. Thanks, Mom.

This summer our daughters, Emily and Piper, moved out of our house and are both attending Dalhousie University. It's strange not having them here, and it tore me apart to watch them go. But we're fortunate; it's not like we're Audrey and Danny, sending our children off to war, wondering if they will ever return. I cannot imagine the agony military parents experience as they send their grown children off. The world can be a sort of battlefield sometimes, and I guess the best we can do is give our children the tools and skills to defend themselves and get the job done. My husband and I are so incredibly proud of who our daughters are and who they are becoming.

And finally . . . More than once I've threatened to put my husband's name on the front cover of my books beside mine. Without him I would most likely have had to take advanced courses in engine repair, mechanics, hunting, trapping, fishing, farming, guns, boating, and map reading ("How can you write historical fiction and not know how to read maps?!"), among other things. Even if I had, my translation of them still wouldn't be as clear as it is after he explains things to me. He gets how my brain works, which makes life much easier. Dwayne is the first person to read any of my books—before my agent, before my editor, before anyone, and he tells me exactly what he thinks every time. I value every one of his comments, questions, and guffaws. If he isn't moved to tears ("It's just allergies!") by the third or fourth chapter, the manuscript is politely returned to sender. And that's really great.

I'm a come from away. I grew up in Toronto, lived almost

twenty years in Calgary, lived a little while in New York, and I have visited beautiful places all around the world. Now that Dwayne and I are empty nesters, we plan to travel a lot more. This life is new, and it's exciting, but no matter where I go, I'll always be at home . . . as long as I'm with him.

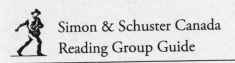

Simon & Schuster Canada
Reading Group Guide

COME
from
AWAY

Genevieve Graham

QUESTIONS FOR BOOK CLUBS

1. In the mid-1930s, memories of the First World War and the devastating Halifax Explosion were not far from the hearts and minds of Nova Scotians like Danny and Audrey Baker. How does their past experience influence their reaction to each of their sons' enlisting?

2. Grace worries that she's not contributing enough to the war effort, but her father reassures her that everything she does helps in some way. What are some examples of how Grace contributes, indirectly or otherwise?

3. Grace describes herself as wearing a mask around those she loves. Do you think this pressure to be cheerful and happy all the time comes from others or from herself?

4. In the novel we learn that German U-boats were patrolling Canada's eastern shores during the Second World War. Did you know this before reading *Come from Away*? Did it change your understanding of the lives of those on the home front?

5. If you were in Grace's place, would you have turned Rudi in to the police? Would you have hidden him? Or would you have done something else entirely?

6. After Rudi's U-boat is bombed, his sole focus is surviving, but when he is discovered to be German, he is immediately distrusted. How does Rudi try and prove himself to the Bakers? Do you think his actions are sincere, a necessity of survival, or both? Why or why not?

7. How do Danny's and Audrey's First World War experiences colour how they treat Rudi?

8. The author uses various flashbacks to tell us about Rudi's past. What was the effect of this throughout the novel? Did it change your opinion of who Rudi was when you learned about his childhood growing up in prewar Germany?

9. Rudi's parents caution him to question what he's been taught under the Third Reich, which was a dangerous idea to express at the time. On the surface, his parents seemed like model Germans. Why do you think they took this risk? What does their decision tell you about the German people during the Second World War?

10. The news plays a central role in the novel, and there are many references to German and Canadian news stories, rumours, and even propaganda. Name a few and discuss how they affect each character differently, particularly Grace, Rudi, Linda, and Tommy.

11. Grace and Rudi are on the opposite sides of a war they never wanted to be a part of. How does meeting Rudi change Grace's understanding of the other side and vice versa? Can you come up with some examples?

12. With Grace and Rudi, the author explores the line between doing one's duty and doing what is right. In what ways do Grace and Rudi struggle with this choice? Do you think one is more important than the other? Why or why not?

13. In *Tides of Honour*, the author describes the effects of PTSD, or shell shock as it was called then, on Danny, and she picks up that thread again in *Come from Away* with Harry, Eugene, Norman, and even Rudi. How does each man's PTSD affect him throughout the novel?

14. When Norman reveals that he deserted the Canadian army, the Bakers see Rudi's predicament in a new light. Did Norman's revelation have the same effect on you? Why or why not?

15. Both Norman and Rudi feel they need to take the identity of a dead man in order to survive. How does either scenario work out for them? What do you think this says about the nature of war?

16. Before reading this novel, had you heard of the phrase "come from away"? Has the novel changed your understanding of the saying?

ENHANCE YOUR BOOK CLUB

1. Have you read *Tides of Honour*? If not, consider reading the novel as part of your book club and discover how Danny and Audrey Baker survived the First World War and the Halifax Explosion of 1917, and became the parents of Harry, Eugene, Norman, and Grace in *Come from Away*.

2. In the note to the reader, the author references the Battle of the Gulf of St. Lawrence, during which, between 1942 and 1944, German U-boats penetrated Canada's coast and came within 300 kilometres of Quebec City. Veterans Affairs Canada has published a short book on the battle that includes black-and-white photographs of ships as well as news headlines of the day. Read more about the battle here: http://www.veterans.gc.ca/public/pages/re membrance/history/second-world-war/battle-gulf-st-law rence/battlegulf_eng.pdf.

3. For a broader overview of the Allied fight against the wolf packs of German U-boats, go to the American Battle Monuments Commission website and use its free online interactive to learn about the Battle of the Atlantic: https://www.abmc.gov/sites/default/files/interactive/in teractive_files/BOTA_Web/index.html.

A CONVERSATION
WITH GENEVIEVE GRAHAM

Come from Away is your third historical romance set in Canada and follows up with the Baker family from your bestselling book *Tides of Honour*. What inspired you to write about these characters again?

To me, the hardest part of every book is finishing it and sending it away for the final stages of publishing. "The end" is like a farewell to my characters, and it feels like I'm saying goodbye to very close friends. The process of writing historical fiction like this is multilayered, but that doesn't change the fact that I become very attached to my characters. And Danny, well, I truly love Danny. After publication, a lot of readers wrote asking what happened to the Bakers after *Tides of Honour*, and I started wondering that myself. What was it like in this neck of the woods when the next world war began? How did the people live, and how did they cope with everything that was going on? Of course, by then the Baker children would be old enough to be a part of that, and suddenly I needed to know all about the different branches of the military, how they worked, where they went, what they did . . .

At the same time, today's world was dealing with a huge refugee crisis. Foreigners were arriving on our shores by the thousands, driven from their own countries by terrorism. But whom could we trust? Could some be an actual part of that threat, using the crowds as a shield? The Western world polarized over the refugee crisis, and friendly conversations became antagonistic. During the Second World War, Adolf Hitler and the Nazis were the epitome of terrorists, unanimously and deservedly hated around the world. What if one of Them was suddenly alone in the midst of all of Us? How would everyone react? It was an interesting idea, considering the varied personalities in the Baker family. How would Danny react? Would his past experience be tempered by his honourable character? How would Audrey and the rest of the family face this new challenge? I could hardly wait to get to know them again.

The premise of _Come from Away_ centres on a local legend that U-boat sailors attended a Christmas dance in 1942. Where did you first hear this story, and what did you think?
When I was first doing research for _Tides of Honour_, I drove up to visit the always welcoming volunteer ladies at our Eastern Shore Archives, about twenty minutes from my house. Actually, it took a little longer that day, I recall, because it was about minus twenty-seven degrees and the road was covered in crunchy snow intent on grabbing my car tires. Their little building is in Memory Lane, our area's historical village, which happens to specialize in the 1940s. So when I started to plan a book set in the early forties, I knew that's where I would have to start.

Since they'd been so helpful the first time, I asked the ladies what they remembered hearing about the Eastern Shore during the Second World War, and as usual they were full of stories from friends and relatives over the years. When the subject of U-boats came up, I was intrigued and asked to hear more. Then one of the ladies asked, "Who remembers the story about the dance?" and everyone did. Someone's aunt had been at that dance and seen the German boys there. Someone heard from their father that they were there. "What happened after that dance?" I asked, but no one knew. No one knew who they were, and no one around here ever saw those boys again.

At the time, I knew nothing about U-boats, but to me the whole idea of a German U-boat surfacing in one of our harbours sounded fantastical. To imagine a German commander permitting any of his men off the boat was practically impossible. Then for those men to happen upon a local dance? But everywhere and everyone I asked confirmed the story. Sounds crazy, but it happened!

All your novels are heavily researched. How do you normally start that process, and where do you find resources? Have particular times been more challenging than others?

When I research I submerge myself in non-fiction. As tempting as it might be, I never read historical fiction when I'm writing historical fiction. I never want to be swayed or misled by someone else's interpretation of the time, and I don't want their voice in my work. So I read only non-fiction, which can be difficult for me because often I find that kind of reading to be a little dry. But it's what I need, so I start at the library; my friends over there are always the first to know what the next book will be about. I'm actually not very good at reading entire history books, but once I understand the major historical framework I've become adept at finding the facts and little known details that bring it back to life. I also do a ton of research work online, and I enjoy that most of the time. My favourite thing about that kind of research is falling down the rabbit hole, taking a little zig instead of a zag and ending up at a whole new *aha!* moment. Online I also come across experts, occasionally re-enactors, who are passionate about details and demand that everything is recorded exactly right. And that is perfect for me.

The periods are quite different in both research and story-line. When I first started writing, my books were based in the 1700s, and I was happy that *Promises to Keep* went back to those roots. Initially I'd thought I would keep writing in that era. I love the gallantry, the adventure, the romance of those dark, difficult years. I love researching it, too.

But when *Tides of Honour* came along, it was as if my brain clicked into a different gear. I feel a closer connection to the early twentieth century, and research is very different. We have newspapers and photographs, not just painted likenesses. We have stories from ancestors. And now that my stories are based in Canada, I can visit those places and see exactly what it is I need to write. And on rare occasions, I can touch them . . . like while I was working on *Come from Away* I was invited on board the (docked) HMCS *Windsor*, one of the Royal Canadian Navy's submarines! I will admit that I remember very little about the instruments and the tour I was given, but I left with a strong understanding of what it would be like living inside those things, and with a pretty good idea of how that kind of life might affect a man's mind after a few months under the sea. Terrifying!

What was the most surprising thing you discovered during your research? Did anything seem more fiction than fact?
The premise of the story seemed more fiction than fact, but the story about the German U-boat sailors at our local dance was true. And when I told people what I was writing about, I was surprised by the many additional stories they told me about U-boats skulking around our shores. I had no idea. I was already aware of most of the historical information, but listening to actual interviews of Second World War veterans and hearing the raw emotion in their voices even after all this time was

intense. Usually when I write I am surprised by little things, and I love when that happens. For example, in *Promises to Keep*, I wanted to write a story that stayed in Canada, but it didn't look promising after all the Acadian ships were sent off to unknown ports. Then I came across the *Pembroke*, the only ship to remain in Canada after the Expulsion. Then I discovered Charles Belliveau, who was the actual Acadian mast maker and eventual captain of the *Pembroke*. The dialogue he had with the captive English captain was taken word for word from journals shared online. Those are the moments I find so thrilling when I'm researching, like I've found the exact puzzle piece I didn't even realize I was missing.

You have a background in music, but you've been writing full-time for more than a decade now. Were you always interested in becoming an author? Or did something in particular spark your interest?

Until I sat down at my computer for the first time in 2007 and began to play around with words, I never had any interest in being an author. I never even thought about it. I have always loved the magic of beautifully woven words, and it was my love of reading that led to this new career. I didn't read a lot when I was a stay-at-home mom—I was always cleaning or feeding or trying desperately to sleep!—until my mother handed me a copy of Diana Gabaldon's *Outlander* one day and gently suggested it was time for me to escape for a while. I'd never read much historical fiction before that, but I was immediately swallowed up by Gabaldon's world. I read that huge series *seven times* and learned something new every time—whether it was about the craft of writing or the reality of history—and the experience was intoxicating. It was after all that reading that I decided I'd see if I could create anything like that myself. I told my husband I was going to try and write a book, and he said, "Okay. See you in a few hours." When I emerged from the basement, flushed and nervous, he read the pages I handed him and said, "You know, this is pretty good," and a writer was born.

You've written several bestsellers now, including *Tides of Honour* and *Promises to Keep*. What's your writing process like? Has it been different for each book?

I am constantly learning, so while I'd say my process is similar with each book, I'd also have to say it's evolving. A huge part of that is because I am fortunate to have an amazing editorial team who have the experience I lack and are very generous in sharing. My process starts when a moment or place sparks my curiosity, and I'll read up on the basics of the era or event. If I'm intrigued enough, and if I can see a story forming around it, I will dig right in. Once I place myself in the time period, I start writing right away, seeing the surroundings from the mind and heart of a character I am just getting to know. I stop writing when I have a question, like *What would she be wearing in this time/instance?* then I dive into the research. I take notes constantly, and when I am done writing, I will plug in as many details as I can without turning the book into a textbook. That is really important, because the story must be told from the characters' perspectives, not mine. They don't know the particulars—or wouldn't take notice of them—like how many inches deep the snow is or how many buttons are on a coat. It's up to me to share the information with the reader in a way that it doesn't interrupt the flow of my characters' actions and thoughts.

When I first started writing, I thought the idea of letting the characters "speak" to the writer was a myth, a fancy way to make the art of writing seem even more magical than it is. But it's no myth. When I let their voices speak to me, and when I follow their lead, the book will flow without too much effort. Other than typing what I see and hear, my job is to do all the research as soon as it's required and integrate it into the story, but they know more of what's going on than I do most of the time. Usually when I run into writer's block, it's because I've stopped listening.

Come from Away, Promises to Keep, and Tides of Honour are all set on Canada's east coast. Would you say that living in Nova Scotia has inspired your writing? How so?

Yes. Before, I had written historical adventures set on an entirely different continent, but suddenly I was living in a place where hundred-year-old houses stand along the highway, where statues and museums tell stories (like the *Titanic* and the Halifax Explosion) that had seemed too removed from real life or simply too far away for me to grab on to before. People here proudly remember the generations past and are more than willing to share the stories. So, yes, Nova Scotia has been very inspiring, and it has also whetted my appetite for Canadian history. Now I am hungry for stories from across the entire country. Canada's history is exciting but mostly forgotten, its adventures confined for the most part to textbooks that are rarely opened. Why is it that Americans and Europeans are so great at telling their own stories and we generally don't dwell on ours? My plan is to change that.

Can you describe the responses you've received from readers of your books? Has anything surprised you?

No matter how many of my books are sold, I expect I am always going to be surprised when I receive notes from readers. When they connect to the stories and are moved enough that they feel compelled to write to me, that means so much. When *Tides of*

Honour came out, I received an email from a gentleman in his eighties who had "nabbed the book from my wife's nightstand" and his sweet letter made me cry. He talked about how five members of his family, from grandfather to sister, had participated in the military in various conflicts, and he said Danny's character and the battle scenes in the book brought it all back to him. He also said he appreciated the care and respect I'd given PTSD, the violence, and the affected family members. Other readers wrote to me about relatives who had experienced the Halifax Explosion, and many shared stories and pictures. With *Promises to Keep* I have received a number of passionate letters from Acadians who are grateful this story is bringing back their history. Best of all are the notes I receive from younger readers (eighteen years old or so) who say they had no idea Canadian history was so exciting and my books have encouraged them to read more about our great country.

Do you have any advice for aspiring writers of historical fiction?
Someone on Twitter asked for help the other day regarding how to write historical fiction. She wondered how she would know if she'd put too much detail in. I say put it all in on the first draft. Everything you can find. Don't edit until you're all done (a rule which is really hard for me to stick to), then read it through. If you are distracted or bored at any point, then your story has just turned into a textbook. That's how I see it, anyway.

To me, the most important rule about writing historical fiction is always to tell the truth. Do not shy away from the ugly truths. Not everything in our history was happy or romantic like we might want, but everything that happened was important to different degrees. If you are writing about something terrible, write it the way it was. Don't make light of it, but don't make it gratuitous, either. Your readers are smart. Don't do everything for them. Let them draw their own images in their minds based on your words.

What are you working on these days?
I'm super excited about my next novel. For the first time I will be shifting my focus to Canada's west, and the more I research, the more there is to write about! When you think of Canada, one of the first symbols to come to mind is the steadfast Mountie, right? What do you know about our famous force? I knew nothing, and that has definitely changed. My book will begin on the rapidly changing Prairies, where our hero will join the early Mounties, who were the North-West Mounted Police. We will ride both horseback and the rails with him all the way to the trials and triumphs of the Klondike gold rush, and eventually he will mosey on down to the coal mines of the Crowsnest Pass—where he will experience the little-known Frank Slide.

The book after that will most likely be one about the British Home Children which I have already begun to write. Somewhere in the next couple of years I want to research the path my husband's grandfather took when, at the age of sixteen, he sailed from Poland by himself, came through Pier 21 in Halifax, then rode the train to Saskatchewan at the beginning of the twentieth century with plans to single-handedly clear the tangled bush and establish a farm—with nothing but five dollars in his pack. Oh Canada. So many stories!

Also by

GENEVIEVE GRAHAM

Globe and Mail bestsellers

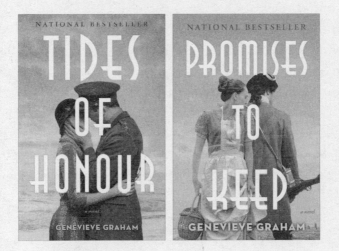

"Graham is a remarkable talent."

MADELINE HUNTER, *New York Times* bestselling
author of *The Accidental Duchess*